THE LAST COWBOY

Written by Ava Armstrong

D1715582

CHAPTER 1: THE UNEXPECTED

When a dairy farm runs on all eight cylinders, there's a distinctive sound – Linc always thought of it as the hum of efficiency. Lincoln Caldwell glanced at the clock on the wall and realized he was right on time. He sang along with the radio in the barn, as he moved with his usual efficient rhythm through the herd. It was the 5:00 PM milking. Everything was going smoothly. Sonny nodded and smiled as he moved past him to attach the milking machine to the next udder. Rob and Chris were feeding the cows and bringing the raw milk to the clean room. Yes, the crew was in the zone.

Linc was thinking about stopping by Bruno's later on for a beer and a pool game. He hadn't been out of the house for two weeks, except to bring his daughter, Clara, for an ice cream last Sunday after church.

The heavy thud in the hayloft was loud enough to cause Linc to stop in his tracks. Sonny cast a worried look his way.

"Damn. What the hell was that?" Linc yelled over the noise of the machinery and radio.

Panic swept through him as he realized his father just went up to the loft. Wasting no time, Linc scrambled to the ladder. Being six-foot two and lean, he had run up that ladder a million times, but this was the fastest ascent he could remember. It occurred to him that his father had just mentioned he was going up to move some hay around.

As soon as he got eye-level with the floor of the loft, his gaze riveted to his father slumped on the floor, in a strange position, not moving.

"Shit.... dad. Are you all right? Oh damn!"

Timothy Caldwell was splayed on the floor before him. His head had a bad gash in it. Blood trickled onto the floor. It appeared he wasn't breathing.

"Linc, what's the matter?" Sonny bellowed from below.

"Call 911, oh God, my father is on the floor. He fell off the top...oh, shit."

The next few minutes were a blur. Linc shook his father and tried to give him mouth-to-mouth. He pushed his fist into his chest, willing his heart to beat, but the big man was unresponsive. Tears clouded his vision as he spoke to his dad.

"Come on, don't do this to me now! Oh, damn it. I can't let you go like this dad, please!"

When the firefighters arrived, they knew Timothy Caldwell was dead. Linc was holding his father, crying and muttering until he felt Sonny's hands pulling him away.

"Let these guys do their job."

But Linc knew. His father was dead. This couldn't be happening. His dad was a six-foot four wall of muscles, healthy as a horse. Linc was thirty-two years old, but hadn't contemplated his father's death. Dad had just celebrated his sixty-sixth birthday. Linc expected him to live to be ninety-five.

He had no idea how much time passed as he sat in a catatonic state in the hayloft. He was aware of the firemen, guys he'd graduated from high school with, tenderly working on his father. Checking for vitals. Doing everything possible to figure out what had happened.

Linc felt like he couldn't breathe as one of his best friends approached him. It was Chet, and he put his arm around him and the look on his face was somber.

"He's gone, Linc. It was quick. He was working up above and that railing gave way. The blow to his head took him out. I'm sorry, man."

Linc jumped up. "Damn. The cows. I've got to get downstairs and help Sonny."

"No." Chet glanced at the other firemen already making a descent from the hayloft. "We're milking the cows tonight, buddy. I just called the medical examiner. It's routine. I'll wait with you until he comes. Then you're going with your mother to take care of things. I'll get your mom and explain what's happened. It's all right, Linc. You've got to take care of your mom tonight. She's gonna take this hard. And, little Clara, too. I'm sorry, Linc."

Linc sat with his father's body in the hayloft and listened to his mother scream the word *no* just once. Katherine Caldwell worshipped the ground his father walked upon. It was a deep abiding love that he watched like a family movie up close and personal for thirty-two years. A love he hoped he would experience in his lifetime. He thought he had that love once, in high school, but she left him.

So many thoughts passed through his mind as he watched his mother climb the ladder. The hayloft had always been a pleasurable hiding place for him, but now he'd never look at it the same way. It was the first place he had kissed Riley years ago. He remembered his father switching on the light and speaking in a stern voice. "Come on down here now, Linc." That was all he said. At least he didn't embarrass him in front of Riley. But later, when Riley was gone, his father sat him down for a talk. One of many.

His mother ran to his father's body and Linc watched with a lump in his throat as she lovingly caressed his face. After a few minutes, he moved toward her and watched as she cradled her husband in her arms one last time. He felt tears sliding down his face, but couldn't stop them. He hadn't sobbed like this since Riley left him. He felt as if his heart was breaking. Somehow, he had to tell his three-year old daughter that grandpa, her favorite person in the world, just died.

Linc descended the ladder and made his way back inside the house. He found Clara at the kitchen table drawing pictures. "Look daddy. I made a picture of your horse, Ranger!" Clara's blonde hair framed her face and her blue eyes looked up at him for approval. Linc couldn't find the words to communicate what had just happened. But Clara read his face and body language quickly. "Why are you so sad, daddy? Are you crying?"

With tears streaming down his face, he scooped Clara into his arms and carried her into the parlor where it was dark and she couldn't see his tears. "Listen, angel. Daddy has something to tell you. There's been an accident. Grandpa has gone to heaven."

Clara looked baffled. "You mean right now? He went to heaven and he didn't say goodbye?"

Linc just nodded. The daylight filtered in through the heavy drapes highlighting Clara's eyes filled with tears, and her blonde hair curled around her innocent face. "Why daddy? Why did Grandpa go to heaven? Can he ever come back?"

So many questions, and Linc had no answers. He was numb from the reality of it, and he knew, in time, Clara would understand. Right now, though, she couldn't comprehend what had happened.

"I'm going to take you next door to see Rachel for a little while. Then, I'll be back to get you. Grandma and I have to take Grandpa to a special place....where he can sleep peacefully."

The visit from the medical examiner and the ride to the funeral home was surreal. Katherine Caldwell, a widow at age sixty-four, had stopped crying. She was made of steel, Linc thought as he glanced at her thick silvery hair pulled back into a pony tail, her blue eyes brimming with tears. When he made eye contact with his mother, it was as if she could read his mind.

"Our lives just changed, Linc." She uttered. "Ain't never gonna be the same."

Linc wrapped his arms around her. There were no words of consolation. He knew she was right. He tried not to cry. He had to be strong for his mom. She needed him more than ever, although she had been his rock always. A registered nurse at the regional medical center for all of her adult life, Katherine Caldwell was familiar with what came next. Linc stood there feeling like a bump on a log while his mother took care of every detail.

Sonny arrived in his truck to bring them home. Leaving the funeral home, Linc felt empty inside. The three sat in the front seat in silence. His mother's hand touched his. Sonny drove without uttering a word, but Linc could tell he'd been crying, too. Sonny was his right-hand man. Native American, he lived on a ten-acre spread that Linc's father had given him for working on the farm. Linc's dad had also bestowed him with the name Sonny. He said he was his fourth son, not by birth, but by choice. Sonny and Linc grew up together, best friends. Linc knew Sonny missed the old man as much, if not more, than he already did.

Scruffy ran out to greet him, but the dog immediately sensed his somber mood. The small terrier trotted next to Linc as he made his way to the next door neighbor's to bring Clara home. "Thank you." He tipped his hat. A good friend of the family, Rachel had tears in her eyes. "I'm so sorry, Linc." Walking home with Clara, he could see her mood was subdued. The gears were turning in her three-year old brain trying to understand what was taking place. Clara mounted the stairs to the porch and went into the kitchen where his mother was preparing something for dinner.

The sun was setting on Clear Springs Farm, a two-hundred acre spread that covered half the county in Gorham, Maine. Scruffy sat next to him and whined. Linc's hand automatically picked the durable little terrier up and put him in his lap. The rolling hills and green forest never looked so desolate, as Linc sat on the stoop waiting for his mother to toss a salad, he allowed his grief to morph into worry. *What the hell am I going to do without him?*

The last family-owned dairy farm in the state of Maine, Clear Springs Farm was now teetering on the edge of demise. The dairy industry, like many other businesses, was turning into large-scale corporate entities. His father had fought valiantly to keep the place running. Every dime of his savings had been eaten up with rising operating expenses and the ever-growing list of governmental regulations.

Linc couldn't imagine life without his father. They were so close they'd complete each other's sentences. The eldest of three sons, he'd promised his father to keep the farm running in his stead. His father called it his legacy. The farm had been in the Caldwell family for over a hundred years. Linc felt strongly about keeping the promise he'd made to his father. He'd keep the place running if it killed him.

His younger brothers had bigger and better things on their minds. As soon as they graduated from college, they moved away from Maine. Grant, the youngest, now twenty-eight, was a Silicon Valley tycoon. Madison, thirty, was a successful airline pilot for Southern Express. Neither of his brothers could believe the old man was gone. Linc choked back the tears when he made those phone calls. They'd be coming home right away to console mom. He sensed their concern. For a moment, he wondered if Riley had heard the news, but was stirred by his mom's soft voice behind him.

"Linc. Let's have something to eat. You need to eat." He felt his mother's hand on his shoulder and moved into the kitchen. As he did, his phone vibrated and he pulled it out of his chest pocket. A text from Riley with the message, *what's going on there? What happened? Call me.*

"I gotta step outside, Ma. Just for a moment."

The screen door slammed and Linc walked to the edge of the barn, as he tapped Riley's number. It rang once and she answered immediately. Her voice was breathless and filled with concern.

"Linc. Thank God. What's going on?" Silence. "Tell me."

Linc choked back the tears. "He's gone. It happened so fast. It was an accident." That was all he could utter. He was sobbing uncontrollably and afraid Riley could hear him, so he covered the speaker on his phone.

Riley could hear him weeping. Her only thought was *I've got to go there now*. She managed to say she was sorry. But wondered if Linc even had his phone up to his ear. "I'll be there in a couple of hours. I'm driving up. Linc, can you hear me?"

His answer was brief. "Yup." The call ended.

CHAPTER 2: BACK TO THE BEGINNING

"Where the hell do you think you're going?" Marcus startled her when she turned around.

"Damn it, Marcus. Don't sneak up on me like that." Riley was tossing clothing into a canvas bag. She tried to avoid his dark piercing eyes. "There's been an emergency. Timothy Caldwell, you know, the family I used to work for in high school? He just passed away….it was an accident. I've got to go home for the funeral."

"Shit, Riley – you haven't even *seen* those people for years! They're in your past, way back to your high school days! Really? You've got to run home to Maine to see this family now? They probably don't even remember you."

Marcus was like that. Riley expected him to say those things. He always hated the fact that she kept in touch with old friends like the Caldwell Family. In fact, three of her best friends had just contacted her on Facebook to let her know about the accident. Word traveled quickly in a small town. Yes, she kept in touch with her friends. Why Marcus couldn't understand that was beyond her. He acted like he was jealous that she even *had* friends who cared about her and contacted her every day.

"I've gotta go, Marcus. I'll be back in a couple of days, when the funeral is over." She touched his arm and gave him a peck on the cheek.

Marcus followed her outside to her vehicle. But she ignored him and tossed the canvas sack into the backseat and closed the door. As she started the Subaru, she could see Marcus moving his lips, but she was done arguing with him. This was always the way he behaved when she visited a friend, even if it was a planned excursion. She pulled onto the street and wound through the late afternoon traffic to Interstate 95 and headed north.

She tapped her steering wheel and the Bluetooth display came up. She spoke the name she wanted to dial, "Conor

O'Neal." The phone rang to her father's shop and she heard his voice boom over the car speaker. "O'Neal's engineering."

"Dad, it's me. You're working late again."

"Where the hell are you? In your car? Where are you traveling now, Riley? You're never home, not even for a weekend lately." Her father obviously had no idea.

"I'm heading up to Clear Springs Farm in Maine. Mr. Caldwell had an accident, it was terrible. Dad, he's gone."

There was silence on the line for a moment. Riley heard her father clear his throat. "Damn, what happened?"

"I have no idea. I just know there was an accident on the farm and he's dead. I've got to go to the funeral, you know. There's Linc and Katherine, and his two brothers. They were like family to me."

"I know Riley. I'm just closing up here. I'll give Linc's mother a call and see if there's anything I can do. They'll most likely need a hand over there. That's a big place. I know Linc's been struggling. I saw him at the grocery store the other day. He didn't look too good."

"Okay, dad, thanks. I'll be staying with you and mom, but I won't be there until later tonight. I want to stop by and pay my respects to the Caldwell Family. You understand. I just wanted to let you know what's happened."

"Thanks, honey." Her father's voice softened, "I'm sorry, Riley."

As soon as the call with her father ended, her phone rang and the Bluetooth displayed the name Sandra Winship. Riley touched the answer button on the steering wheel. "Hey Sandy...."

"You're in your car driving to Maine, aren't you?" Sandy asked.

"Of course I am – I've got to go to the funeral. You'll be there, right?"

"Yes. We'll all be there. Gosh, I can't believe this happened. I feel so sorry for Katherine. How many years were they married? I feel badly for Linc, too. Running that farm will fall to him. That's a lot to put on a guy. He's dealt with enough the past couple of years, with Jenna running off and all."

"Hey, look, I'm driving. I'm staying at my parent's place."

"Shucks, I thought you'd stay here with me. I've got the spare room all ready." Sandy huffed.

"I should be there in a couple of hours. But, I'm going to stop to see Linc as soon as I arrive. I'll text you. And, thanks for the offer, Sandy."

As the call ended, Riley's mind flooded with memories of working at Clear Springs Farm. She remembered the first time she met Timothy Caldwell, a handsome giant of a man, wearing denim overalls. The thing she remembered most were his clear blue eyes and how they twinkled with mischief, as if he knew something she didn't. *He knew something, all right.* He knew that Riley and Linc were an item long before he let on.

He'd watched them work together in the barn every night at milking time. Linc was a patient teacher and Riley a willing and enthusiastic student. Riley smiled as she remembered the first time Linc showed her how to scrape cow manure into the trench so the barn cleaner could carry it out to a giant waste pile. The stench was pretty bad, but Riley had to buck up. That's what Linc had said. At the time, she had no idea what that meant. She was fifteen years old. Riley was a mess on that hot summer day, but Link took her out behind the barn and hosed her off. It had to be 80 degrees and the cool water in the hose had turned warm lying in the sun. The cow manure was crusted onto her clothing. She now smelled just like Linc did. He had the smell of a working man, sweat mixed with leather and a little bit of manure. She remembered what he said, "Those will be your workin' clothes from now on. I have a whole bin full."

Bonding over manure. That was the first moment she knew she loved him. Even though she'd never had a boyfriend before, by age fifteen she noticed things like his muscled forearms and his gorgeous blue eyes. She observed the tiniest details about Linc. How he squinted when he looked at her, the stride he had in the barn when working, and how he sang along to songs on the radio.

https://www.youtube.com/watch?v=aLfWqog76q0

https://www.youtube.com/watch?v=fefu8tca4EY

https://www.youtube.com/watch?v=924Ryk0jW7g

Country songs. And, he had a pretty good voice. Before long, Riley was looking forward to listening to him in the barn, brushing by her at a good clip, winking and smiling, "Excuse me, ma'am."

Linc caught her looking at him several times causing Riley to blush and turn away. How could she ignore his lean rugged body in those Wrangler jeans? They fit his rear end just right. When he saw her in the hallway at school, Linc always nodded and smiled. Even if he was talking to one of his friends, Riley felt his eyes lingering on her when she passed him in the hallway. And, when she walked by, he left his friends and fell into step beside her.

One day she found a note inside her locker on Valentine's Day. She knew it was his handwriting. It simply said, Be Mine. Riley saved the handmade valentine. She wasn't sure why, but she saved everything Linc ever gave her. The first photograph of her standing in front of the barn, taken by Linc. Her favorite was the photo of her first time horseback riding on Star. Everything was in the cedar chest she called her time capsule. The story of her life resided in scraps and pieces bundled up, like buried treasure waiting to be discovered. Sometimes on a rainy day, she'd sit and sift through it all. Happy memories.

The first year she worked on the farm was physically challenging. Riley learned about milking cows and growing vegetables, and ran the antique cash register at the farm stand. Her favorite task was taking the newborn calves into a separate pen to feed them from a huge baby bottle filled with the mother cow's first milk. She remembered the calves' eyes with big long lashes gazing into hers as she fed them. Linc told her they were bonding with her. For the first time in her life, Riley felt a motherly instinct.

By the time Riley turned sixteen, Linc was waiting outside of her classes to accompany her to the next one. He walked her to homeroom in the morning and gave her a ride to the farm in his old truck right after school. He said it saved her some shoe leather. Riley kept her farm clothes in her locker and couldn't wait to change into a flannel shirt and rolled up jeans.

Forever etched in her memory, was the night Linc's mother asked her to stay for dinner. It was a warm day in late May, just before school let out for summer break. Riley helped Mrs. Caldwell in the big farmhouse kitchen as she prepared a meal for the three boys and her husband.

The table was set by Mrs. Caldwell and she had Riley seated directly across from Linc.

"Hey, Linc. You've got a girlfriend?" his brothers teased.

Riley's eyes locked with Linc's and he smiled.

"What's the matter, you jealous?" Linc shoved Grant. Linc took his appointed seat.

"You guys getting married?" Madison chimed in.

"Linc and Riley up in a tree...K-I-S-S-I-N-G." Grant sang loudly.

Linc reached his long arm around and slapped his brother on the back of the head.

"Enough!" Timothy Caldwell said with a stern tone. The boys froze. When their father spoke, they listened. "We have a guest here tonight. Let's treat this young lady with respect. Now who's gonna say grace?"

"I will." Riley offered.

Mr. Caldwell's eyes rested on her. "Thank you, Riley. Go ahead."

Riley knew she scored points right there. She actually enjoyed the gentle teasing of Linc's brothers. Being an only child, she enjoyed the banter because it was a novelty. That dinner was an important event in her life in more ways than one. That was the night that marked the beginning of a love affair with Linc Caldwell that became the talk of the town.

After dinner, Riley helped with the dishes, but as soon as she was done Linc pulled her outside to go for a sunset walk. The May weather was comfortable, warm days and cool nights. They meandered down through the pasture and up to the vegetable garden as the sun was setting. As she stood next to Linc, she sensed he was trying to tell her something. When he took her hand in his, she felt a tenderness and warmth in his touch. Linc had big rough working hands that seemed to swallow hers. When his deep blue eyes met hers, it was if she was staring into his soul. He led her to the barn and up the ladder to the hayloft in the fading sunlight.

"We gotta be quiet..." he put his finger up to his lips. Once in the hayloft, Riley watched as Linc took an old horse blanket and spread it atop a few bales of hay. Only a sliver of fading daylight illuminated the space and she could barely see Linc as he awkwardly took her hand again. This time drawing her closer to him, he shyly nuzzled her neck. She felt a hot flash go through her as he pulled her even closer. She curled into his six-foot two inch frame as if she was made for him. His muscled body felt solid. She had never been this close to a guy – any guy – and her body reacted instinctively. Her nipples hardened, her breathing almost stopped. She felt his finger lift her chin slightly as he placed his lips upon hers. Every hormone came alive inside her at that moment. She closed her eyes and enjoyed the soft wet warmth of Linc's lips on hers. His strong hands roamed over her body and his kiss became urgent. Riley felt his tongue as it

tentatively explored the seam of her lips, as if begging her to let him in.

"Linc, you up there?" Mr. Caldwell was at the bottom of the ladder. Linc snapped to attention at the sound of his voice. The bright fluorescent light hanging above them suddenly came on and Riley screamed when she saw the spider's nests in the ceiling of the hayloft. But more than that she remembered Linc's face turning beet red, as he mouthed the word, "Sorry."

"Coming, Dad." Linc said loudly as he pulled Riley toward the ladder and they sheepishly descended. Linc gave Riley a ride home that night in his 1950 Chevy truck, a project he'd worked on for years with his father in the garage. It was completely dark when they got to her house. The moment he shut off the engine, he pulled her closer to him on the bench seat. She tilted her head toward him, eagerly accepting his mouth this time. She wanted to learn how to kiss. He was her first.

Linc was more eager than she. Riley felt his hot breath in her ear when he spoke, "You have no idea how long I've wanted to do this." His mouth covered hers, causing a wave of longing that started from her lips and spread like wildfire to every cell in her body. Riley had a pretty good idea how long he'd wanted to do this. Linc had been following her around at school like a love-sick puppy. Secretly, she loved the attention. The other girls in her class thought Linc was a pretty good catch. They'd all go out with him if he asked. In fact, some of her girlfriends were downright jealous. The senior prom was coming up, and rumor had it that Linc was going to ask Riley. She'd be the only sophomore at the senior prom. That was a big deal.

When he asked her that night in the truck to go to the prom with him she was breathless from kissing him. "Yes." was all she could manage to utter gazing into his blue eyes. Riley's parents were standing on the porch watching as she got out of the truck. "Bye, Linc." she murmured. He tipped his hat and nodded at her parents. They didn't look too happy at the moment. Riley was three years younger than him. Riley knew *they would have concerns. But, she also knew Linc would put those all to rest. His intentions were honorable.*

That was the beginning of it all.

CHAPTER 3: WRITTEN ON HIS HEART

It was sunset by the time Riley arrived at Clear Springs Farm. Friday night traffic was thick on the interstate. Tourists were flooding into Vacationland, her home State of Maine, aptly named on the license plate. When she pulled into the gravel driveway, it seemed every light was on inside the old farmhouse. She thought she saw the outline of Linc's figure sitting in a rocking chair on the porch. She could hear Scruffy, Linc's little side-kick, whining at the porch door. It seemed Scruffy could hear her coming a mile away.

As she stepped out of her vehicle, the figure rose from the chair and the screen door opened. As Linc stepped onto the gravel, Riley ran to him and she folded into his embrace automatically. Tenderly, his head dropped onto her shoulder and his breath warmed her face as he exhaled. It was a distinct sigh of relief. She could tell he hadn't shaved for days. As she closed her eyes, she detected the aroma of leather, hay, and the pine tar soap Linc always washed with. His familiar scent surrounded her and she couldn't stop herself from reminiscing for a long minute.

"Riley. I'm glad you're here." When he spoke, she detected the odor of Sam Adams pale ale, too.

She pulled him close with her arms around his mid-section. Lean and muscled, Linc was rough and tumbled on the outside, but tender on the inside. He seemed to be unaware of the effect he had on her when he held her like this. As Riley enjoyed the warm embrace, she realized this was the first time she'd hugged Linc since she could remember. There was that one time she saw him at the grocer's with his wife, Jenna, and newborn Clara. That was a quick hug. *This was different.* Linc was holding her, as he used to. She could tell he'd been crying. She could also tell he didn't want to let her go, not just yet.

Their faces touched, cheek to cheek. Riley whispered, "I'm so sorry, Linc. Oh God, I know everyone probably says that. I'm truly deeply sorry. Your dad was such a wonderful man. I loved him..." Riley's words trailed off and she felt a lump in her throat. Now she was the one breaking down and she felt Linc's hand smoothing her hair, like he always did.

"It's okay, Riley. Don't cry. It'll be okay." She felt Linc's face pressed against hers. She sensed his breathing changed, almost stopped. She turned her face toward him, the lamplight from the house painted his handsome features. His face was the same, even though it had been a decade. His deep-set blue-green eyes met hers and she watched his manly brow furrow ever so slightly. His full lips were so close, she imagined kissing him. *Damn.* She'd had dreams like this, but she couldn't allow it to happen -- not now that she was married and Linc was freshly divorced. No, it was wrong – but being in his arms felt so right.

Scruffy, started bouncing off her leg and barking. Riley glanced down, breaking the intimacy of the moment. "Hey, Scruffy!" She crouched and the Jack Russell terrier licked her face. "He remembers me..." Riley's hands were shaking.

"Who could ever forget you?" Linc said softly. "I'm sorry, Riley. I don't know what got into me just then. I've been so emotional today."

The door to the porch opened and Katherine Caldwell waved Riley in. "Come on. We've got baked beans in the oven and hot dogs on the griddle. I have homemade bread, too, and coleslaw."

Riley ran to Linc's mother and gave her a solid hug. "I'm so sorry, Katherine."

It was a homecoming, of sorts, being at the farm like this. Seeing Linc and his mother, and even little Scruffy. He was just a pup the last time she stopped by the farm a few years ago. It was on a trip home during the summer and the vegetable stand was open. She couldn't resist stopping. She was hoping to get a glimpse of Linc. However, it was Jenna, Linc's very pregnant wife, who sold the vegetables to Riley that day.

Jenna was tall, dark, and gorgeous with the features of a super-model. Riley expected no less. He was a handsome guy, after all. Women tripped over themselves to dance with him at Bruno's Tavern. At least that's what her girlfriends reported to her. Riley always figured he'd end up with a gorgeous woman for a wife. That was the first time Riley laid eyes on Jenna. It was the first time she saw the dog, at Jenna's feet. He was a tiny puppy.

"What's his name?" Riley had asked.

"Scruffy." Jenna said flatly. Her demeanor was emotionless. Her eyes scrutinized Riley in a way that made her uncomfortable.

"Oh, that's a cute name." Riley gushed as she knelt and caressed the puppy.

Jenna just stared at her and put her cigarette out in an ashtray near the old cash register.

"Yeah. Linc named him. He's cute. You can have him if you want him. I don't like dogs."

Riley was taken aback by her casual nature of her remark. "Oh, gosh, no dogs are allowed at my condo. But, if I could take him, I would."

"You're that girl that Linc used to run around with in high school, ain't ya? Riley-- right?"

"Yes. That was a long time ago..."

"I saw pictures of you. Linc has an old thing that looks like a sea captain's trunk. I got into it one day thinkin' he had some sort of treasure in there or somethin'. I figured it had to be somethin' valuable, the way he kept it to himself. But when I opened it, it had shit like yearbooks and pictures of you an' him. Everything you ever gave him. Junk, really. Scraps of paper and such. Old photographs. Damn, you even made him a gum-wrapper chain that was six-foot two, exactly his height. That's *some talent, right there!" Her words dripped with sarcasm. Jenna knew how to put the needle in and hit just the right spot.*

Getting into the car and driving away, Riley wondered what Linc's life was like now, married with a baby on the way and a puppy. She had watched his Facebook page from afar. There were the typical farm photos and some of Clara with Jenna, but most were Clara with Linc. That was three years ago. Things had changed a lot in that short span of time. Jenna was gone and Linc was raising little Clara on his own. Scruffy had proven to be more faithful.

Meanwhile, Riley received a blow-by-blow description of everything about Linc from Martha, Sandy and Anita – her high school chums. About a year ago, Riley had sent a friend request to Linc's Facebook page and he accepted it. But she imagined he was way too busy for social media right about then. Heck, he probably didn't have time for any sort of social life.

Linc's mother was one of the most gracious people Riley had ever met. She made Riley feel like she was part of the family, even though they hadn't been in the same room for years. "I remember when you first came up here looking for a job on the farm." Katherine reminisced. "And, look at you now, Riley. You're a successful engineer and more beautiful than ever."

Riley blushed as Linc smiled and looked away for a moment. Riley should've been the one saying nice things and condolences to Katherine. But, as usual, Katherine Caldwell was the caretaker of everyone, leaving herself last in the equation.

"Damn, I wish I would've stopped by this past Christmas." Riley uttered. "I loved Tim. He was a father figure to me. Oh, you all know that. I remember everything he taught me here on the farm. I feel so lucky to have known such a wonderful man." She felt her words catch and couldn't stop the tears stinging her eyes.

That night Riley sat cross-legged on the floor in the parlor. She joined in with Linc and his mother and brothers talking for hours about the man they called dad. Timothy Caldwell left a legacy, three sons and a wife who loved him more than life itself. His life was lived with integrity and devotion. That night Linc made a promise to keep the farm, no matter what happened. Riley saw the raw determination in his eyes and knew this was his life's purpose. He was the spitting image of his father. Riley had never heard Linc speak with such passion and conviction.

Her cell phone buzzed. Her father's text said: *Are you coming?* She'd forgotten all about the time. It was 11:00 PM. Riley stood and grabbed her purse. "Gosh, I lost track of time. I'm sleeping at my parent's tonight." She felt Linc's eyes on her as she spoke. Sensing he wanted to walk her out to her vehicle, she turned and dashed toward the door. "See you folks in the morning."

Her parent's home was a five minute drive and the moment she touched the door handle, it opened quickly. "What took you so long?" Conor O'Neal asked with an all-knowing smile. He reminded Riley of the Cheshire cat with that grin.

"Oh, you know. Catching up with Linc and his family. I lost track of time talking with them. This whole thing is devastating for them. So unexpected."

"And..." Her mother was standing there with cold cream on her face, wearing her flannel robe, tapping her slippered foot upon the tile floor. "Hmmm....anything else to tell us? Like how was it to see Linc after all these years?"

Riley could feel herself blushing a little under her mother's watchful and way too observant eyes. "Yeah, it was good to see Linc. Real good." She averted her eyes from her mother's big brown inquisitive ones.

"And, did he hug you and say how happy he was to see you?"

"Yeah. Something like that. I spent the night having dinner and talking with his brothers and Katherine. We talked about what a great father he was – a great man."

Seemingly satisfied for now, her mother led her down the hallway to the small back bedroom. A beautiful fresh bouquet of flowers filled the room with a heady fragrance. "Roses! Oh, those smell so lovely!" Riley said breathlessly.

"Fresh from the backyard garden, for you, my dear. They bloomed early this year with the unexpected warmth. You look tired. You know where everything is. Help yourself. We all need a good night's sleep." Mom hugged Riley tightly, turned and walked toward her bedroom.

"Wait." Riley stepped into the hallway. "I didn't give dad a hug." She bounded like a school-girl toward her father and gave him a bear hug. "You're the best father anyone could have." She could feel her father laugh. He slapped her rear. "Get that skinny butt of yours into bed. Lights out! Got work to do tomorrow."

After the early morning milking and feeding, Linc was asked to put together a collage of photographs, with the help of his brothers. These would be representative of his father's life, his mother told him. Thank God, Riley showed up on the porch bright and early. She had on a flannel shirt and jeans. When she lifted her Ray Bans, her blue eyes sparkled. "Hey cowboy -- need some help?" She always made him smile when she called him *cowboy*. It was her special nickname for him from day one. He kept that name all through high school -- and when they were crowned king and queen at the prom, his banner said "cowboy" and Riley's said "queen". The photograph in the yearbook was priceless. Linc looked at it often, noting the big grin on his face as he held Riley's hand. That was when he believed he would marry her and live happily ever after. How naive he was at that time.

"Yes, I'd love some help." Linc responded. "I'm not good with photographs and arranging them on a board. In fact, I'm just about helpless right now. My brothers are doing all of the work, along with my mother. I'm so glad you're here, Riley." There. He said it. It was the truth. He was tickled pink to see Riley again, to have her all to himself. Even Scruffy was happy. He licked her face when she picked him up.

"You need coffee, right?" Linc knew how she liked it, light and sweet.

"That'd be great." Riley smiled, and Linc marveled at how beautiful she was. Her golden hair framed her face and those pale blue eyes still held the vestiges of innocence. He took her hand into his remembering the first time he did so. Her hand was the same -- delicate and feminine -- but she kept her nails short -- the sign of a working woman. Fighting an overwhelming urge to hug her again, he pulled her into the kitchen and poured a steaming mug of coffee. Hazelnut, her favorite. Damn she smelled good. She always did. It was somethin' just standing next to her like this again. Coconut. That's what she smelled like. He leaned a little closer trying not to be obvious.

"Mornin Riley. You two can tend to other things. We've got this." Katherine Caldwell lifted her head long enough to observe Riley and Linc together. "Rachel, next door offered to keep Clara tonight. We think she's too young to understand what happened to grandpa."

Riley watched as Linc leaned down to kiss his mother's cheek. "Thanks, mom. I'll stop over to give Clara a kiss and make sure she's okay."

Riley moved toward the table filled with photographs. "I can help. Just let me know what you need done."

"Here's a list. If you can get to the florist's and pick out some pretty flowers. Don't worry about the money. I gave him a credit card on the phone. I know your taste will be impeccable." Katherine Caldwell touched Riley's hand.

"Consider it done." Riley smiled. As she turned away and finished her coffee, she could hear their voices reminiscing about each photograph. Linc's brothers were talking softly, there was occasional laughter and Riley imagined plenty of tearful moments.

"Riley, walk with me for a bit." Linc opened the screen door and they moved to the porch.

His voice had a serious tone. "I spoke to the estate attorney this morning early. Apparently, my father left this place to me, exclusively...and, he left this letter." Linc's voice stopped for a moment. Riley saw the folded piece of paper in his hand. She touched his arm and steered him toward the rocking chairs and he sat next to her. His eyes locked with hers for a split second and she saw they were brimming with tears. "Dad...wrote this letter saying he wanted me to keep Clear Springs going as a dairy farm. We're the last family-owned farm in the state. He said he never wanted any of the land sold. The place is to stay within our family. He wanted my children to have it and so on..."

Riley could see that Linc was overwhelmed. She covered his big hand with hers. "That's no surprise to me. Both of your brothers have successful careers. You were special to your dad, the apple of his eye. I hate to say it, but it was obvious to me you were his favorite son."

At that remark, Linc stared her right in the eye. "You think so, huh? Oh, I don't know about that. My brothers lived a charmed life. They were in and out of trouble all the time and managed to get all of my parents' attention. It seems I remember them saying, *oh, let Linc do that. He knows how to do it.* My brothers were masters at gettin' out of chores. That's just how it was, always. I did all the work, they got all the attention and accolades. It's okay. I got used to it. I know my dad loved me. He never actually said the words, but I knew."

Your father loved this place and worked hard all of his life here. Two-hundred acres, Linc. That's an estate. And, with some tender loving care, this place can be fantastic!"

"I've got to tell you, Riley. Dad's bookkeeping skills were not exactly the best. He was taking money from one account to pay another. This farm is not self-sustaining. In other words, he's been going in the hole for a while, but he never said anything about it to us. The estate attorney told me to get a financial guy to go over this." Linc put his head into his hands, and Riley watched as he tried to get the words out. "The attorney said I'd probably have to sell some of the land off right away. That was his opinion, anyway. I *can't* do that, Riley. I promised my father. You understand."

"Yes. I do understand. And, I will help you."

Linc's head popped up. "Damn. I can't put this on you. You've got your own life in Boston with Marcus. And, I know you're busy traveling all the time as a civil engineer. Heck, you're up and down the entire Eastern seaboard. Hell, you're never home." Just then, Riley wondered how Linc knew so much about her comings and goings. Instead, she focused on telling him the good news.

"Well, I've got a little surprise for you. I'm moving back to Maine. That is, *we* are moving to Maine. We'll stay at my parent's house until we locate a piece of real estate that meets all of Marcus' criteria, you can just imagine how long *that* list will be. He just got a job here working for the government. You know, the DEP."

"Wow, that's a step up for him, huh?"

"It's a big promotion. He will be heading the office here in the state of Maine. He's not too excited about leaving the city. He's always been a city boy, being born and raised in the Big Apple. But, I'm thrilled to be coming home. And, I'll be able to help you out with the farm. I'm creative, you know, even though I'm a boring structural engineer." Riley smiled, hoping she could brighten his mood. "I'll be working with my dad. He wants me to take over his engineering firm someday. He's sixty-five, but doesn't look it."

Linc seemed to come alive with her words. There was a brightness in his eyes. She felt like she'd tossed him a life-preserver and he'd grabbed on. "Now, let's go downtown and get the flowers. I promised your mother." Riley's eyes met his and held them.

"Damn, Riley. I don't know if I can ever thank you enough." Linc muttered as she led him to her vehicle. Riley gave him a little push. "Get in. We've got a lot to do. Starting with breakfast. You haven't eaten. I can tell."

The diner they went to in high school was still there. The Palace. A little old-fashioned place where the omelets were made to perfection. Once they slid into a booth, Linc never stopped talking and Riley listened with rapt attention. She realized this guy had a lot on his mind. He was raising a three-year old on his own. He was concerned about overworking his mother, as she helped out with Clara and spent long hours as the head of nursing at the regional hospital. The farm was not only a dairy business, but there was a huge vegetable garden to be tended with a dilapidated greenhouse and roadside stand. When he wasn't taking care of that, he was haying. When he wasn't milking cows, haying, tending the gardens, and taking care of

Clara, he was at the feed store or blacksmithing. After listening to him for an hour, Riley wondered when the hell this guy *slept*. The only time he got away from the farm was when he went to Bruno's Tavern, to shoot pool and drink beer with some friends -- and that was on rare occasion.

She now had the picture of Linc's life before her – he worked himself into the ground and was incredibly lonely. He loved Clara more than anything in the world and was trying to be both mother and father to his daughter. For the first time, Riley looked at Linc through a different lens. He'd always seemed boyish and charming to her. The man sitting before her today was worn out from worry and just plain hard physical labor. His heart had been not only broken, but trampled upon. He wasn't taking care of himself. All of the pent up worry and frustration spilled out and Riley soaked it in. She knew she had to change what was happening to Linc. But how?

After picking out floral arrangements, Riley didn't let Linc see her when she slipped her credit card to the florist. "This is on me." She spoke softly to the clerk as Linc was staring out of the front window. "Yes, ma'am." The clerk responded. She'd be damned if she'd let Katherine Caldwell pay for funeral flowers. Riley knew she went overboard, but Tim Caldwell deserved the best. The church would be filled with flowers and so would the gravesite. And she even added the planting of a cherry tree from the nursery at the farm in his memory.

Linc held the door of her Subaru and she got in. She felt his eyes on her. "Thank you for doing that." He spoke softly. "You didn't have to."

"Damn, I didn't." Riley countered with a smile. "It's my contribution."

"Do me one more favor?" Linc implored her.

"Anything." She smiled. He slid into the passenger's seat. "Take me to see Clara for a few minutes. I just want to give her a kiss and check on her. I didn't tuck her into bed last night."

Riley felt her heart break just a little at this request. In his deepest grief, Linc was thinking of Clara and worried about her welfare. She wound through the tree-lined streets and stopped a few houses down from Clear Springs Farm. "Come in with me, Riley." Linc asked softly.

She followed him to Rachel's back door and saw Clara playing with dolls on the porch as Rachel was cutting out something from construction paper. The older woman looked up and smiled, "Well, hello. Come in." Clara jumped up and ran to her father. "Daddy, I missed you last night."

"I know, baby. I'm sorry. But, I'll bet you had fun with Aunty Rachel." Linc held her on his knee so the two were eye-to-eye. Clara's expressive face showed no sign of distress. Riley heard Linc as he let out a sigh of relief. "Daddy, I saw grandpa last night in my room. He smiled at me and said goodbye." There was a pause in the conversation. Then Linc hugged Clara. "Grandpa loved you, that's for sure." Linc kissed her cheek tenderly.

Rachel smiled. "It's all right. She slept really well last night." Linc let Clara slide off his knee and she went directly to Riley. "Who are you?"

Linc smiled. "That's Riley. She's my friend." Riley sat down on a chair so she could be face to face with Clara. "Hey Clara. It's nice to meet you." She couldn't help but notice the strong resemblance between Linc and Clara. "You look just like your daddy."

Clara surprised her. "You're pretty, Riley. And, I think my daddy likes you." Clara giggled. Riley noticed Linc turning a little red-faced.

He ruffled Clara's hair as he spoke. "We're off to do some errands for grandma and she might be the one picking you up. At least that's what she told me."

"No worries." Rachel said. "You folks got lots to tend to right now. Everything's fine here."

CHAPTER 5: CHAMELEON

"Hey, babe. It's me. Are you free tonight?" Marcus Reed left the voicemail message and hung up quickly. He poured himself a Johnny Walker Red into a crystal glass tumbler. For a brief moment, he wondered what Riley was doing, but decided not to call her while she was with her high school chums. Boring, red-neck country-folk. Yeah, real down home shit. He wanted no part of that. In fact, he was dreading the move to Maine.

Marcus Reed met Riley O'Neal at Cornell University in upstate New York, right after her painful break-up with Linc. He was a rebound, no doubt. He detected she was frightened and lonely at the campus. She'd never been away from home before. It was her physical beauty that caught his eye and he remembered the first time he saw her. It was during orientation. He had volunteered to be an ambassador for the new incoming freshmen. He had found it to be a great way to date new chicks. Fresh meat. The minute he laid eyes on Riley, he knew she'd be his. He also knew he had to be on his best behavior to win her over. She was a smart girl, not like most of the others he dated. This one was pretty *and* had brains. A beautiful but dangerous combination. Marcus was attracted to both of those characteristics.

Now a successful environmental attorney, it had taken him a full year before Riley finally acquiesced to marry him. After a small wedding in New York City, they moved into an apartment off campus in Ithaca, New York, while she finished her engineering degree, and he completed a lucrative paid internship with a prestigious law firm. After two years, they moved to Boston where Marcus had a worthwhile job offer working for the government's Department of Environmental Protection. It took a lot of favors and pressing of flesh, but he won the position.

In Boston, Riley landed a job as a civil engineer with a top firm. She was at the bottom rung of the ladder, thus she had to travel often. In their first year together, Marcus made a rapid ascent through the ranks of the federal bureaucracy. He was tagged with the nickname "pit bull" known for sinking his teeth into a case and winning it, no matter what. In fact, he worked many hours, nights, weekends, and holidays, in order to shutter non-compliant companies.

And when he wasn't shutting down companies, he was fighting to reduce global warming. He had become a staunch champion running educational conferences on the side, educating wealthy business owners about the benefits of alternative energy sources, and he earned a tidy sum doing so. Chinese companies paid him handsomely to peddle their solar panels and wind turbines. Even though he knew, scientifically, what he was handing out for information at his conference wasn't proven, he was more than happy to join the elite cabal of so-called experts, sucking money off the ignorant public.

There was plenty of money to be scooped up, and what made it even sweeter was the profits weren't taxable. He had set up a charitable foundation called Fight Global Climate Change, or FGCC. It had taken a couple of years, but he was making a name for himself. China alone was investing seven billion into this cause. India and Mexico utilized his sales talents, as well. If he kept going at this pace, he'd have enough to invest with his hedge-fund buddy who required a minimum of two million. Meanwhile, he focused like a laser beam on shutting down non-compliant companies and climbing the federal ladder of opportunity.

"Don't you feel terrible causing lay-offs, altering peoples' lives like this?" Riley had asked him several times.

"They're breaking the law." Was his standard answer. "I'm just bringing their violations to light. The government has strict standards in this country. We're not India or China, thank goodness." Lately, Marcus Reed had found another lucrative pastime: lobbying those in congress to vote for the Environmental Protection Agency to have much more power. He viewed this job in Maine as a stepping stone to the EPA. He didn't plan to live in Maine long. His objective was to get a high level job in Washington D.C. The DEP was only the watchdog for the EPA. The big money would be in the highest rungs of the Environmental Protection Agency, and that was his goal.

His phone buzzed with a text. The answer he was waiting for. It was Vanessa, his latest playgirl. She wanted to meet him for a cocktail and then an evening of sheer pleasure. Vanessa liked him more than the others; he knew this because she lingered with him afterwards. He always left her a big tip for her extra time. He sent a message back asking if Nicole could join them, too. Nicole was younger, nubile, not yet a pro like Vanessa. He'd only met her once, but was captivated by her youthful charms.

Vanessa was on top of her game. She answered back within minutes. *Sure, Nicole will be there, too*. Marcus smiled and gazed at his image in the mirror. Not bad for thirty-five years old. He could satisfy two women at once, and sometimes more than two. He poured another Johnny Walker and hit the crushed ice button on the fridge. As he sipped his drink, he reached into the medicine cabinet for the bottle of little blue pills. He'd need these tonight for sure. But, the pleasure would be all his.

When they returned to the farmhouse, Riley and Linc were surprised that the photo collage for the funeral had been completed. As Linc scrutinized the photos, he felt his chest constrict as he fought the urge to shed tears. His brothers managed to portray the man their father was – they captured the essence of Timothy Caldwell. Handsome, rugged, a tall imposing figure, the type of guy who filled up a room when he walked into it. Women would turn to gaze at him and men stood aside, hoping he'd talk to them. The one detail that Linc noticed and never had before, was how much his father smiled. In every photo, whether it was candid or posed, he noticed his dad's demeanor – happy.

"Great job." He turned to Grant and Madison. They were sitting on the sofa eating sandwiches and drinking beer.

"Thanks, bro." Grant nodded.

"I knew my boys would come through." Katherine Caldwell came into the room handing a beer to Linc. "I know it's the middle of the day, but I figured we'd probably all need a beer right about now." Linc handed one to Riley and shrugged his shoulders. "Yeah, a beer would be good today."

As he gazed upon his two younger brothers, Linc felt the sting of shame that he always did in their presence. It wasn't anything they did or didn't do. They always included him in their antics and treated him exactly as they always had. Linc was the older brother, the responsible one. He was the peacekeeper, Mr. Fix-it, the quiet workaholic. He couldn't put his finger on it, but Linc felt like a lesser person when he was in the same room with his brothers. He figured it was because they were so successful and happy whenever he saw them. They'd left Maine and escaped the lowly life of a dairy farmer. *They'd made it.* No longer living a small-town existence, they were wealthy, without a care in the world. And he, well -- he was still shoveling cow manure, milking the herd, feeding chickens, tending the garden and selling fruits and vegetables. It was as if time stood still for

Linc, but his brothers moved on to another realm, a much happier place.

Over time, his brothers came home less and less as their lives filled with women, friends, and busy careers. Linc envied the fact that they had escaped and made their fortunes while he whittled a piece of wood behind the barn watching the sunset, or took a ride with Ranger down to the pond. Neither of his brothers were interested in farming. In fact, they both moved quickly to college and careers, never looking back. There were times that he questioned his decision to stay. What had it gotten him? He knew the answer – the love of his dad. Even though the farmhouse was built in 1902 and needed lots of renovation, that house represented his father. The farm, itself, was insolvent, soon to go bankrupt if Linc couldn't figure out a way to save it. But, he couldn't let his father down. He'd made a promise, and he was the guy who kept his promises. A man of his word. Just like his dad.

His brothers had no idea he felt so insignificant next to them. But a pang of jealousy crept in when his mother would tell the townsfolk about his successful siblings. Just last week, he was with his mother at the grocer's when she ran into some friends who asked about Grant and Madison.

"Oh, Grant, he's my baby, only twenty-eight. But, he's working for a big technology company out in California! Can you imagine? He developed some sort of app, whatever that is. He's in development for the company, a project manager. He's a genius, they say." His mom was so enthusiastic when she said that, and Linc had heard these lines spoken many times.

"Oh, Madison, he's an aviator! Yes, he served in the Navy. He was a fighter pilot in the Iraq war. Then Southern Express hired him. He's a pilot for them out in Arizona now. He's doing very well. No babies yet, but getting married soon. Yes, he's just turned thirty."

Standing behind his mother, staring at the groceries on the shelves, Linc could feel the eyes of the folks on him. It was almost as if they wanted to say: *How's Linc doing*? But, they simply ignored him, as if he didn't matter or suffered from a low intelligence quotient. They never actually *said* it. He just felt it. Their eyes ran over his work clothes and he knew they were judging him on how he looked, the fact that he'd forgotten to shave for a few days, that he might not have had a shower before coming to the store. He needed a haircut. Snap judgements. Those were the worst kind.

His brother's question snapped him out of his reverie.

"So, what are you going to do about the farm?" Madison asked pointedly.

"Not sure just yet." Linc answered.

"You need some sort of plan." Grant added. "We've already funded dad to the tune of $25,000 each. We knew he was in trouble."

"Workin' on it." Linc avoided their eyes.

Mom came to his rescue. "Linc needs to meet with a financial guy. I'm sure we can manage. Right Linc?"

Linc nodded and took a long pull off his beer. Riley's eyes met his, serious-like.

Mom spoke again. "I plan to continue working at the Regional. As head of nursing, I've put away a good amount of money for my retirement. Five more years and I'll be done."

Her comments were just matter-of-fact, but Linc felt like the biggest loser in the world. He should be supporting his mother in her time of need. She shouldn't have to work any longer at age sixty-four. Katherine Caldwell had put her forty years into nursing and raising three sons. She should be retiring, taking it easy. Instead, she was soldiering on, taking care of him. At age thirty-two, the eldest son in the family, Linc felt he should have accomplished *something*.

His only claim to fame was marrying Jenna. No, scratch that. Getting Jenna pregnant, then marrying her. At least he produced the first grandchild. But it all went downhill and Linc blamed himself for that, too. He never gave Jenna the attention she needed. No, the attention she craved. He was always too busy with the physical demands of the farm. Milking, feeding, blacksmithing, tending to crops, working in the greenhouse, getting the hay in – working side by side with his father every minute of every day. And, he watched helplessly as Jenna pulled away from him, little by little, over the past two years, talking to some dude on Facebook. Then, she left him. Just like that. Left Clara, too. Clara still asked where momma was, but she was asking less frequently now. Probably because she knew what his answer would be. He couldn't bear to tell her the truth, so he made up a story saying Jenna had to go take care of her sick granny in another state far away. He always said she'd be back. But wondered if that was a healthy thing to do.

His mother and brothers had no idea he felt this way, nor would he want them to know. These were his deepest feelings. Hell. He wouldn't even tell Riley he felt like a big nothing. Besides, what woman wanted to listen to a grown man whine? Not many, he reckoned. Time to buck up. If anyone had to do it, it was him. But the hole in his heart was just made larger by his dad's passing. The hole was already there from Riley's leaving. But he didn't want to think about that right now. She was here. That was all that mattered. He had her for another day, maybe two, if he was lucky. And the sheer fact that she was moving back to Maine buoyed his spirit. *She's coming back.* The thought was in his pocket like a touchstone. That's what she was to him, his center, his happy place, a quintessential part of him as a human being. She always would be – she was his first love.

Gazing at Riley as she engaged in conversation with Grant and Madison, he watched her laugh and take a sip from the beer bottle. She was careful not to smudge her lipstick. She hadn't changed except to become even prettier, if that was even possible. Her blue eyes were big and expressive. Her sense of humor and wit were sharp. Although she was a tall, beautiful blonde, there was so much more to Riley O'Neal than just being attractive. It was what was in her heart that drew him to her from the very beginning. And, looking at her right now, Linc knew that none of that had changed. *He loved her, always had*. But, she was married now. He couldn't tell her how he felt. It wouldn't be right. He couldn't tell her he still loved her, but he'd lay his life down for her. Riley deserved happiness, a man that loved her, and eventually children. She always said she wanted children. That was a major thing with her. Linc wondered why she hadn't had one yet, she was twenty-eight. But, he didn't dare to ask her that particular question. Not yet, anyhow.

"I have news for you guys." Riley smiled at Grant, Madison, and Katherine. "I'm moving back to Maine next month. My husband has accepted a position here working at the DEP. And, I've decided to throw in with my dad at his engineering firm. He said he's got more than he can handle."

The room erupted with comments. Grant exclaimed, "Wonderful! Katherine Caldwell's eyes lit up. "That's great, Riley. Don't be a stranger. You come out here to the farm and visit regular-like."

"Oh, I will." Riley responded eagerly.

Linc felt everyone's eyes on him. He felt obliged to say something, anything.

"Hell, yeah....come on by. I need all the help I can get." He felt himself blushing. Shit, what the hell was he thinking? Riley here at the farm. Riley living nearby. Linc had never felt so lonely in his entire life. Then he promptly reminded himself: *Riley was married*.

"I've gotta go milk the cows." Linc excused himself and headed to the barn.

"I'm helping him." Riley announced and followed closely behind Linc.

As the screen door slammed, Grant and Madison exchanged an all-knowing look. Katherine Caldwell shook her head. "I hope this doesn't lead to anything."

Her sons laughed. "Come on, Ma. You saw the way Linc stares at her. He's still in love. Puppy love. It never ended for him."

"But, there's just one thing....she's *married*." Katherine Caldwell said. "And, Linc knows that. And, he ain't never gotten over her. He regrets ever lettin her go. Lots of regret right there, bottled up in that young man. I hope this doesn't lead to anything...complicated."

Riley followed Linc into the barn. It was karma that she'd worn a flannel shirt and jeans today. She hadn't planned on barn work, but she was dressed for the job. Riley pitched in and started carrying the raw milk to the clean room as Linc moved from udder to udder in the barn. Chris, Rob, and Sonny showed up. Chris and Rob got into their clean suits. Then Sonny fell into a rhythm with Linc on the milking machines. Passing her in the barn, Linc stopped briefly. His blue-green eyes met hers and his request was softly spoken. "You can get feedin – they're pretty hungry." Riley stepped into action placing hay, grain, and soybean meal in front of each cow. Linc had taught her long ago, a milking cow needs about one hundred pounds of feed daily. So feeding was a continual job through the day, usually morning and night. The herd fed on grass during the day.

After three hours of hard work, Riley was scraping manure into the trench and the manure conveyor was cranking the stuff out of the barn. Once that was done, she hosed down each stall to keep everything clean. She was wearing her old rubber boots, surprised that Linc had left them there all those years in the barn. Linc walked by her as he cleaned the last milking machine. "Come on, Riley. Supper's on."

"Yeah, I'll be right in." she said. "I'm almost done."

She heard the barn door close and everyone had left except her. Memories flooded her mind as she watched the water flushing each concrete stall. Good Lord. The memories were beautiful and painful all at the same time, bittersweet.

The first time Linc kissed her was in the barn right after chores were done. He'd been wrestling with her all day playfully. But, he finally caught her and pushed her gently up against the wall in the barn and covered her mouth with his. She was sixteen and he was nineteen then. They'd been workmates for a full year and knew one another well. She didn't struggle to get away. In fact, she kissed him back. Once that happened, the chase was on. Linc dogged her during chores to get a quick kiss, anywhere he could, trying not to get cat calls from the other guys. Riley flirted with him, too, making it worse....or better, depending upon your point of view.

The real romance got kicked up a notch on a warm evening in July. Linc was into haying and exhausted. Between haying and milking and feeding and the garden chores, there was little time for a farm boy to have any fun. But Linc surprised her after milking that night. He'd managed to pack a picnic lunch and, unknown to her, he had plans. He started up the old '50 Chevy pick-up. She remembered telling her parents she was having dinner that night with the Caldwell Family and there'd be fireworks later. It wasn't completely a lie, she just stretched the truth a little.

"Come on, hop in." Linc held the door of the truck and she got onto the seat. Riley noticed he was all sunburned from haying, and his blue eyes twinkled with a sense of adventure. He drove the truck hard down through freshly mown hayfields until he came to a hill. The sun was setting later that time of year. She remembered the colors as they crested that hill -- pink and gold, then once the sun slipped below the horizon, the sky remained gold for a while longer. "There." Linc gave her a look like he was sharing a secret with her. "That's where we'll have our picnic tonight." As the truck coasted down the bumpy terrain, Riley tried to figure out why she'd never seen this beautiful pond on the property. She had cruised around out there in the truck with Linc many times in the daylight but she never noticed it. But, then, maybe she'd never gone beyond this hill.

By the time they parked the truck at the edge of the pond, it was almost completely dark except for the stars and the moonlight. The headlights of the truck attracted all sorts of insects. Linc shut off the engine and took an old blanket out of the back of the pickup truck. He spread the old quilt on the ground right at the edge of the pond. Riley thought she heard coyotes howling. The moonlight lit up Linc's tall figure as he put the picnic basket on the quilt. "Mom doesn't know, but I have a six-pack in here for us."

Riley had never had alcohol. Lots of her friends drank, but she was not one to participate in adventures of that sort. But, tonight she felt a little bit reckless. Why not have a beer? Maybe it would be fun. They sat together on the blanket and had a few snacks, then drank a few beers. She was fascinated as fireflies surrounded them. There was lots of giggling and Linc skimmed a stone across the surface of the pond.

Then, both of them had to pee, and Linc closed his eyes when Riley dropped her jeans, or at least she thought he did. But when Linc took his turn, Riley pretended she wasn't looking, but she was. Everything about Linc gave her butterflies in her stomach. She'd never felt that way before and didn't know if she was nervous or attracted to him, like seriously attracted. Some nights she spent time in bed thinking about what he'd look like naked and would have the wildest dreams.

But this wasn't a dream. She was standing at the edge of the pond and it was a hot night, ripe with humidity and sexual tension. Linc tapped her shoulder. "I'm dyin' to go swimmin'; want to?" As he finished asking, he slipped off his boots, jeans and shirt, tossed his hat on the ground and dove into the pond head first, completely naked.

"Come on, Riley." Linc's voice resonated. She had never done anything this daring before. But she had consumed two beers, they were all alone, so -- what the heck? She slipped off her clothes and did a cannonball leap into the pond. When she surfaced, Linc was right next to her in the darkness. "Feels nice, doesn't it?"

As Linc put his arms around her in the cool water, Riley let out a nervous breath. "We're skinny-dipping, aren't we?" she asked.

The two climbed out together and Riley didn't expect what happened next, but recalled how pleasurable it felt. She remembered moving closer to Linc as he embraced her, naked under the stars. It was the feeling of his muscles against her chest, his hardness against her softness that took her breath away. Her soft curves molded to the contours of his lean, rugged body. She closed her eyes and remembered the smell of leather and pine tar soap, then his warm wet lips on hers. His tongue urgently probing the seam of hers, softly at first, then with more urgency. Her lips parted slightly and his tongue darted in. The kiss lasted for what seemed like an eternity. As Linc skimmed her feminine curves with his hardened hands, Riley experienced feelings stirring in her she never felt before. Kissing Linc like that brought her to the point of no return. Shivers of delight traveled through her. Her pulse was beating wildly. She was excited, turned on, and wanted Linc to touch her.

Mosquitos buzzed around their heads and suddenly she was lifted by the cradle of his arms. Linc put her into the back of the pickup truck onto an old mattress and got underneath the quilt with her. As she reclined, he moved above her, touching her breasts with his strong hands, kissing her lips, sucking her bottom lip into his mouth as if he wanted to devour her. He whispered, "Oh Riley, do you know how much I want you?"

Her hand touched his erection in the darkness. This was the first time she had ever touched a man in this way. Her body tingled from the contact. He held her hand there firm and persuasive, inviting more. She was filled with excitement and fear at the same time. "Yes. I know." She managed to whisper. "Cowboy...go easy. Okay?"

"Oh yes, I will. I won't hurt you." Linc exhaled. Riley didn't know it then, but it was Linc's first time, too.

Her mouth eagerly invited his kisses. A sense of urgency drove him. The idea of his eagerness excited her. He kissed her like he was starving and she was the last morsel of food. His tongue explored the soft fullness of her lips. His hands explored every plane of her body. His lips devoured her neck, her breasts, and she closed her eyes and enjoyed the wild sensation cascading through her body as he suckled her erect nipples. Pure pleasure. It felt as if he had unlocked her heart and soul.

But when his finger slid between her legs, she let out a gasp. It felt good. Whatever he was doing felt so damned good. He guided her hand to his pleasure spot and showed her how to move it. She heard him groan with delight and wanted to please him more. Linc stopped for a moment and his eyes searched hers. "You're a virgin, aren't you?" Riley closed her eyes. "Yes."

He inhaled sharply and let his breath out. "Damn, I want you, Riley. But, it's got to be a gradual thing. I don't want to hurt you, babe." His hardness was straining and the more she touched him, the closer he was getting to doing something explosive. Exactly what that would be like, she wasn't sure. She'd only heard about it from girlfriends, seen it in movies, or read about it in a book. She knew about the anatomy of a man and how things worked. She'd done plenty of research, just no field work. She was definitely out in a field right now in the middle of the biggest experiment of her young life. Fiery currents raced through her. She wanted him.

In exasperation, Linc put his body atop hers and allowed his stiffness to move between her legs, against her pleasure spot in a beautiful soft rhythm that brought them both to heaven. She gasped and he groaned as they rode a wave of ecstasy together.

Linc covered her with the blanket and kissed her again. They kissed a lot that night. He exploded more than once rubbing against her like that and she received pleasure from it, too. Riley felt his lips on her ear. "I love you, Riley. I want to marry you."

A noise in the barn startled her from the erotic memory of her first time with Linc. She turned off the hose and saw Linc standing in the doorway. "You okay?" he asked.

"Yes." She smiled and blushed.

"What were you thinkin about just then?" Linc probed.

"Oh, nothing....much." Riley turned away.

"Aw, come on. You were thinkin' of somethin – I know you, Riley."

"I was just thinking of you and me, and that mattress in the back of that old truck."

His eyes narrowed and his lips curled into a cute little grin. "Really? You think about that stuff, too?"

"Why?" she rolled the hose up.

"Because I think of it constantly. There isn't a day goes by that I don't think about that first night with you. The first time we kissed at the pond. The first time...."

"We gotta go inside, cowboy. Seriously. I'm hungry." Riley knew she'd better nip this conversation in the bud. It had already gone way too far.

CHAPTER 8: A REAL GOOD MAN

Riley expected Timothy Caldwell's funeral to be well attended, but never did she expect the whole town to turn out. The Methodist church was overflowing. People stood on the lawn in the front. Friends and neighbors, guys who went to school with Tim Caldwell, people he did favors for, they were all there on a sunny day in May. The type of day you'd expect everyone to be mowing their lawns or cooking on the barbeque. This was Sunday, after all. The whole service that morning had been about helping your neighbor and loving one another. Timothy Caldwell's life personified that and so much more.

Driving to the cemetery behind the hearse made Riley feel like she was in some sort of parade. The funeral had its teary moments, but for the most part it was an uplifting experience. Riley sat with her parents in the church, but they got separated as the cars wound their way through the flowering trees to the grave site. Riley wondered how Linc was taking this. Her biggest concern was the depression she'd witnessed in him. He had hit a low point.

Before getting out of her car, her good friend, Martha approached. "Quite a crowd."

"Yes." Riley stood next to her as the enormous throng of people gathered around the burial plot. "He was well-loved, that's for sure."

Martha Blakely was a high school friend who now had a thriving psychotherapy business in town. Riley enjoyed her company immensely. Martha was like hanging out with Buddha. *No, better.* Her sense of humor was sharp and sarcastic. She could always make Riley laugh. Martha had this magical calming effect on Riley, no matter what was on fire at the moment in her life -- Martha had a way of talking her through it.

"You okay?" Martha asked as they strolled toward the mass of people.

"Yeah. I'm good." Riley shot her a side-long glance, but made eye contact. She looked around as the cars kept coming and parking. "I don't think I even *know* this many people."

Riley spotted Linc standing with his family. His eyes were roaming over the crowd as if searching for someone in particular. Sandy, Martha, Riley and another girlfriend, Anita, stood opposite the Caldwell Family, on the other side of the grave. Riley realized she had on black dress slacks and a while sleeveless top. She could've sworn she threw a black cardigan into her bag when she packed it, but now she imagined she stood out like a sore thumb. She was the only dolt wearing a white sleeveless top in this whole crowd. When she glanced up, Linc's eyes were fixed upon her.

Damn, her cowboy looked good in a suit. He'd shaved, too. He had on a Navy blue blazer, with matching pants, and a white shirt and red tie. He removed his ever-present white cowboy hat and was holding it by the brim with his hands in front of him. His greenish-blue eyes were squinting in the sunlight, but he was staring directly at Riley's face, she could feel the intensity of his gaze as the sunlight glistened on his dirty-blonde hair.

Both simultaneously bowed their heads in prayer as the Methodist minister said a few words. When his head came up, Linc's eyes met Riley's again and he stayed focused on her until the graveside service ended. Slowly, people moved to their vehicles and filed one-by-one out of the cemetery in the direction of Clear Springs Farm.

Riley followed the long line of vehicles. A whole parking lot was created in the field adjacent to the old farmhouse. Outdoors in the side yard, Katherine Caldwell stood with a flock of neighbors who'd laid out a banquet feast. The canopy of big elms and maples shaded the setting. Riley noticed a pile of folding chairs had been delivered by the church. She began to open them one at a time and found Linc right next to her, pulling chairs out of the pile.

"Thank you." He said in a measured tone.

"For what?" Riley hit him with her elbow.

"You know." Linc said softly. "For being *you*. For showing up. For making me feel so damned happy all of a sudden. I've been crying. I'll admit that. But, when you said you'd be moving back here, well, it was like someone turned on a light. Everything felt different."

Riley stood facing him and Linc awkwardly touched her hand. "I feel blessed." He whispered.

She was moved by his words. But wondered if she just filled a void at the moment, the big gaping hole that Jenna had left. Riley felt the urge to change the subject. She didn't want her cowboy feeling indebted to her. "Let's get something to eat."

Linc followed her to the tables filled with every salad imaginable, along with meatballs, pot roast, and several freshly roasted chickens. Mrs. Evans, a neighborly helper, filled their plates and they moved to some chairs underneath an old elm tree. Riley felt her girlfriends watching from afar. She imagined the townspeople were having a heyday while they observed her sitting with Linc alone eating lunch. But she quickly forgot about the townspeople or her friends. She was wrapped up in listening to Linc and how much he wanted to keep the farm, improve it, even. Whenever he talked about the farm, he seemed upbeat, hopeful and his blue-green eyes sparkled.

"Hey. I've got an idea." Riley spoke when Linc seemed all talked out.

"What?"

"You know that appointment you have with the financial guy?"

"Yeah, that's tomorrow at 9:00 AM." Linc reiterated.

"Would you mind if I went with you to that appointment?"

"Would I mind? Hell, no! I'd love for you to come. You're so smart, Riley. You have all this college learnin and -- well, I've got none of that. I'm just a simple country boy, with the emphasis on simple." Linc exhaled.

"Don't say things like that." Riley chastised him.

"It's true, you know it is. I don't know the first thing about financial stuff. Hell, I don't even keep my checking account straight most of the time."

"Get rid of your debit card." Riley said flatly.

"What, what?" Linc laughed a little.

"I'm serious. If you want control of your checking account, cancel your debit card."

"Gee, Riley, I live with that debit card in my pocket. I use it for everything, just about." Linc smiled.

"I'm just sayin'....get rid of it. And, balance your checkbook. You can do it right on-line."

"Well, I'll be damned. How about showin me that." Linc stood.

"Okay, inside, to your computer. I hope you've got good security software." Riley found herself in business-mode.

After an hour on Linc's computer, Riley had updated his software, removed programs, installed new banking security, and balanced his checking account. Yes, he was close to being in the red. She also cancelled his debit card.

"There. No more debit card. From now on you'll do everything in cash and keep every receipt....right here in this shoebox." Riley felt a little bit like a school teacher just then. Even so, she could see Linc felt like a weight had been lifted from his shoulders. She even set up a way for his savings account to be tapped if he ran short in the checking. Problem was, he had very little in his savings account right now, too. "You're a little low on cash right now, cowboy."

"Yeah, I know. The dairy deposit will go in automatically in a day or two. That'll put me in the black for a short time. Meanwhile, I need to find a way to make more money." Linc swallowed hard, obviously more than a little embarrassed to have Riley see how badly in the hole he really was.

As Linc stood up, he moved behind her in the office chair. Riley's hair was pinned into a loose pile on top of her head. She felt the barrette holding it all together slip out, and her blonde hair tumbled down. "I like it better like this..." Linc murmured.

Riley stood quickly and took the barrette out of his hand. "I'm a mess, Linc."

"No, you're not." He responded. "I think you're more beautiful now than you ever were."

Katherine Caldwell stuck her head around the door. "Hey, guys – there are relatives who've traveled from far away. You coming?"

"Yup." Linc answered. "I'll bring super-woman here with me, too."

Riley smirked and put the barrette back into her hair. Within minutes, Linc was swallowed up by the crowd, and Riley strolled toward her friends hanging next to the beverage table.

"Lemonade?" Martha smiled holding a glass full of ice and a lovely lemon concoction.

"Yes!" Riley sighed.

"Okay, what were you two talking about?" Sandy asked pointedly.

"Yes. We saw you go into the house with Linc." Anita added.

Riley felt like she was in an interrogation room for a moment. Three pairs of eyes were staring at her, waiting for some sort of answer.

"I was helping Linc with some stuff on his computer. That's all." Riley uttered with all the dignity she could muster.

"And..." Sandy prodded her. "There's got to be more to it than just *that*..."

"I'm going to the financial appointment tomorrow morning with Linc. I think it's just a downright friendly thing to do. He's sort of lost in the details, if you know what I mean." Riley offered.

"Yeah, right." Anita whistled. "I think he's lost all right, but in something else." Riley detected a hint of jealousy or sarcasm in Anita's comment. A stunning red-head, Anita was an X-ray technician at a local orthopedic clinic. She spent a lot of time on dating websites trying to find the right man, and hadn't been successful as of yet.

"All right, ladies. I get your drift. I'm not getting too cozy with Linc. He's mourning the death of his father right now. Come on. Have some sympathy for the guy. He's thrilled that I'm going to this appointment with him. He needs my friendship right now." Riley didn't know if she was trying to convince her friends or herself, but she was doing a great job of justifying everything she did with Linc. It was nothing, really. Helping a friend in need like this. She'd do it for Sandy, Martha, or Anita. *Why shouldn't she do it for her cowboy?*

CHAPTER 9: LOVE, THE DEEPEST KIND

In Riley's opinion, Marcus didn't seem affected by her absence. She phoned him Sunday night to let him know she'd be staying one more day. As it turned out, Marcus had an out-of-town trip planned for Monday, so he'd be gone anyway. He ended the call saying he would see her on Monday night or Tuesday at the latest.

As Riley clicked off, she felt as if a weight had been lifted from her. She'd imagined Marcus was going to throw a fit. But, he hadn't. Business prevailed and he was off doing whatever it was he had to do as an environmental attorney. Probably shutting down someone's family business or hurling a grandmother off a mountaintop.

She paused for a moment and looked at her image in the vanity mirror. The job she did, as an engineer, was building things, creating magnificent projects that benefited mankind -- or so she thought. But as much as Riley was a creator, Marcus was a destroyer. In fact, what Marcus did sometimes made her wonder how he could sleep at night. It didn't affect him one bit, however. A few times, they'd had death threats because of a case he'd won. The losing side lost *everything.* Everything they'd worked their whole lives for. One guy even had a heart attack and died. She tried to put herself in her husband's shoes on more than one occasion, but couldn't imagine it. He was so very different than her. Sometimes she marveled at the fact that they were even married. Who was it that said opposites attract?

In fact, it had been many days, maybe weeks, since they'd gone to dinner together or even slept in the same bed. With her traveling schedule and his busy caseload, they rarely spent time together at all. In fact, the more Riley thought about it, the more she realized they lived more like roommates. She couldn't remember the last time Marcus held her hand or kissed her, let alone made love. Many months had slipped by and she felt like she was dying a little bit inside with each passing day.

In the quiet of her high school bedroom in front of the vanity, she stared at herself. She was twenty-eight years old and wanted a baby. But that wasn't in the cards for Marcus. The last time she'd brought the subject up, you'd think the world had ended. He was adamant that he didn't want children, *period*. End of discussion. Yeah. Easy for him to say. Riley felt something missing from her life. It wasn't just the hand-holding and dinners together, it was the feeling of being loved. Completely loved. Worshipped. Adored. Wanted. Desired. Call it what you would, but every ounce of romance had disintegrated from her relationship with her handsome husband. And, lately her interactions with him weren't even friendly. He bristled at her touch and moved away from her in bed at night. Almost as if he was closing himself off intentionally. But why?

She ran the brush through her hair. Tomorrow morning she would wear her hair loose. Linc made a big deal about that. Glancing at herself in the mirror, she held her hair up, then let it fall down. Her cowboy was right, she looked better with it down, more youthful. She rummaged through her canvas sack to find something to wear. Damn, all she had was that flannel shirt and jeans and the dress slacks she had on.

"What're you doing?" Her mother was standing in the doorway. "Did you lose something?"

"Yes. My sanity." Riley laughed. "I could've sworn I packed more than this. I'm looking for something to wear to that financial meeting tomorrow morning. I just have this flannel shirt and jeans. And, I'd raid your closet, but you're two sizes smaller than me, and petite to boot."

"What about the pants you have on now?" Mom asked wide-eyed. "You look great in those."

"Oh, gosh, they're dirty from wearing them for two days. They're dry clean only. Hey, there's a shop I used to go to, Boho or something like that, it had a French sound." Riley tilted her head.

"Yes. That's still there. I think they're open on Sundays during tourist season. I'll call." Mom offered. *She was such a wonderful mother.*

Just then, the doorbell rang. Mom ushered Sandy to Riley's bedroom and let her know. "They're open."

Sandy asked, "Who's open? Where are we going?"

"Boho." Riley said as she gathered her purse and car keys. "A quick shopping trip."

Sandy smiled. "Let's go. I love that place, too. And, I've got some money to burn."

Riley spent late Sunday afternoon shopping with Sandy, then met Martha and Anita at La Belle Restaurant. Sandy owned La Belle, a tiny little place by the sea. Surf and turf, and the most delicious lobster pie anyone could imagine. And, the drinks concocted by this place were world-renown. There were only fifteen tables and tonight the place was humming. Tourist season was in full swing.

Anita found a corner table for the four of them. "Okay, I want to see what you girls bought today. Give us the goods."

Sandy and Riley were both laden with bags. First Sandy, then Riley, went through each garment, explaining why they bought it and what they'd wear it with. A mini fashion show took place in the corner of La Belle, while the girls ordered drinks called the Wham-Bam and the Cocky Rooster. "Where the hell do you come up with these names?" Riley laughed as she sipped a coconut, pineapple, and rum mixture.

"Don't ask." Sandy winked. The bartender, Santos, a handsome dark-haired gentleman looked away, but Riley knew he was eves dropping on their conversation and getting a kick out of their comments.

Riley's back was to the door, but she knew someone special walked in the moment Sandy's eyes rose above her head. Anita and Martha were staring too, with their mouths slack-jawed, gaping. As Riley turned around, she saw Linc. He pulled up a chair and turned it backwards, straddled it and sat next to Riley.

"Hey, Riley." She felt his arm draped across the back of her chair.

"Hey, cowboy." Riley said, wondering why he was there. Scruffy was at her feet.

"Saw your fancy Subaru outside. I was ridin' by in the truck with Scruffy, bringin the chairs back to the church. I just wanted to thank you -- all of you -- for comin to my dad's funeral this morning." Linc's demeanor was not one of gloom, but genuine gratitude. "I got a reprieve from milking tonight. My brothers, Grant and Madison, and Chris and Rob are going to pitch in. Damn. I don't get too many breaks like this. Gotta take 'em when you can get 'em." He placed his hat on the table and asked, "What are you girls drinkin?"

Anita was already a little bit inebriated, "I've got a cocky somethin'..."

Everyone at the table burst into laughter. Oh God, Riley thought. We must look like a group of lushes, sucking down drinks like this on a Sunday, no less, and after a funeral.

"Well, I think I'll have a beer..." Linc waved to Santos. A cold Sam Adams was placed in front of Linc with a frosted glass. "Thank you, sir."

After a few sips of beer and some raucous laughter about something or other, Linc tapped Riley on the shoulder. "What's in the bags?"

Riley was feeling a little light-headed. "Nothing special. Just some clothes. I didn't pack much."

"Aw, heck. I'd have loaned you my britches." Then, in an exaggerated fashion, he scrutinized her physique up and down and said, "Nah, that wouldn't work. I'm a helluva lot bigger 'n you are. And, your shape, it's....."

All of a sudden there was silence at the table. Riley was in the mood to poke Linc. "My shape is what...Linc?"

"Well, your shape is *womanly*....oh damn. I'm making a horse's ass of myself here. You know what I mean."

The fact that Riley got Linc to blush made the whole table laugh, and the comments came fast and furious.

"You mean she has a nice ass." Sandy chimed in.

"Or, the figure of a dancer." Anita blurted.

"She's built like a brick shit house." Martha almost choked on that one.

The smile on Linc's face said it all. "Yes, yes, and yes. She is all of that, and more."

Riley felt her face reddening. And she began to regret toying with Linc. She'd forgotten how he could give as good as he could get.

Linc changed the subject. "Is that old juke box still in here?"

"Yes, it is." Sandy smiled. "Over there on the wall."

"I'm right in the mood for some music..." Linc stood up and walked over to the juke. Riley allowed her eyes to follow his fine rear in those Wrangler jeans.

She watched as he dropped in quarters and made a selection. By the time he got back to the table, Linc scooped Riley out of her seat and started swaying with her in his arms on the wooden floor of the restaurant. "I love this song." He spoke softly into Riley's ear. It felt so natural to fold her body into Linc's. He pulled her closer and her face rested against his soft flannel shirt. His jeans rubbing against her were worn to the point of fraying. His scent delighted her. She closed her eyes and listened to the words of the song... *Miss Me Baby by Chris Cagle*--

Sandy danced with Martha. Santos came from behind the bar and danced with Anita. The song was soulful and slow, and immediately filled Riley with emotion. Stuff she had bottled up for a long time was beginning to surface. Being in Linc's arms, listening to the words of the song, she could barely breathe. Her face was against his chest and he was singing the words. Tears were stinging her eyes as she closed them.

An incredible sadness swept over her as the song ended. Linc sat next to her at the table for a while longer, laughing and talking, cracking wise with the girls. He nursed that one beer for the whole time. Riley realized he didn't come there for the beer; he came for the company. After an hour or so, there was a lull in the conversation.

Linc took his hat and put it on. "I need to go check on Clara. She's with Rachel for tonight. You ladies have fun." Scruffy followed him out to the old pick-up truck and Riley watched through the plate glass window as the little terrier hopped inside with Linc. He pulled away slowly without looking back.

"What the hell was *that* all about?" Anita asked, now tipsy. "Miss me, Baby?"

"He's still in love with her." Martha hiccupped. *Thank you so much, Riley thought.*

"He's madly in love with her, always has been." Sandy added.

"Oh gosh. It was only a song and a beer. You guys are getting too mushy for me." But, in reality, she knew her friends were perceptive – and dead on. In fact, they could read Linc like a book. Not to mention their psychic powers with *her*. The way they were staring at her right then, she imagined they were reading each thought as it appeared in her brain. "Come on, guys. I've got to go to bed. Let's walk home. Tell Santos I'm leaving my vehicle in the parking lot overnight." Riley collected her bags and Sandy followed. *Thank God we live in a small town, Riley thought. We're all liquored up and feeling no pain. Couldn't drive.*

As the girls stepped into the parking lot, darkness had fallen. The 1950 Chevy was there in the corner and the lights came on. Riley couldn't believe her eyes. Linc pulled up beside her. "Any of you ladies need a ride home? I can fit two in front here and two in the back."

Sandy said thanks, but she was already home. She lived above La Belle. Anita lived two blocks away and Martha lived on the same street. They said they wanted to walk, it was such a beautiful night. That left Riley, standing there feeling no pain, clutching a bunch of shopping bags to her chest. Linc examined her with his eyes. "How many have you had tonight, missy?"

"Who, me?" Riley smiled. "Two, I think. But, I'm not used to rum." As a gentleman would, he hopped out of the truck and took her bags and offered his arm for support. "I think I'm driving you home tonight. How about that?"

Riley was exhausted and she knew Linc must be, too. He waved at the girls as he drove out of the parking lot toward her parents' house. "I must look like an idiot." Riley mumbled.

"Nah. You look like a mess all right. A beautiful mess." Linc kept glancing at her but kept his eyes on the road. When he stopped, he ran to her side of the truck, took her bags -- and then slipped his arm snugly around her. "Yes, you are a beautiful mess tonight. I wish I was takin you home with me, but that ain't gonna happen. Damn, Riley. Your dad's waitin at the door. Just like the old days."

"Thanks, Linc." Conor O'Neal sounded relieved. "I figured she was gabbing with her friends somewhere. She never drinks. This just isn't like her."

"Oh, I know." Linc replied as he helped Riley up three steps to her father's arm. "She's a right sensible girl. Always. I think she just needed a little fun. Today was hard on her, too.

Heck, after today, we should all examine our lives and live in the moment, 'cause that's all we really have."

As Linc got into his truck, he tipped his hat to Conor O'Neal and for a moment the elder man wondered what Riley might be getting herself into. It was beyond obvious to him that Linc cared for his daughter. Not just in a physical sense, but a deep caring, like that of a good friend – a lifelong friend who'd do anything for her, no matter what. Linc loved her.

For some reason, this reminded him of the night Linc asked him if he could meet with him to talk about Riley. It was a poignant memory that only surfaced once in a while. It was nine years ago or more, Linc had called him at work. He needed to meet with him alone -- it was important. The first thought that flashed through Conor O'Neal's mind was, oh God she's pregnant. But when he met Linc at Bruno's Tavern, he seemed nervous and waved him to a corner table. He spilled his guts right there. "I'll get these words out right away because I can't hold 'em in any longer." Linc had said. "I want permission to ask for Riley's hand in marriage."

Conor remembered looking at Linc, wondering if young men even did these things any longer. But here was one young man who did, and he was sitting in front of him sweating bullets. Linc was a throwback, a Renaissance man, a true gentleman. Conor O'Neal knew the love was strong between the two, but Riley was young, only eighteen. And, Linc was only twenty-one at the time. He also knew if love was strong enough, even at this tender age, it could weather anything. Proof of that was his own marriage to Erin. Conor nodded his head, and gave his permission. He listened as Linc told him about his plans to take Riley to dinner and surprise her with the ring. It was a ring she had favored in the window of Pratt's Jewelry Store on Main Street. Five thousand dollars' worth of ring. Way out of Linc's price range, but then Linc had told him that Riley was way out of his league. She deserved that ring, or one better. There wasn't anything he wouldn't do for Riley. Every father wanted to hear those words.

The next day they were officially engaged. Riley was beaming, showing off the ring to all of her friends. There was an engagement announcement in the local newspaper. The other guys in town knew she was off the market, so to speak, according to Linc. But he never saw Tom Simpson coming. How could he? It was two weeks before Riley was to move to Ithaca, New York, for college. Tom met up with Riley at a party. There was beer drinking that night, too. Somehow, Tom managed to get Riley alone. Her father knew Tom sweet-talked her and maybe stole a kiss. But that was the extent of it. He figured it was best not to say a word to Linc.

Riley was young, only eighteen. It could've been a passing fancy or just friendship. When he asked her about it, Riley explained she had brushed Tom off. And, Riley had never lied to him about things like that. Funny thing was, a few days later, Tom drove Riley to dinner one night in-town to a fancy pub. Her friends had set up a surprise farewell party before she left for New York for college. Conor O'Neal knew very little about Tom Simpson or why Riley even let him drive her that night. But, later found out Riley's girlfriends asked Tom to bring her there to be her designated driver. And Tom was only doing as he was told. They didn't ask Linc because they were afraid he'd spill the beans to Riley. Plus, he was too busy with chores on the farm. He generally didn't finish up until 8:00 PM some nights. So, this thing was set into motion. Thinking back on it -- that was a dark time. Linc took it hard. He lost it.

As Conor watched Linc drive away tonight, all calm, cool, and collected, he remembered how he brutally attacked Tom, putting him in the hospital for a week. Then came the long, dark depression that followed Riley's leaving him. The worst night was when she gave him back the diamond ring. Linc's parents called and said their son was suicidal. He had spoken of killing himself if he couldn't have Riley. He didn't want to live without her. Tim and Katherine Caldwell begged Riley to stay engaged to Linc, not to do this to him.

A week later, Riley was in Ithaca and Linc Caldwell spent a year trying to get her back. He called her so much she had her

phone number changed. Then, he drove to Ithaca several times.
Riley refused to see him. He got on Facebook and stayed in
touch with all of her friends. Martha, Sandy, and Anita all
attempted to fill the void left by Riley, but didn't quite make it.
Finally, after two years, Linc gave up and practically became a
hermit. He never left the farm, except to go to the feed store.
He never dated other women, although he had plenty who were
interested in him. His parents were so worried, they locked up
all the firearms and kept the key from Linc. He spent a lot of
time alone, riding Ranger down to the pond and sitting there for
hours alone. The only person he spoke to was Sonny.

That was when Linc started drinking, just beer at first.
Then hard stuff. A pretty little waitress by the name of Jenna at
Bruno's caught his eye. Or, he caught her eye. Conor wasn't
sure how it happened, but the two ended up together, pregnant
and married in a matter of months. Two years after the birth of
their baby girl, Jenna walked out on Linc. Left her baby girl, too.
Linc took it hard. His mom pitched in. Word had it around town
that Linc was an excellent father. He poured himself into little
Clara. It was as if all of the love he had stored up for Riley was
now bestowed upon her. He seemed to be doing all right the last
year or so.

And now this. Riley was married and coming back to
Maine. There was no question in his mind that Lincoln Caldwell
was still in love with his daughter.

******

That night, lying in bed, Riley couldn't get that song out of
her mind -- *Miss Me, Baby*. Nor could she stop thinking of her
cowboy. Oh God. It was all coming back to her. There was the
bitter and the sweet. Thus far, she'd only thought about the
sweet. In bed that night she remembered the bitter, horrible
pain of leaving her cowboy -- the most agonizing moment of her
life. Even though she closed her eyes and tossed and turned,

she could still see Linc's face twisted with pain, crying. Even though it was ten long years ago, she could remember the details like it was yesterday.

"Don't turn on that light." *He'd said in a strange voice when he came to her house a week before she was to depart for New York.*

"Why? What's wrong, Linc?" She had asked him, like an idiot.

He'd been crying. He found out about the guy that took her to dinner at a pub. Riley had been trying to distance herself from Linc, knowing that going to upstate New York for four years would unravel their relationship. It would be impossible to see him with his work schedule and her class schedule. She didn't have the backbone to sit him down and tell him they'd have to separate. But she felt it coming, the parting, and dreaded it. If their bond was to be broken, she knew it would be painful for both of them. She wanted it to end quickly, sort of like ripping a Band-Aid off. The faster you did it, the least amount of pain -- or so it seemed. She had to go away to college, even though her heart was breaking, too. She was still wearing the engagement ring Linc had given her.

"I want you to stay here; don't leave." Linc choked out the words in the darkness on her parent's screened porch. "Don't do this, Riley. Don't go to New York. I can't....I can't live without you. I love you."

"Stop this, Linc." she answered sternly, hoping she could snap him out of whatever was happening to him. She expected him to step off the porch and leave in a huff.

Surprisingly, he embraced her. She felt his chest rising and falling. He was sobbing uncontrollably. It was as if she had plunged a knife into him and he was dying right there in her arms. Riley cried, too. She didn't know what else to do. She felt she was on a freight train with no brakes and it was about to careen off the tracks.

"Don't go out with any other guys." Linc said desperately.

"I've got to go away to college, cowboy. I'm going to miss you so much. I've got to get used to being without you. I've got to get used to being with other people. I'm too dependent on you."

"No." he implored. "No, please, I'm begging you."

She stood there for two hours consoling him. Crying, off and on. Feeling like she was losing her best friend. Wanting to die herself. Wishing she hadn't gotten a scholarship and she could become a hairdresser in town and live with Linc happily ever after. But that wasn't the situation.

He walked off that porch a changed man in the dark and drove away. He refused to take the diamond ring with him. She later sent it special delivery and his parents signed for it. Riley couldn't sleep that night. She didn't go to the farm.

She was shopping for college stuff and ran into Tom, or he ran into her, conveniently. She figured he was probably following her. Tom talked her into going to the pub that night. This time Tom wanted to pick her up and drive her there. He was insistent. Riley gave in.

There was a surprise farewell party for Riley at the pub that night. Later, she realized that's why Tom insisted on driving her there. He was her designated driver. That night at the pub a large group of friends had gathered to say goodbye to Riley. There was a lot of beer drinking going on. As she emerged from the brick building, Tom was already at his car. He was opening the passenger side door for her. As he did so, someone leapt out of the car behind his at the curb. The attack was swift and violent. The aggressor was big and tall and he punched and kicked Tom until he was unconscious. Riley crouched in the stairwell filled with fear as she watched Tom's head get crushed -- the car door was being slammed against him with great force. When the attacker turned, she caught a glimpse of his face. It was Linc. She froze on the spot and watched as his car sped away.

Tom's jaw was broken and his eye socket, too. He had internal injuries and a serious concussion. Someone called an ambulance. One of Riley's friends brought her home. Tom recognized his attacker and pressed charges against Linc. It got very ugly.

Linc's parents called Riley, begging her to talk with him. He was out on bail, but would be prosecuted for the incident. His parents had gotten him an attorney. But Linc had isolated himself. He wasn't talking to anyone, just working from sun-up to sun-down. Riley's parents got involved. They asked her why she saw another guy. How could she hurt Linc this way? A week later, Riley was in upstate New York on the campus of Cornell. Even though she was far away, her cowboy was still in her mind, in her heart, every waking moment and sometimes in her dreams.

She half-justified her leaving -- telling herself that Linc would be unhappy being tied to someone for four long years dedicated to getting an engineering degree at Cornell. Sure, she could go home on holidays and school vacations, but that wouldn't be enough to keep them together. Linc would be lonely and she would be lonely. She kept telling herself it was inevitable, but was it – really? She would never know the answer to that. That's what really got her. She second-guessed what she did a thousand times. She could never forgive herself and wondered how Linc forgave her. He was a good man. A real good man, just like his father.

Her girlfriends kept in touch with her through Facebook giving her updates daily on Linc. It wasn't good. Assault and battery with intent to harm. The attorney was a good one and pled the charge down to aggravated assault. Linc was to serve three years' probation. Riley could tell from her girlfriends' descriptions of him, Linc was depressed, angry, frustrated, hurt. Riley would often cry herself to sleep. She was the cause of all of this pain. All because she won a scholarship and left for college, she ripped Linc's world apart. He was her cowboy and now he was miserable, all because of her. She wanted nothing more than to run home to him, fold into his arms, and tell him *everything would be all right. But, inside she knew their parting changed everything, in her life as well as his.*

CHAPTER 10: RAW AMBITION

A throbbing headache woke Marcus Reed in his hotel room at the Ritz-Carleton in New York, the city of his birth. He stumbled to the bathroom and brushed his teeth. The meeting was at 9:00 AM and he hadn't even taken his shower yet. His grooming was usually methodical and slow, but today he had to hurry. The hangover from the night before didn't help. It really threw him off his game. He shaved and used eye drops to reduce the redness in his eyes. The new Brooks Brothers suit hung neatly on the valet before him. This meeting was critical. He was taking down a large farming business in Massachusetts, the biggest family farm in the state. They had broken a few regulations, but through some undercover work he also discovered the family hadn't been disclosing all of their revenue. Thanks to an inside helper at the IRS, Marcus had them audited. They had a pony ride for children and didn't report the income.

If he won this court case, it would enhance his notoriety in legal circles. He very much wanted a big win. Meetings like the one this morning were critical to strategically plan his attack. The IRS was a powerful weapon in his arsenal. And, he had others, too, in government positions everywhere. They all owed him favors. At the meeting today, he had legal experts who would advise him, for a substantial fee.

Vanessa was gone, but Nicole stayed with him last night. She had fallen asleep in a drunken stupor after hours of uninhibited sex.

He picked up the phone and ordered room service, pronto.

Nicole was still asleep in the king sized bed. Her blonde hair covered her face. Just like Riley. But she was much younger than Riley, and very beautiful – and she did things with him that Riley would never do. Submissive things, kinky fun things, with Vanessa and handcuffs. His mind drifted back to the drunken orgy last night with the two girls. He didn't want to wake Nicole, but he was hoping she could stay with him tonight. Already, just watching her sleep, he was getting excited again.

Maybe it was the aftereffect of the Viagra. Or, maybe he just wanted her again. He showered and dressed quickly. No time to spare.

Nicole's eyes opened and she still looked a little drunk. "Where are you goin'?"

"To a meeting." He caressed her face with his hand. "I'll be back in a while. Can you stay tonight?"

"I don't know. I'll have to look at my schedule. Where's Vanessa?" Nicole mumbled as if her head hurt.

"She's gone. Listen, Nicole – I just want *you* tonight – not Vanessa. Okay?" He lifted her chin slightly as he eyed her lovely features. She was young, but if she kept drinking like this, her physical beauty would be gone in a few years. Her eyes closed again.

"I don't know. I'll have to talk with Vanessa." She whimpered.

Room service came and Marcus ate a few bites of breakfast. "I'll take the coffee with me." He kissed Nicole on the cheek. "Eat. You need something. You're too thin. I'll be back later. He paused in the doorway before leaving. "Nicole, stay tonight. I'll pay you double."

The door closed and Marcus was gone. Nicole called Vanessa. "He wants me to stay tonight again. But not you. Ah, you are free."

"He's an ass." Vanessa retorted. "I'm busy with appointments all day and night anyway."

"Who's on your agenda?" Nicole asked.

"I've got that guy on the 12th floor in the Amherst Building. You know, he's a regular. Then three others in a row. Last one is Andrew, late tonight."

"Do you think I should stay with Marcus tonight?" Nicole asked innocently.

"Only if he agrees to pay you more – a lot more. He's sweet on you. Charge him plenty." Vanessa advised.

"I'll think about it." Nicole murmured weakly. She pulled on her clothes, finished the breakfast left on the tray, and was gone.

*****

Marcus was not in top form that morning. He left his notes in his briefcase which he left in the hotel room. He tried to call Vanessa to bring it to him, but she had left the building. Nicole did not answer. Damn. He'd have to wing it. He had some notes on his iPhone, so he put that in front of him to use for an outline.

Six suits filed into the conference room and the door closed. "Are you ready, Mr. Reed?"

"Yes." Marcus could feel the sweat trickling from his forehead down to his neck. The collar of his freshly starched shirt felt too tight. He smiled and waited for each person to be seated. One of the lawyers was a woman, her hair was wound into a French twist. She was scrutinizing him too closely. She sat next to Marcus at the conference room table. Marcus hoped she didn't smell the booze on his breath and prayed he used enough mouthwash to mask the odor.

As soon as his presentation was finished, each attorney in the room gave him their opinion. One of the men seated at the table was a retired judge. These people carried a lot of weight in the legal arena. Each one methodically shot holes in his case. His legal reasons to shut down the largest family farm in Massachusetts was not strong enough. *Not yet, anyway*. The female attorney found the most flaws in his case. His head was aching and he wished he had taken a pain reliever.

After the meeting ended, Marcus had a headache that just wouldn't quit. And, he was feeling nauseous. He called his family physician and made an appointment for the next day. He had the sinking feeling this could be more than just the run-of-the-mill hangover. He spent the night on the phone with various business associates, at least that's what he liked to call them. Actually, they were operatives in the underworld. People who could hack information for him for the right price. He wanted more information on the farmers he was trying to shut down in Massachusetts.

He finally made the right connection. The guy wouldn't talk on the phone, however. He insisted on meeting in person. Marcus met him in the alley next to the hotel. The guy called himself Victor, no last name. He wore a hoodie and slipped a bandana over the lower half of his face when he met with Marcus near the garbage cans. Marcus thought he detected a slight Russian accent. Victor said he could hack computers and security systems. He would record everything for a few days and give the flash drive to Marcus. This would allow Marcus to listen in on their personal lives. It was the quickest way to get what he wanted. But Victor wanted a bundle of money to do the deed, $20,000. Victor told him not to contact him on the phone. If he wanted to do it, he could drop the money. The two men parted.

Marcus had to think for a little while. But in the end, he decided to go for it. Nothing ventured, nothing gained. As ordered, he left the cash tucked into a backpack in a locker at the train station at 5:00 PM when it was busiest. Wearing a hoodie and sweats, he knew he'd not be recognized on security cameras. He made the deposit into locker number 1348, as Victor instructed, then headed back to the Ritz-Carlton. Maybe if he spent the night with Nicole, alone, he'd feel better in the morning.

Driving back to the hotel was a challenge. His headache had gotten worse. His doctor appointment was for 2:00 in the afternoon the next day. Not only was his head throbbing but now his vision was impaired. He began to think he had the flu. Once he arrived at the hotel, he pulled off the tie and suitcoat and sucked down a bottle of water to steady himself. He called Nicole's number but no answer. After the tenth try, he decided to drive home. He stopped to order take-out from an Indian place on the way. The food was unappealing and he picked at it while driving. An idiot in front of him stopped short causing him to jump on his brakes. The food was propelled onto the seat, then the floor of the car. "Screw you!" Marcus screamed as he flipped his middle finger.

The drive was uneventful after that. His head continued pounding. When Marcus flopped onto his bed at home and stared at the plaster detail in the ceiling of the expensive condo. He hoped Riley's venture to the backwoods of Maine with her clodhopper friends got it out of her system for a while. She was always talking about the people there, and Marcus dreaded moving to Maine. Even though he knew it would benefit his career, he also feared Riley would constantly be focused on her family and friends. She would end up neglecting him. *He hated to be neglected*. Marcus Reed needed constant care and feeding. It was time that Riley understood that. She needed to be a more dedicated wife. They had been married for nearly nine years. He knew it was time to be more forceful with her. He would lay things on the line as soon as she got home. He wondered where the hell she was and why she didn't call him to say she'd be late. He tapped his phone and it rang through to Riley's voicemail. Tossing his cell phone to the other side of the bed in exasperation, he rolled over and promptly fell asleep.

CHAPTER 11: FEMALE INGENUITY

When Riley picked up Linc to drive to the financial appointment, she was wearing the clothing from her Boho purchase. A long flowing soft blue skirt and a top with a matching cardigan sweater topped it off. A vision in blue, and feeling feminine for once, she stood on the farmhouse porch and listened to Scruffy barking as she buzzed the ancient doorbell. Linc came to the kitchen door, opened it, and wolf-whistled softly. "Wow, you're a sight for sore eyes, right there." Linc snapped a picture of her with his phone. "I've got to keep that for inspiration."

Riley could only imagine how that picture came out. She was tilting her head and urging her cowboy to get a move on. Riley opened the screen door and tugged at him. "Come on, cowboy. We'll be late if you don't get into my vehicle. These financial types don't like waiting."

It had been a long time since anyone showered her with attention as Linc was doing at that moment. She had to admit, it was fun to have someone flirt with her instead of nit-picking. Lately, that's all Marcus did – and she tried to put the thought of Marcus out of her mind. She was here to help Linc right now. Marcus and his admonitions could wait.

Linc was wearing a freshly pressed red plaid shirt and jeans, topped off with his white hat. She noticed he had a fresh shave and smelled wonderful. He fastened his seatbelt and shot her a dimpled smile. There were times he could look so innocent. She felt his blue-green eyes on her all while she was driving. "Damn, you smell good." Linc said quietly. Riley couldn't help but smile.

"I don't have perfume on." She informed him.

"Then it's *you* that smells good. Your skin, your hair." Linc was making her chuckle.

"Honestly, cowboy, I'm driving. Don't get me laughing now." Riley gasped.

As they pulled into the parking lot, Linc hopped out of the vehicle and attempted to open her door for her. But she was already out. He walked closely to Riley and opened the door to the building, removing his hat. The financial office was on the first floor. The receptionist announced their presence. An older, pudgy man in a gray suit that looked too tight came out to meet them.

"Hello. I'm Greg Smith. Come on in. I have your paperwork here."

Linc shook his hand and Riley did, too. Smith's fingers looked like little sausages. Riley walked in and took a seat. Linc pulled his chair closer to the desk and to Riley.

"I won't beat around the bush, Mr. Caldwell."

"Call me Linc, please."

"Okay, Linc. I won't sugar coat any of this. The farm your father left you and the 200 acres has a tax bill and operational costs that exceed the revenue. In other words, financially, it is not a self-sustaining business." Mr. Smith paused. "Your brothers, Grant and Madison I believe their names are, donated $25,000 last year to your father, to keep things running. That barely kept his head above water, so to speak."

"Just how far in the hole am I?" Linc asked the question and it hung in the air for a moment.

"Right now, it's $40,000 -- but the bills are mounting and the revenue just isn't keeping up." Mr. Smith reiterated.

Linc felt impatience sweeping over him and wanted to get to the solution. He already *knew* what the problem was. "What can I do to change this?"

Smith took a deep breath, as if he was about to dive underwater. "Well, there are several possibilities. First, you could sell off some of the land..."

"No." Linc interrupted him. "Not happening. I promised my dad I'd keep the place intact."

"Okay." Mr. Smith continued. "You could lay off some of your farm workers. Rob and Chris are making $12 an hour and they are paid for six hours of work per day, that's costing you $144 a day."

"Nope. I can't do that. These guys have been with me for years. They have other jobs, too. But this is part of their income. And, they're hard workers, reliable." Linc countered.

"Then, there's Sonny Black. You're paying him $25,000 a year." Mr. Smith exhaled. "Any chance you could let him go?"

"Not a chance. Sonny is like a brother to me. We go way back. He's my right-hand man on the farm. He runs things if I have to skip out to buy feed or take my daughter somewhere. I couldn't function without Sonny."

"Then there's the feed. You're buying organic and it's the best there is. It is very expensive." Mr. Smith posed.

"Can't change that." Linc said flatly. "I'm an organic farmer, everybody knows that. It's one of the reasons our farm stand does so well in the summer and fall. It's the reason we have a contract with the premier milk retailers."

Mr. Smith mopped his forehead with a handkerchief, visibly frustrated and sweating a little. He took a deep breath. "Mr. Caldwell, you've got to give on something here. You either decrease costs or increase revenue. And not just a little bit. I'm talking about increasing your revenue substantially. Got any ideas?" Smith put his hands on the desk as if he'd given up.

"How about this..." Riley interjected. "A good portion of Clear Springs Farm is heavily forested. Could we utilize that acreage as a tree farm and get the taxes reduced?"

Smith looked puzzled. "Well, I never thought of that. Yes, it's a possibility."

"How about setting up a wholesale connection for local restaurants to buy Linc's organic produce?" Riley offered.

Smith was jotting everything down. "Good idea. What did you say your name was?"

"Riley O'Neal."

"What else do you have, Miss O'Neal?"

"Linc has more than one barn. He keeps the milking cows in one. The other barn is for his two horses. But there are empty stalls in there and plenty of room for more. What if Linc boarded horses for folks?" Riley suggested.

"Yes. That's a possibility. He'd need to increase his liability insurance, but it could net him a fair amount of money in the long run." Smith almost smiled.

"One more thing..." Riley was on a roll. "The house. It was built in 1902 and needs upgrades, you know like electrical and plumbing and a kitchen remodel and bathrooms, too. Would it be possible if we had a big event at the farm to raise money to make these repairs, tax free?"

"I've never heard of anything like that." Smith pondered. "But, I could look into it."

"Well, there's this thing on Facebook called Fund Me." Riley explained. "I can set up the event and explain what the money would be used for. There's lots of people who'd come and donate. In fact, I'll bet there might be thousands of people."

"You've given me a lot of things to research, Riley. Thank you. Those are wonderful suggestions." Smith nodded to Linc. "What do you think Mr. Caldwell?"

"I think she's a genius." Linc said as he gazed at Riley. She felt his eyes on her all while she was talking. "Not only is she a genius, but she's beautiful, too."

Now she felt the heat creeping up from her neck to her face. "I'm having a hot flash, I think." Riley fanned herself. I think we'll be back in a couple of days. Is that long enough for you to do your homework on these things?"

"Yes. Let's meet on Friday. I'll have answers for you by then." Smith stood and was ready to walk them to the door.

"Wait." Riley turned to Smith. "Linc, would it be all right if I took a copy of your deed and some other legal documents? I want to do some research of my own. No offense to you, Mr. Smith."

"Fine. Yes. Give her copies of all of that stuff, please." Linc asked Smith. The pudgy man ran to his secretary and she started photocopying.

"It'll just be a few minutes." Smith said when he returned.

Moments later, a large envelope was handed to Riley and she was outside with Linc.

As Linc opened the door to Riley's Subaru, he took her hand and brought it to his lips, right there in broad daylight in the parking lot. "I don't know what I would have done without you in there. I was tongue-tied. I felt like this guy was brow-beating me. I got my back up. You know?"

"You don't have to thank me, Linc. I'm glad to help." Riley gushed.

"Let me take you to lunch...oh darn...I've got to pick up Clara from pre-school. I've got a cow that's ready to calve at any moment." Linc got into the front seat and glanced at Riley. "Can you stay a little bit longer?"

"Can I watch the birth of the calf?" Riley inquired.

His eyes lit up. "Would you? Damn, let's go. She's due any moment and I wanna be there to assist, you know."

"Sure, cowboy." Riley glanced his way and noted the grin that had spread across his boyish face. *He's hopeful. He's happy right now.*

Katherine Caldwell said not to worry. She'd pick up Clara from pre-school when the time came. This gave Linc the window of time he needed to tend to urgent matters in the barn.

Riley had witnessed Linc assist with the birth of a calf at least ten times -- maybe more. But, she'd forgotten what a momentous occasion it was on the farm. Rob and Chris were there, Sonny had arrived before them, and once Linc stepped into the stall where the cow was laboring, everything swung into action. Clean blankets were brought in, warm clean water, gloves, and other items in a black leather bag.

Linc washed up to his shoulders, then put on clean rubber gloves to help his grip. Riley watched in amazement as Linc put his arms in up to his elbows as the mother pushed what looked like a huge bubble out. The amniotic sac ruptured and the cow's contractions almost broke Linc's arm. But he remained calm and collected.

"Come on, Harriet, you can do it girl..." he said in a low soft tone. For a moment, Linc relaxed and the cow relaxed with the calf's hooves and nose protruding. One more grunt by the animal pushed the baby completely out. The mother's breathing was labored and Linc protected the baby from her rolling onto it. Once the calf was out, Linc attempted to get it breathing right away. Riley watched as he cleaned out the calf's nose with his fingers to get all the amniotic fluid out. He tickled its nose with a clean piece of hay. But the calf wasn't breathing. Without wasting a second, Linc bent down and performed artificial respiration, and Riley saw the baby take its' first breath.

He gently moved the baby to the mother's face and she licked the tiny calf clean. Everyone moved back and gave her space and time to complete this tender task.

The cow's eyes gazed upon her baby and after about twenty minutes, she got on her feet. "Here's the less glamorous part." Linc smiled. The sac had moved out and dropped to the floor. Linc cleaned everything up with the tub of warm water. The baby started nursing immediately. Riley knew it would only be a few days and then someone would be milking the mother and putting her special milk into an oversized baby bottle to feed the calf. Weaning the baby was critical. The process usually took about a week. Linc practiced the partial weaning method, where the baby could suckle the mother for the first few days, and was introduced to water and grasses early.

Without hesitation Riley offered, "I want to bottle-feed her, when the time comes. Can I?"

"Sure." Linc responded with a smile. "Just like old times. "Will you have time for that, in the middle of moving and all?"

"I'll make time." Her eyes met Linc's and he knew she meant it.

"Maybe you can start showing Clara how it's done. She's only three years old, but catches on quick." Linc said softly.

"Yes. I'd love to." Riley sighed. The crew just stood there having witnessed the miracle of life before their eyes.

CHAPTER 12: COMING HOME

Marcus was pacing the floor waiting for Riley to return. She had left a voicemail message saying she expected to be home Monday by dinner time. It was now 7:00 PM and he imagined she was somewhere in the snarl of traffic that seemed to swirl around Boston twenty-four hours a day. One thing was for sure -- he planned to have a long talk with her about the move to Maine. And, he would let her know how neglected he felt lately.

He heard the sound of the elevator and opened the condo door. Riley was carrying some bags in addition to the canvas bag slung over her shoulder. "Welcome home." He said flatly.

"Gosh, the traffic is crazy." Riley stepped into the condo looking frazzled.

"I thought the funeral was yesterday." Marcus started.

"It was. I wanted to see some of my friends and had lunch with my parents before I left."

"Oh. I see. You didn't think to call me at all while you were there?" You must've been *really* busy." Marcus spoke with a tinge of sarcasm.

"Marcus, I was with a grieving family. They're heartbroken. I helped with the funeral. I'm sorry I didn't call you, but I was tied up." Riley explained. Why was she even making an explanation? She attended a funeral. This was her welcome home. No groceries in the cupboard, no dinner cooked, not even a simple *sorry to hear about Mr. Caldwell's untimely death*. Nothing.

He was spoiling for a fight, Riley could sense it. "And, by the way. This move to Maine to stay with your parents. I've changed my mind about that." Marcus turned away as he said the words.

"Why?" Riley asked, shocked he was bringing this up now.

"We need a place where we can be alone. I don't want to live underneath the nose of your parents." Marcus avoided her eyes.

"Staying with my parents would only be for a week or two, until we locate a place we want to buy." Riley said softly.

"Well, that's the other thing." Marcus retorted. If he didn't look at her when he spoke it was never a good sign.

"What do you mean?" Riley took the bait.

"We won't be *buying* a property in Maine." Marcus informed her.

"What will we do? Live in a tent?" Riley felt impatience rising in her.

"No. We can live in a nice rental while we're there. I don't anticipate being there for years and years, you know." Marcus said with a note of finality.

Riley said nothing. After a moment of silence, Marcus continued. "So, it's settled. I've located a beautiful property right in our price range and we can lease it for a year at a time. You'll love it. It's on the ocean." Marcus slid a piece of paper in front of her with a photo and description of the place.

"I don't like the ocean. I wanted to live on the lake." Riley challenged him.

"What do you mean you don't like the ocean? Are you delirious from the long drive or something? *Seriously?* Riley, people would give their right arm to live on the beach in Scarborough Maine. This is a beautiful stretch of beach, seven miles, to be exact. The home we are leasing is a million dollar cottage."

Riley studied the photo of the cottage. Pleasant Point. She pondered the name for a moment and tapped the GPS on her phone and put the address into it. It was exactly five miles from Clear Springs Farm. Was Marcus doing this intentionally?

Or, didn't he realize she had just returned from that very point on the map.

"Yes, it is lovely." She conceded. "How much is it – for the lease?"

"Don't worry about that. I've already paid it for the first year." Marcus smiled. It wasn't so much as a smile as it was a grin. He looked a little bit like the Joker on Batman when he smiled like that. It gave her the creeps. Riley realized this had all been planned and done without her involvement.

"So, this decision was all signed, sealed, and delivered before you even told me." Riley stared at him.

"You were gone. The opportunity came up. I had to make the decision immediately. It's late May, Riley, almost Memorial Day. Someone backed out at the last minute. These things don't happen very often. I needed to jump on it. You understand."

Maybe she was being too hard on him. The cottage was lovely, after all. And it was so close to her cowboy. And, she wanted to help out at the farm so Linc could keep it.

"Riley, I just asked you a question. Are you listening to me?" Marcus seemed perturbed.

"Sure. What was it?"

"The move will take place next week. I've hired a moving company to pack everything up. So, whatever you don't want to take – you should drop it at Goodwill. I've boxed up most of my stuff already. I managed to stay pretty busy while you were away gallivanting with your friends." Marcus moved from his chair to the phone. "I'm ordering take-out. Anything special you want?"

"Yeah, chicken salad on rye." She said absentmindedly. This was her life with Marcus. They never cooked dinner. It was take-out or eating in a restaurant. Condo-living in Boston had taken its toll on Riley. She was sick of the city. Tired of traveling for her job. Her mind drifted back to her cowboy.

Although Riley hadn't seen a lot of Linc in person over the last decade, she was friends with him on Facebook. On rare occasions, she'd messaged him privately, like on his birthday or Christmas. Tonight when she opened her laptop, she looked at his Facebook page. There were photos of Clara there and his mother. He seemed to post at least one photo of something going on at the farm every day. She noticed his posting was usually late at night, after milking, chores and dinner, right around 9:00 PM.

Today he had a photo of a new baby calf born right in front of Riley's eyes just before she left to drive home to Boston. That's what her cowboy did after he had his financial meeting. He delivered a baby. Then he fed and milked the herd, watered the garden, and did some weeding. Riley scrolled through each photo. There was a cute one of Clara feeding the chickens. She looked so innocent and adorable. One photo of Jenna was amongst the pictures and she opened it and zoomed in. She was definitely pretty. No two ways about that. The pendant she wore was unique, it looked Native American in its design. Definitely handmade. The stone was green and the beads that made up the necklace were stunning.

Riley noticed she had a private message from Linc and opened it, a little bit surprised. "Thanks for everything. Can't wait for you to be living back in Maine."

She poised her hands over the keyboard ready to compose a message back, but then thought better of it. Instead, she located the song he played in La Belle for her, *Miss Me Baby* by Chris Cagle and sent it to him in a private message. She had added the song to her playlist and whenever she heard it, she thought of her cowboy. He was struggling and she wanted to help him in any way possible. She owed him this.

Riley swallowed hard as she glanced at Marcus across the room on his computer. He wasn't going to take this well, her helping the cowboy. The more she thought about it, she realized Marcus didn't take many things well. But she wasn't going to let that stop her. Marcus would be busy in Maine and Riley had a score to settle. A debt to repay. A heart to mend. She had so many emotions running through her as she stared at her cowboy's photograph on the page before her. That was the only regret she had in her twenty-eight years on the earth. She had hurt another human being so badly he almost didn't make it. She had to save the last cowboy.

Life had a way of pushing forward. The next day, Linc ran to fetch Clara from pre-school at 3:00 PM and Mrs. Eldridge, the teacher, motioned to him, crooking her finger. "Let Clara play for a few minutes. We need to talk." Worried, Linc followed the older woman to the edge of the room where the children couldn't hear them.

"Linc, I'll be right up front with you. The other day you were late picking Clara up and she was crying. There have been other times you've been late, too. And, I haven't said anything because, well – I know – she has no mother and you're doing everything yourself."

Linc felt he had to explain. "That's the day I had the vet come to examine a pregnant cow. I called and left a message but you might not have gotten it."

"I got the message. That's not the point. The fact remains, Clara watched every child leave here and she was the last one alone with me. I explained you'd be late. She sat by the window alone and I noticed she was crying. I tried to comfort her, but she told me to leave her alone. I've noticed other things, too. She's withdrawn. Other children are making fun of her unkempt hair. I don't even think I can get those tangles out with a comb. And, I hate to mention this, but I have to: her shoes are too tight. She has completely outgrown them. I don't know if you have noticed these things or not."

Mrs. Eldridge was right. Fact was, Linc often didn't come inside the building to get Clara until most of the other kids were gone. He felt embarrassed in his work clothing. The other parents stared at him and he knew he smelled like cow manure. He needed a haircut and often hadn't taken a shower. He usually reserved that pleasant ritual for the very end of his day. Most of the other parents picking up their children wore business attire and were well-groomed. They looked like successful, well-to-do, responsible parents – the exact opposite of him. Their stares sometimes made him feel inadequate, even though he knew he was doing the best that he could. When he looked at those other parents, he felt he had to somehow do better.

His biggest concern was what Mrs. Eldridge said about Clara being withdrawn. That was something new he hadn't noticed. "Tell me more about being withdrawn, what did you mean by that?" Linc encouraged the teacher. "I'm more concerned about that than I am her shoes at the moment. I can get her some shoes right off, but I'd like to know what's going on with her feelings."

Mrs. Eldridge took a deep breath. "Well, I don't know how to put this delicately. But, the other children make fun of Clara. They say she smells funny. I don't know if you are bathing her every night, but that needs to be taking place." Linc, who could fix just about anything couldn't fix the way he was feeling right now -- totally inadequate as a parent. He was letting Clara down. He didn't tend to her bath time every night. Sometimes his mother did it, sometimes he did. There were certainly times when Clara skipped her bath.

Mrs. Eldridge continued. "If you're going to keep her hair long like this, you need to wash it every day and put it in a ponytail or braid it. She has so many tangles, I'm afraid you might need to take her to the beauty parlor and have them cut out. I tried combing her hair, but she won't let me. She cries and said she wants *you* to do it." Another punch to his gut. Linc knew this was probably true, too. He couldn't fault Mrs. Eldridge for pointing these things out to him. In fact, he should be shaking her hand right about now and thanking her.

"Well, you've given me a lot to think about, and I thank you, ma'am." Linc tipped his hat. "I'll get on this stuff right away. Especially the bath at night. As for her hair, I'll talk to my mother and see what she wants to do."

Mrs. Eldridge touched his arm. "I'm sorry, Linc. I know you have a busy job running the farm, especially now with your father gone. I didn't want to tell you these things, but I *had* to. You understand. I love Clara, too."

Linc saw the genuine kindness in Mrs. Eldridge's brown eyes and nodded. "I know. I am thankful you took me aside and told me." He strode across the room and picked Clara up sideways underneath his arm. "Come on. Time to go home and feed the chickens." Clara squealed and the remaining children laughed. One said, "I wish my dad was a cowboy." Linc smiled as he put Clara into her car seat. "We're gonna go shoppin." He smiled at her lovely little face.

"You mean at the feed store?" Clara's eyes lit up.

"No. We're gonna get some girly stuff. Like shoes and clothes and maybe even get your hair done like grandma does. Would you like that?" Linc tested the waters.

"Yes!" Clara reacted enthusiastically. Good, he exhaled. He hoped it would be this easy. "How about tomorrow? It's Saturday and I can get Sonny to watch the farm for me."

"Okay, daddy." Clara said as she pushed her tangled hair out of her face. "I love you, daddy."

"I love you, too, buttercup." Linc said glancing at her. That's what he always called her and she was his buttercup – his ray of sunshine – when everything was gloomy or overwhelming. She was the apple of his eye. He felt like a lucky man to have a wonderful daughter like Clara.

∗∗∗

The next day Linc yelled to his mother, "Clara and I are going to the mall. She told me about a place called The Jungle. We need some new britches."

"Okay." Katherine Caldwell was on the phone with someone.

"Sonny will take care of things for a while." Linc added, and the screen door slammed.

He put Clara in her seat in the pick-up and they made their way to The Jungle. They named this place right, Linc immediately thought when they arrived. The place was packed and he had no idea where to start. Right away he was approached by a saleswoman and she asked him what size Clara was. Linc was embarrassed that he had no idea. The saleswoman eyed Clara, then measured her. "She's big for her age. She will be tall, I think. Let's see – we're looking for a size five, maybe even a six."

It was difficult to maneuver through the store, it was so crowded. He felt a tap on his shoulder and wondered if he was in someone's way. As he turned, Riley was smiling up at him. "Shopping without me?"

Clara spied her and ran to her side. "Hi Riley. Can you help me find some clothes?"

Linc felt like he was seeing an apparition. He had wished someone young and hip could be with him, someone with a sense of style, like Riley. It was almost too good to be true. He thought about her and she appeared.

"Sure. I'd love to look at clothes with you, Clara. But, there's another place I'd like to take you, if it's all right with your father." Riley's eyes met Linc's.

"Yes. Lead the way." Linc chuckled.

The three made their way to a different store. Riley was speaking to Clara. "You don't want to wear what all the other kids wear. You want to stand out, and be a little bit different. Right?"

Clara nodded her head in agreement. Riley took them into a store that had unique brands, all American made. "It's Cabela's for kids." Riley smiled. Clara skipped alongside Riley as they picked out shirts and pants, jeans and shoes, and finally a hat and some hair doo-dads. Linc had never seen Clara so focused as she was with Riley.

On the way home, they followed Riley to a restaurant and had lunch. In the truck, Clara was bubbly. "Daddy, I like Riley a lot. She's fun."

At the restaurant, Clara kept a running conversation with Riley. When they finished eating, Clara's voice, filled with sincerity, made a request. "Riley, can you come back to the farm with us?"

"Sure, if it's all right with your dad." Riley answered glancing at Linc.

"Heck, yeah." Linc uttered. "I mean, please, yes, please do."

The expression on his face said everything she needed to know. Riley was impressed with little Clara. She was an inquisitive child and asked many questions. "Will you braid my hair, Riley?"

"Well, I think your hair needs a little trim. There's a shop on the way home. Would you let a nice lady trim your hair a little bit? Not too much, maybe just a half an inch." Riley held her fingers up showing Clara how much that was.

Clara was excited. "Yes. Will you have your hair done, too?"

"Sure." Riley agreed. Linc drove to the Hair Express and waited in the truck as Riley and Clara went inside. He could see them through the large window. Clara was all smiles and had a booster seat. The hairdresser washed her hair first in the sink, then wheeled her over to the mirror. For a moment, he envisioned Clara all grown up. She was only three right now, but he knew how quickly time was flying by. In ten years, she'd be a teenager. He wondered what his life would be like then, and dreaded the thought of raising a teen-aged daughter alone.

Riley had her hair done, too. Damn, she looked beautiful with wet hair. She was stunning with messy hair, or hair pulled up with a barrette. He couldn't take his eyes off her. Clara and

Riley had their hair trimmed then braided. Clara skipped outside and wanted him to look at her.

"Surprise, daddy!" Clara exclaimed as she twirled around.

"Wow, you look all grown up." Linc said.

"Just like Riley." Clara was exuberant. He hadn't seen her like that in a long time.

"Yeah, just like Riley." He said as he buckled her into the car seat.

"Thanks. I can't say that enough." He touched Riley's arm as she got into the Subaru.

"How'd you know I was at the mall anyways?"

"I called your mother. I had to ask her a question about something." Riley responded.

"See you back at the farm." Linc tipped his hat. "You're gorgeous with that braid. You look like Rebecca of Sunnybrook Farm. I always did have a crush on her."

Riley followed Linc back to the farm. There was a strange vehicle in the driveway when Linc and Riley pulled into the yard. A rental vehicle. When Riley parked behind Linc's truck, she watched as he took Clara out. Not wanting to intrude if he had visitors, Riley stood next to the Subaru as she watched a tall dark-haired woman open the screen porch door. Linc stood still as he stared at her, sort of like he was seeing a ghost. But Clara broke into a full run and jumped into the woman's arms. *Jenna.* She was at Clear Springs Farm after being away for a full year. What could be the purpose of her unannounced visit?

Riley turned around and got back into her vehicle and drove away. As she glanced toward the gravel driveway, she saw her cowboy talking with Jenna. For a moment, she felt a wave of jealousy engulf her. But then quickly realized she had no right to be jealous. *Her cowboy wasn't hers any longer.* Riley was married. Her cowboy had been married for nearly three years to the lovely Jenna. What right did she have to feel anything? Easy enough to rationalize, but her heart still sank.

She stopped at La Belle and Sandy waved her in.

"What's up with you? You look like you've just seen a ghost."

"I have." Riley sat at the bar and dropped her head into her hands. "I just came back from Clear Springs Farm. I'm here because it's moving day for me. I called Linc's mother because his truck was gone from the yard when I drove by on my way to the mall. She said he was at the mall buying clothes for Clara. I figured he might need some help, so I went there. We had a great time shopping. When we got back to the farm --- who was in the driveway? *Jenna.*"

"No!" Sandy covered her mouth with her hand.

"Clara ran to Jenna. She is her mother, after all. I just pulled away and left. Linc was standing there as if he couldn't believe his eyes. Oh God, Sandy. I don't know what this means for Clara. She's gone a whole year without her mother and now – wham -- she's back. But, for how long?"

"And, what about Linc?" Sandy pondered. "How the heck do you think he feels? His heart's been on a yo-yo with this chick. I never liked Jenna. She's a selfish, cold-hearted bitch."

Riley lowered her eyes. She really didn't want to think about Jenna being with Linc right now, or ever. Changing the subject, she muttered, "The moving trucks will be at the beach house in a few hours. I'm going to be busy arranging furniture for the next few days. I'm heading there now. Stop by if you have some free time. Marcus is away giving a seminar. He relegated all moving chores to me. Aren't I lucky? Ha!" Trying to be lighthearted, Riley felt she was failing miserably.

She waved goodbye to Sandy and started driving toward the beach. Her route would take her right past Clear Springs Farm. She swallowed hard when she rounded the bend and saw the farmhouse. She slowed down enough to see the rental vehicle still in the driveway. Linc's mother was at the hospital working. That meant Linc was alone with Jenna and Clara. She imagined it could be a tearful and poignant reunion. *Maybe even a happy one.* She kept going toward the beach house. It was time to deal with boxes and bags of stuff, and furniture arrangement. Not her favorite chore, but it would take her mind off her cowboy for the time being. Maybe.

CHAPTER 14: BY THE SEA

Riley arrived at her new home. Her father was going to meet her at the beach house at the end of his workday. He promised he'd be there by 4:00 PM. Her mother, a busy district attorney for the county, worked long hours and wasn't available, ever. Ah, well, having her father there would be helpful. Plus, he might shed some light on Jenna's reappearance at Clear Springs Farm. Or, maybe not. But, at least she could talk with him about it. Riley could talk to her father about anything. They were close. He always wanted a son, even had the name "Riley" picked out for one. But, when she was born, her father treated her just like she was the child he always wanted. Riley knew he wanted a boy. It was sort of a running joke, now. But, Riley had met and exceeded his wildest expectations. He often told her he doubted a boy could have done as well as she did in college. He showered her with compliments and was in her corner, rooting for her success. And, he'd never hesitate to take her down a notch if she was doing something wrong, too. Even though she was a twenty-eight year old accomplished adult, she still sought her father's approval. That, she knew, would never change.

Talk about timing. The moment she arrived at the cottage, the moving van was coming down the narrow sea lane to the charming bungalow. And, right behind the van was her father's truck.

Conor O'Neal stepped out of his vehicle and embraced his worried looking daughter. "Lots to do here, I see. I brought you a few snacks." He put the grocery bag on the kitchen counter and she watched as his eyes took in the place. "Wow, this is nice – *really nice.*"

"Yes, it is beautiful." Riley responded. "I suppose I'll spend lots of time walking on the beach. It's right here." The two stepped in unison through the French doors onto a screened porch overlooking the most beautiful beach in the State of Maine. White sand for as far as the eye could see. Conor O'Neal smiled at her. "I'll be coming over for a swim sometimes on hot days. You don't mind having your old dad around, do you?"

"No. In fact, I'd love to have you here visiting often, and mother, too, before she works herself into the ground." Riley smiled.

Back inside, Riley was instructing the movers where to put the bedroom pieces, the living room furniture, and dining room items. For a moment, it seemed like they were taking items out of a clown car, with a never-ending stream of stuff. But, after a couple of hours, everything was unloaded and the huge tractor trailer pulled away.

Riley was now surrounded by unopened boxes, but at least the rugs were down and the furniture was placed. That was half the battle. For the next two hours, her father helped her unpack each box and put everything in its place.

"Did you know Jenna showed up at Clear Springs Farm today?" Riley started.

"No, kidding. Really?"

"Yes. I was with Linc and Clara at the mall. When we got back, she was there. I left in a hurry. I didn't want to be in the way." Riley stopped short.

"That's gotta be hard on Linc." Her father said after a quiet minute.

"Do you think he will be happy to see Jenna?" Riley asked, probing.

"I don't know, to be honest with you. I just know he took good care of Clara this past year. He's a caring father. People around town saw how he stepped in. It had to be difficult for him. Jenna ran off with a guy she met on Facebook. I mean, imagine how embarrassing that was for him? It was a shock, really. Linc had no idea she had a guy on Facebook who wanted to have a relationship with her. That's gotta leave a mark."

"Yes. I think I left a mark, too." Riley whispered.

"Yeah, I know. You were Linc's first girlfriend. So, this thing with Jenna had to have a déjà vu feeling to it. Because, you know, in a way, when you went out with that guy while you were engaged to Linc -- that was borderline infidelity." *There. Her father said it. Oh gosh, she was guilty of infidelity, herself. She had broken her cowboy's heart. And now, Jenna had done the same thing. Riley felt like she was in the same category as Jenna – not to be trusted.*

"I'm sorry, honey. You weren't married to Linc when you went out with that Tom guy, but it was just as painful for him. In Linc's mind, you were *his* – pledged to him. He had already planned it all out. It was devastating for him. I'm sure you remember. I don't need to tell *you*." Her father was right. Riley remembered every horrible detail about that time, and pummeled herself every time she turned it over in her mind.

"Dad, I have a question for you. It's one of those uncomfortable ones." Riley glanced at him as she put the dishes into the kitchen cabinet.

"Shoot. I'm not embarrassed about anything. I'm tough. I can handle it."

"Do you think it's odd that Marcus and I aren't having....*intimate relations*." Riley presented the words, almost regretting them. She sounded so desperate.

"Nothing?" her father asked.

"Not for six months." Riley answered matter-of-factly.

Her father was silent for a few minutes. He was busy putting things away. When he stood up, he put his arm around Riley. "Is this something that you want to talk about with me or your mother?"

"I don't know." Riley hesitated. "Actually, I'd like a guy's point-of-view. How do men think about such things? Why would Marcus ignore me this way? He kisses me on the cheek and gives me a hug, but we hardly ever see each other."

"That might be the problem, right there." Dad pondered. "It's difficult to have an intimate relationship if you're not in the same zip code. You two are running off in opposite directions and have been since you got married."

Food for thought, Riley contemplated. It might be true. Marcus was running his conference for the next two days. She'd be alone again. The odd thing was, she was beginning to create a life *without Marcus*. She relied more and more on her friends for companionship and now that she was home, she'd be working with her father. She'd see her family and friends even more. She might possibly miss Marcus less, if that was even possible.

Her father kissed her goodbye. "We've done all we can for today. See you tomorrow at the shop, bright and early."

"Thanks, dad." Riley put her arms around her father's neck and kissed his cheek. "I'm so lucky to have you." He waved goodbye and smiled as he pulled away in his truck.

The sun was setting and Riley grabbed a hand knit shawl her mother had made for her years ago. She ran her fingers over the soft cotton yarn. The shawl was well worn, but precious to her because it made her think of her mother. The air was warm but the wind had picked up. Riley walked barefoot along the front of the bungalow. At this time of day, there were one or two people walking their dogs. One man approaching was tall, and Riley squinted as she tried to see the details of his face. He had a familiar stride. The closer he got, the more he looked like her cowboy. Was he coming straight toward her with Scruffy on a leash? Her expression must've given away her surprise. Linc removed his hat and acted like he had come upon her coincidentally. "Good evening, ma'am."

"What...what are you doing here? What happened with Jenna?" Riley's thoughts were scattered. She wasn't planning to see him so soon.

"She's gone. Just stopped to see Clara and she wanted to talk with me. We talked." Linc said.

"And, what did she want to talk about?" Riley prodded. Linc didn't answer right away. Instead, he changed the subject. "Can I see your new place?"

"Sure." Riley took his arm and walked him onto the porch of the bungalow. Riley unlocked the French doors and Linc stepped inside. Scruffy ran around, his nose glued to the floor, as he started to sniff every inch of the place. An old-fashioned shingle-style cottage, the 1937 oversized bungalow was filled with charm. Everything was painted white, except for the old pumpkin pine floors that had aged to a soft golden color. "This place is awesome!" Linc smiled as his eyes roamed over the beach house. "You'll love it here. Who wouldn't?"

"I'm sorry. It's a mess. My father just left. He helped me organize things, sort of."

Linc's eyes didn't linger on the rooms for long, they were fixed on Riley. "I'm really here to say I'm sorry about what happened earlier. You probably felt uncomfortable with Jenna there."

"Yes." Riley avoided his face. "I thought maybe there'd be a reunion. I didn't want to interfere with Clara's excitement...or yours, for that matter."

"Jenna's boyfriend in California broke it off with her. She's regretting the whole thing, I think. At least she said so. She wants me to forgive and forget." Linc spoke in a quiet somber tone. He paused for a moment, then continued, as if it was difficult to do so. "She said she heard about my father's passing and was sorry. She told me how much she missed Clara. It was painful for me to watch Clara with her. It was as if Jenna had never left. Clara was thrilled to see her. Little kids don't know the meaning of the word forgiveness, because they always have a forgiving nature. They haven't learned how to protect their hearts yet. So, they're wide open. Sort of like me when you left ten years ago. I'd never experienced that kind of hurt before. I'd have forgiven you and taken you back right up until I got Jenna pregnant. I knew right then, I was tied to her forever.

We had a child together. I knew the right thing to do was to marry her. I tried to make her happy. It just wasn't enough. I'm not what she wanted."

"I'm sorry, Linc." It was all Riley could say at the moment. Her cowboy wasn't hers any more. He had a child with another woman who was once his wife. A lot of water had gone over this dam, and she had no right to expect anything from Lincoln Caldwell. Friendship, maybe. But, even that would have to be on his terms. Riley understood how deeply the wound went. She also realized how he was tied to Jenna for the rest of his life because of Clara.

"Don't be sorry." Linc moved toward her and took her hand gently. "It's done. Can't go back and change the past. All we can do is move on. Live in the moment. Be grateful for what we have."

Riley instinctively leaned against him and when his arms wrapped around her, she felt as if she was safe, in a cocoon of warmth and love. Linc's pine tar aroma made her swoon just a little. She was exhausted from the events of the day, but wanted more than ever to linger in his embrace. *How she missed him all these years*. She missed the chance to be his wife, have his baby; she missed simply being in his presence. It was at that exact moment Riley knew she loved her cowboy with all of her heart. She always had. She was like Dorothy in the Wizard of Oz – *she always had what she needed – she just didn't know it*. Linc's lips brushed against her forehead as she whispered, "There's no place like home."

She felt his lips on her cheek. "Yes, Dorothy, there's no place like home. And, you're here."

"And, here's my little dog, Toto!" Riley scooped up Scruffy and cuddled him against her chest.

"You happy?" Linc's eyes met hers.

"Yes. As long as you and I can be friends."

"We can." He said with certainty. "Don't you worry about that -- no matter what happens, we'll be friends, always."

Riley breathed an audible sigh of relief. "I'll be at my dad's engineering firm tomorrow. But, I'd like to stop by the farm to see the calf and talk with you about some of the ideas I have."

"By all means." Linc slapped her bottom playfully, like he did a thousand times in the barn when passing her.

"Hey, watch yourself cowboy. I'm a married woman now."

"Yeah, and how's that goin? I see you're all alone here. And, I noticed on your Facebook page, your husband is gone again for a couple of days. I noticed the word *again*. Sounds to me like he's gone a lot and from the photos on your page, you spend most of your time with your girlfriends."

"You're a little too observant for your own good." Riley looked away. He was right, exactly right. She didn't know if this was the time or the place to reveal her deepest insecurities about her marriage to Marcus.

"I've got a barn full of cows waitin on me, girl." Linc put his hat back on and moved toward the French door. "I parked back a ways in a paved lot. Scruffy likes to walk on the beach here. I'll see you tomorrow, Riley." The door closed and Riley ran to it and watched his lean rugged form move along the beach. Cowboy boots and all, he walked Scruffy along the shore until she couldn't see him any longer. She wished he could have stayed with her for a while, but knew he had a grueling schedule and a lot on his mind right now in regards to the farm, and Jenna.

She wondered about Jenna and his comments regarding her. Was he thinking of allowing her back into his life? If so, how much? Would he ever take Jenna back as his lover? Would he remarry her? Riley knew how selfless Linc was. Was it possible he'd remarry Jenna for Clara's sake? She closed the curtains and took a long hot bath, all the while wondering about Linc and the feelings that were probably bubbling up inside of him. There was no telling what he'd do. She knew what she *wanted* him to do, but the time for her telling Lincoln Caldwell what to do had come and gone long ago. As it stood, she had no right to stand in the way of any bit of happiness he could salvage for himself and little Clara. She knew that, but it didn't make her feel any better.

CHAPTER 15: FULL CIRCLE

That night Linc milked the cows and found himself thinking of Riley as he sang the country songs on the radio in the barn. https://www.youtube.com/watch?v=BteQP6dhiGk

Sonny noticed he seemed distracted, but didn't want to interrupt what appeared to be a happy reverie while it lasted. Sonny didn't know if Linc was smiling and singing because of Riley or because of Jenna. But it didn't matter right now. This was the first smile he'd seen since his father passed away. Sonny just wanted Linc to be happy.

When the chores were finished, Sonny was hosing down the stalls. Linc passed by and Sonny sprayed him with the hose to get his attention.

"Hey, if you want a water fight, it's 85 degrees today – you're on!" Linc laughed.

"Nah, I just wanted to ask you – about Jenna. What was that all about?" Sonny inquired.

He turned the hose off and wound it around his arm, noticing Linc didn't answer right away.

"She wants to get back together." Linc exhaled and hesitated before speaking again. "The problem is, she said all of this stuff in front of Clara. So, I had these big blue eyes looking up at me saying -- daddy, can mommy stay?"

"So, what *did* she say, exactly, if you don't mind my asking?" Sonny held his breath a little as he waited for the answer.

"Well, she said the dude in California was a loser. That's all, pretty much. She said she was sorry. She told me she loved me. And, said she missed Clara more than she ever thought possible." Linc paused for a moment. "The part about hurtin me, yeah -- she hurt me...I don't care any longer about that. But, the hurt that Clara has suffered, that's unforgivable in my book."

"That's tough, man. But, what do you think? You gonna make a go of it? Do you want to?" Sonny was asking questions Linc didn't have the answers to. So, Linc turned the question back to Sonny. "What do you think I should do?"

"Oh no. Don't put this decision before me. You have to do what you feel is right." Sonny looked him in the eye. Linc didn't have passion in his voice when he spoke about Jenna. There was only leftover hurt and shame.

"I don't know." Linc said with a despondent tone. "I'll admit, I'm lonely. You have a wife and three kids. You have someone to go home to at night, to eat dinner with, who wants to make love to you. Your kids are great. Maggie has been a wonderful mother to them. That's what I've always wanted, a woman like that. Someone who can commit to me, love me for who I am. Someone content to live a simple life filled with hard work and good lovin. Damn, I need a woman, Sonny. I'm a normal man, you know. I've got needs. Lately, I've been a farmer, a horse whisperer, a father to Clara, and pretty much a workaholic. But, I've not been with a woman since Jenna. And, she is mighty pretty. She is stoppin by tonight after chores. I told her I'd let her see Clara again and maybe we could go for a walk and talk private-like."

Sonny could see where this was going. Jenna was pretty all right. She was downright seductive. She had dated half the county before she hooked up with Linc. But Sonny wasn't going to tell him that. Hell, no one had the guts to say that to Linc. Sonny couldn't tell his best friend who to love. Guys didn't do that. But, he'd support him, no matter what decision he made. "Okay, listen, you know where to find me if you need to talk. I'll be in my shop tonight. Got a great cabinet order. I'm gonna make some serious money, cowboy."

"Make hay while the sun shines, Sonny!" Linc slapped him on the back. "You lucky bastard. Go home to Maggie and give her a kiss for me. You've got the world right there, man. Just sayin".

Sonny knew he was right. He started up his old Silverado and drove to the far edge of the land to his ten acre lot. Maggie was outside with the children playing softball. He watched his sons hit the ball and run around the bases and felt a sliver of joy. The boys were catching on. As he watched them, he knew he was blessed. He only wished he could somehow help Linc get past this rough patch in his life. He had a feeling Riley might be the key to that.

It was the money that worried him more than the female problems, when it came to Linc. After talking with Riley privately, Sonny was wracking his brain to come up with ways to make a fast $40,000. But, damned if he could think of anything just yet. That was a fortune to him. And, right now it was a fortune to Linc.

But just speaking with Riley, Sonny got the feeling that things might work out. He couldn't put his finger on it, but she was a positive force. She had some great ideas. If those things could be put into action, Linc would be breathing easier. He figured he'd know where things were going in a few weeks, anyhow. Riley was on a tear. She was poking and probing every inch of Linc's property, looking for ideas, ways to save money or make money. She was one smart young woman.

And, Sonny couldn't help but feel she was still sweet on Linc. She still called him cowboy and her eyes lit up whenever she was with him. These were things Sonny noticed, along with her body language. She was drawn to Linc like a magnet. She blushed in his presence. How many women even *did* that today? He smiled to himself. Riley and Linc. One big roadblock there. Marcus Reed, Riley's husband. Sonny imagined he'd not be too happy to meet Linc Caldwell. He knew the two had never met and had a feeling of dread whenever he contemplated the face-off. Because that's what it would be. Linc still had feelings for Riley, whether he would admit it or not. And, from what Sonny knew about Marcus Reed, he wasn't the type of guy to give up anything easily, not with the nickname *pit bull*.

***

In the morning, Riley O'Neal had never been as thrilled in her life as she was today, working with her father in his shop. For the first time, she was glad she kept her maiden name, even though Marcus was upset with her for doing so. She wouldn't even hyphenate it. It was as if she knew she'd be back here working for O'Neal Engineering someday.

"I'm a project engineer." Riley smiled putting on a hardhat and getting her tool box set-up on her truck. "What will my first project be?" she asked her father.

"You'll go with me today to a manufacturer of drilling rigs. It's a big place. Lots of machinery and moving parts. They're doing an expansion. I bid the job and got it. Now need to get into the meat of the thing. I'll introduce you to the people there." Conor O'Neal beamed with pride. "I'm sure they'll like you."

Being in the shop felt like going home to Riley. She spent her entire childhood at her father's knee and her very first memories were of his workshop. The aroma of WD40 and cutting oil were the first things she noticed. The wide-plank wood floors were rough-hewn, still the same. There was the noise of someone cutting metal with a grinder in the far corner. The smell of axle grease wafted by. The natural daylight from the tall reinforced windows cast a sunny glow across the building. Her favorite odor was that of molten metal from MIG, TIG or stick welding. Burning smells triggered happy thoughts of her being there with her father working on all manner of projects. There was the scent of wood cut with a blunt power tool, blackened edges, and all that. Warm steam oil mixed with hot copper and iron and a roaring steam-coal fire, and yes -- bacon and eggs done on the wood stove atop the firebox in a cast iron pan. Heaven!

"Riley – you coming?" Her father interrupted her sensory homecoming to his shop. "Yes, just grabbing some gloves. Are these boots okay?"

"Steel toe, right?" her father asked.

"Yup."

"Okay, let's go." Conor O'Neal swept by the man at the front counter, Henry. "We're going to Brigham, be back later. Got the cell phone."

Henry nodded. "Okay. Got it."

The ride to Brigham was long enough to have a conversation with her father. Riley had no idea he wanted to get her alone to talk about things. He started right in. "I've been thinking about what you said – you know – about you and Marcus....not being close and all. I'd like to stop by and hang around when he's there, that's if you don't mind. I'd like to get to know him a little better."

"Oh gosh. I'd love to have you there, dad. Please, stop by. You don't need to call. The door is always open." Riley said happily. Being away from home for the past decade made her realize how much she missed the simple company of her dad, and the easy friendship that had grown between them now that she was an adult.

"I just want to get a feel for Marcus. I've never had the chance to really get to know him. He's sort of a mystery man to me. You know." Her father was planning to do a little reconnaissance. Riley was fine with his method of assessment. Stopping by to get closer to Marcus, he could have at it. She had gotten as close as she figured anyone ever could. Marcus wasn't wide open like Linc. In fact, she was noticing the stark contrast between the two. But, she wanted her father to get to know Marcus without being tainted by her opinions and thoughts, so she kept them to herself for now.

"Great." Conor O'Neal nodded. "I'll be by this week some night for dinner."

"Good." Riley declared. "Bring mother, too. I'll supply the lobster pie from La Belle. No one will know. She'll think I made it."

"Yeah, right." Her father laughed. She loved it when he laughed.

The plant they visited made drilling rigs for artesian wells. The rigs were used to drill for spring water all over the world. Riley sat next to her father throughout the initial engineering meeting. This was going to be different than the civil engineering projects she was accustomed to. Lots of new things to learn, she was always up for a challenge. Before leaving the plant, the chief engineer, Rob Adams, struck up a conversation with them as they walked toward the parking lot.

"You folks live around here?" Adams asked.

"Yes, just a few towns away." Riley's father answered.

"I have a question." Riley interjected. "These wells that your rigs drill. They're very deep. Do you have a hydrogeologist that you work with on a regular basis? You know, someone who knows the lay of the land in this area?"

"Yes, I do." Adams stopped for a moment. "He's on my phone actually. Let me see..." Riley waited as he scrolled through names and tapped one. "Ah, here he is. His name is Winston Foss. He's actually the head hydrogeologist for a company called Pure Nature, that's a big spring water place about ten miles from here. Riley entered the name and phone number into her cell phone. Then Adams rifled through his pockets. "Ah, here's his business card. He's the best. No doubt about that."

She planned to contact Winston Foss about the possibility of looking at Clear Spring Farm's aquifer. The water was clear and clean and bubbled up from a deep old well that seemed to be bottomless. The spring created the beautiful pond where she first made love to Linc. The pond that had been there for generations, possibly a hundred years or more. The farm was named after the spring.

Later that day, Riley was on the phone with a woman from the historical society. She wanted to take a look at plot plans of Clear Springs Farm dating back to its inception. She also contacted the State of Maine to get a topographical map of the property. While on the phone with the state, she asked about the Tree Growth Tax Law Program and asked for paperwork to be sent to her so she could make the application for Linc's property, or at least the forested portion of it, to be a tree farm.

Lastly, she planned to contact Winston Foss. Before contacting him, she needed to check around at other spring water sites to see what the owners of the properties made by selling spring water rights. If it worked out, Linc could possibly be sitting on a gold mine.

Linc Caldwell was milking cows when Jenna's rental car pulled into the gravel driveway. While working, he watched her step out of the car from the corner of his eye. She was dressed to kill. He saw Chris and Rob exchange a look. Sonny gave him an elbow. Linc nodded. Her jeans were painted on, Linc wondered if she could even sit down in those. But as his eyes swept over her body, there was no sign she ever had a baby. She had the body of a stripper, minus the implants. Her breasts were perky and real -- just the right size, as most guys would say. And, they were well exposed as the shirt she wore was cut clear down to her navel. She was still wearing the pendant he had given her when Clara was born. A Native American piece handmade by Sonny's wife, Maggie. It looked good on her. But then, it seemed everything looked good on Jenna.

"Don't let me interrupt you, Linc. I just stopped by to see Clara. Maybe have dinner." She spoke over the noise in the barn.

"Yeah. I'll have mom set another place at the table. It's okay. I can run in for a minute." Linc nodded to Sonny and moved toward the porch with Jenna. Damn, Jenna smelled good, too. He was a mess, covered with milk, and an odor from the barn that probably wasn't too pleasing to her nostrils right about now. He stepped inside the porch and opened the kitchen door. "Hey, mom? Jenna is here. Please set a place at the table for her...." No answer.

Then he heard Clara's panicked voice. "Daddy...grandma is hurt! Come quick!"

Linc ran to the pantry at the far end of the kitchen. His mother was on the floor, unresponsive. "What happened?" he asked Clara. "Oh God, Jenna, call 911."

Jenna knelt beside him and handed her phone to him. "You call 911. Let me check her out. I worked in a hospital in California while I was out there. I think she's had a stroke. Quick, Clara, get me the baby aspirin. Can you find it?"

"Yes, grandma keeps it in the bathroom cabinet."

Clara ran to the bathroom while Linc called 911. He watched as Clara handed Jenna the baby aspirin bottle. Clara's eyes were filled with tears. "Will grandma be all right?"

Linc gave the address on the phone and hung up. Jenna was cradling his mother and trying to check for vitals. "She's breathing! Her body is limp and her breathing is irregular. I'm guessing she's had a stroke. I'm almost certain of it. I've seen this before." Jenna fingered another chewable baby aspirin into her mouth and gave her a sip of water.

Linc stood by watching helplessly. The first responders arrived right away and agreed with Jenna's assessment. "You may have saved her life by giving her this aspirin." One of the attendants said. Jenna stepped back and hugged little Clara. "It's okay, little one." she murmured and stroked Clara's golden hair. Linc kissed his mother as the guys loaded her into the back of the ambulance. "We got this, Linc."

"Hell, I'm goin with you guys." Linc yelled, and hopped into the back end of the ambulance.

The last image Linc viewed through the back window was Jenna hugging Clara as tears streamed down her tiny, innocent face. Then he turned to his mother. She opened her eyes and was breathing in the oxygen. Linc held her hand. "It's gonna be all right, Ma."

The moment they arrived at the hospital, his mother was whisked away to a triage unit and Linc slumped in an uncomfortable chair in the waiting room. He forced himself not to cry. She was alive and appeared to be well when his eyes connected with hers. She was made of steel, tough as nails. He bowed his head and said a silent prayer, not knowing what else to do at that moment. He hoped the good Lord hadn't forsaken him.

"Lincoln Caldwell." A doctor's voice called his name. He stood and the doctor walked to him. "Your mother is all right.

She had a stroke, but we think the quick ingestion of the baby aspirin may have saved her. There's some residual impairment, however. We need to keep her for a few days for testing. But, she is one lucky woman to be alive. You can see her now."

A young woman in a pink uniform took him to his mother's bedside. Katherine Caldwell looked fragile lying there in the hospital bed, with tubes and machines hooked up to her, beeping and humming. The woman in pink gave Linc an overview of his mother's condition. "She's got a normal heart rhythm and good blood pressure. The imaging we did is called an MRI with angiography. It shows us the clot and exactly where it's located. We've given her a clot dissolving drug and need to observe her for the next day or two. Right now she has impaired movement on the left side of her body. But that could change in the next 24-48 hours. We just have to hope for the best. Do you have any questions?"

Linc was dumbfounded. A stroke, and she could barely move her left side. Oh God. He hoped she would recover. He then closed his eyes and thanked God she was alive. "I'd like to be alone with her for a moment. Can she speak?"

"Yes, I can speak." It was his mother's voice all right, but soft and a bit slurred. Her blue eyes focused on Linc's face.

"Hey, Ma, I'm sorry about all of this."

"Not your fault." She managed to say. "I'll get better. Give me a chance."

"Oh, I know you, Ma. You're not one to give up. I talked to the doctor. You're gonna be okay. Don't worry about a thing. I've got everything covered." It was all he could think of to say while his heart beat wildly and every thought careened through his brain. God, he couldn't lose her now. Not right after losing his father. And, Clara needed her, too.

"You go to the farm. There's work to do. Take care of Clara." Her hand reached for his. "Linc...thank Jenna for me.

The doctor here said whoever gave me baby aspirin may have saved my life. It was Jenna."

"I know, Ma. She did a great job. I'll tell her." Linc held her hand for a few seconds, and she squeezed his. "Love you, son."

"I love you, too, Ma." Linc moved back to the waiting room and Sonny was there.

"She's okay, she's had a stroke, but she's okay." Linc muttered to Sonny.

"Let's go home, Linc." Sonny opened the door and they walked outside and got into the truck.

"Jenna saved her." Linc said staring straight ahead at the road as Sonny drove. It was dark and well past dinnertime.

"Yes. Jenna told me what happened. She's made your dinner, Linc. Jenna's waiting for you in the kitchen." Sonny informed him.

"How's Clara?" Linc asked, glancing at Sonny.

"She's fine. Worried. But she's with Jenna. She seems to be all right." Sonny answered.

As he ambled into the farmhouse kitchen, Jenna ran to embrace Linc, then Clara embraced them both. "Daddy, you're home, how's grandma?"

"She's doin better." Linc said as he nodded to Sonny through the kitchen window. "She'll be just fine. She's tough and solid, comes from good stock."

"Have something to eat." Jenna put a plate filled with shepherd's pie in front of him. Then a salad and a glass of milk. He began to eat like a linebacker realizing the gnawing feeling in his gut was pure hunger. He hadn't eaten since noontime or thereabouts. Jenna and Clara placed a piece of homemade apple pie in front of him.

"Look, daddy. Mommy made an apple pie for you, too." Clara pointed out.

Linc's eyes connected with Jenna's gray-green ones, fringed with thick dark lashes. She held his gaze for a long moment. "Is it all right if I stay tonight, Linc?" she asked with an innocent tone.

"Yes!" Clara shouted enthusiastically. "Please, daddy? Can mommy sleep over?"

Linc had a mouthful of food, which gave him a moment to assess the situation. But only a moment. He swallowed and took a big gulp of milk. His eyes moved to Clara. "Sure, buttercup."

"It's late. I'll give Clara her bath. And, I'll wash and braid her hair for bed. Then she will have curls in the morning when she wakes up." Jenna knew exactly what to say and just how to say it. The two scampered upstairs to the big cast iron bathtub and Linc listened as he heard Clara's excited voice talking to her mother. It sure was good to see the smile on Clara's face tonight. She was happy. That was the happiest he'd ever seen his little girl. And, she was all his, legally, anyway. But Linc knew that legal stuff didn't much matter to a three-year old. Clara just loved her mother. Worshipped her, really. He could see it in the way she looked at her tonight.

As he finished eating, he contemplated what this all meant. Jenna here, sleeping at the farm. Clara happy to be with her mother. Sleeping arrangements had to be made. After all, he wasn't married to Jenna – not any more.

After Clara's bath, he could hear Jenna reading a bedtime story to her. Mother of the year, he thought, as he took a shower in the downstairs bathroom. His boots were a mess and he'd tracked stuff all over the house. After showering, he pulled on boxer shorts, grabbed a bucket and mop and cleaned the kitchen floor. He stood in the pantry for a moment, thinking how his mother could've met her demise right there in the scullery where she'd prepared thousands of meals. He owed Jenna *something* for her quick reaction. He had seen Jenna in a different light for the first time today. He almost jumped out of his skin when she tapped his shoulder and he turned around.

"Linc. You okay?" Jenna had on a bathrobe slightly parted. She clearly had nothing on underneath it. His eyes lingered a little too long on her, giving away the fact that he was still physically attracted. It had been a long time. *Too long.* He felt an involuntary reaction taking place in his boxer shorts.

"Did you miss me, Linc?" Jenna moved toward him and the robe parted.

"Yes. I did." He closed his eyes for a moment to steady himself. "Damn. You smell good." He inhaled while trying to avert his eyes, but couldn't quite manage.

"I was your *wife*, Linc. You know *everything* about me. How I smell, how I kiss, how I love you..." her voice was sultry and Linc's erection had become obvious. However, the moment she said *that* – how he knew *everything about her* – Linc's hormones stopped racing. In fact, they came to a dead halt.

"No. I *thought* I knew you, Jenna. But, in reality, I know very little about you, even now." He couldn't stop the words springing from his lips. He'd waited a whole year to say them, and it felt damned good. "Right now, I think it's best if you sleep in the guest room. We'll have breakfast right here in the kitchen tomorrow and have a long talk."

Linc watched Jenna's eyes change from sultry and sexy to hard and cold. That didn't take long. He felt certain she was putting on an act to get cozy with him again. He had to ask himself as she pranced up the stairs to the guest bedroom, *is this what he wanted?* Would it be fair to put Clara through this again? What if he remarried her? Could he ever trust her again?

With his head in his hands sitting at the kitchen table, he thought about that word, *trust.* It meant everything to him. Although, Riley violated his trust, he still loved her with all his heart. But that was different. Riley really loved him. He moved to the small room he called his office where Riley worked on his computer the other day, and opened the closet door. On the floor sat an old sea captain's chest. His father had given it to him years ago. It started out holding an old baseball glove, and some memorabilia from games, but soon the chest was filled with things from Riley.

He fingered the first note she had written to him in high school and touched the yearbook with the prom pictures in it. She was his at one point in time, completely his. But now – she belonged to someone else. There was still something there between them, however. A spark that never died.

She had married Marcus Reed, but Linc figured Riley was lonely in that marriage. *She had to be.* She saw very little of her husband in the past nine years she'd been with him. From what Linc could tell on Facebook, Marcus was a player. One of those guys who was never happy, never satisfied, always trying to keep up with the Joneses, whoever the hell they were. And, Riley – well, she spent most of her time traveling for that civil engineering company. She was always flying off to someplace to build a bridge or something else. Even though she was married, she was still Riley.

Linc marveled at how much he and Riley had enjoyed one another's company since she came back home. In fact, he thought about her every day and wrote to her on Facebook every night. Sometimes she'd answer him back with some lengthy philosophical response. Other times, she'd post some old photos she had scanned. Photos of the two of them way back in the day. She had tons of pictures that he'd never seen, or couldn't remember. As he closed the chest, he noticed his computer was still on. He touched the mouse and thought about Riley. He didn't tell her about his mother and what happened today. He knew she'd want to know. It wasn't something he would tell her on Facebook. He slipped his phone out and tapped her number. It rang once, twice, and she picked it up on the third ring.

"Linc?"

"Yeah. It's me." He exhaled.

"What's wrong? I can tell something is. You'd never call me at this time of night."

"It's my mom...she had a bad spell today and fell in the pantry." He forced the words.

"Oh, God, Linc...is she all right?" Riley sounded alarmed.

"She had a stroke and is resting in the hospital. But, I think she's gonna be okay."

"I'll be over in the morning to help you with Clara. She must be very worried."

The connection ended right there. Linc couldn't tell if it was Riley's phone or his. But the connection cut off. He decided not to call her back. When he looked at the time, he had no idea it was 10:00 PM. He was usually in bed by 9:00 PM at the latest, unless, of course he was in the company of a female.

It dawned on him he'd be in the company of three females in the morning. Oh damn. What had he gotten himself into?

Some people lived their lives with no goals in mind, they just lived in the moment. As Linc shaved and studied himself in the mirror, he so wished he could be one of those folks. But he couldn't. It was always important to have goals. His father had taught him that long ago. You need a roadmap, son.

Well, he had a roadmap and plenty of goals, but not a dime to make things happen. His checking account had sucked out all of the money in his savings account. He was dead broke. He'd pulled up his banking information on-line before going to get his mother flowers at the grocer's. Last time there, he'd bounced a check and felt awful. The sting of embarrassment and shame was still with him. Today, he ran out to the garden and took a handful of wildflowers growing nearby and put them into a canning jar filled with water. It was simple, but would hopefully brighten her bedside table in the hospital.

Jenna traipsed down the stairway with Clara in tow. Both were dressed and ready for breakfast. He had already cooked the bacon and had the eggs ready to go into the pan. He slid the bread into the toaster. "Well, good mornin, ladies." He said with a smile.

Jenna and Clara both hugged him. "Daddy, can mommy stay here again tonight?" As her words hit his heart, he thought the pain might never stop. Did Jenna tell her to say that or was it just the unedited request of a three-year old? He didn't know the answer to that.

A knock at the kitchen door drew his attention away from Clara. "Riley's here." Clara shouted when she saw her in the doorway. Clara ran to Riley and embraced her. "Look at my hair, Riley! Mommy braided it last night after my bath and when I took the braid out, my hair was curly. Do you like it?"

"Yes. It's beautiful." Riley's eyes roamed over the kitchen and landed on Jenna sitting at the table. "Did I interrupt anything?"

"No. Come on in. You like bacon and eggs, right?" Linc asked with a wink and a grin.

"Yes. I'm starving." Riley sat next to Clara at the kitchen table. Linc could see Jenna's eyes as they took in Riley, the same way a cat eyed a bird that's unaware.

"Mommy stayed with me last night." Clara announced.

"That's great." Riley tried to sound exuberant, although her first thought was *where did she sleep?*

"So, what are you doin here?" Jenna asked Riley point blank.

"I heard about Linc's mother. I thought I could somehow help out while he goes to visit her today at the hospital. Maybe take care of Clara or help Sonny with the chores." Riley answered. "How is she doing – your mother?" Her eyes rested on Linc.

"Good. I called this morning. Nurse said she's in physical therapy already. Her left side is weak and not responding completely." Linc looked worried as he slid the fried eggs onto each plate. He buttered the toast and avoided Riley's eyes.

"Well, look Riley." Linc started, "Jenna's here. She can take care of Clara today and help Sonny with the chores. You haven't seen mom yet. Why don't you ride in with me? Or, you can give me a ride in and drop me off when you go back to your engineering work."

Jenna's eyes flashed. Riley sensed this wasn't part of *her* plan for the day, taking care of a three-year old and getting sloppy in the barn. But Linc insisted.

After eating, Linc walked outside with Riley. Just before he did, he kissed Clara goodbye and told her to be good for her mother. Jenna just glared at him.

In the car with Riley, Linc let out a sign of relief.

Curiosity got the best of Riley. "What was *that* all about? Is she staying here?"

"You mean Jenna."

"Yes, of course. I know Clara lives here. Are you messin' with me, cowboy?"

"Nah. Jenna just wants me back, is all."

"And, you – how do *you* feel about that." Riley pressed.

"Don't know just yet." Linc shot a glance her way. "She came onto me last night. All cuddly and cozy and naked."

"Naked?"

"Yeah. She thought she could just get naked and everything would be all right."

"So, what happened?" Riley didn't look at him. The thought of her cowboy with Jenna was....awful. It was disgusting. *He was too good for her*.

"Nothing happened. I don't know what to do right now, so I'm gonna do nothin. Jenna saved my mother's life yesterday. I guess I owe her for that. She's tryin to be a mother to Clara all of a sudden. But, I don't know what her motives are. I just don't trust her, you know?"

"Yeah, I know." Riley sighed. "I think you need more time." Her eyes took him in as they pulled into the hospital parking lot. "What's that you're holding?"

"Flowers for her. Why?"

"That's just sweet." Riley's heart melted as she remembered similar floral arrangements left for her in the barn, many years ago, with a simple note.

As they walked into the hospital, Linc stopped by the nurse's station. "How's things goin?"

"Slowly." The nurse in pink answered. "She needs rehabilitation. There's an excellent facility nearby. They specialize in stroke patients. I'll give you the information."

For an hour, Riley and Linc sat with Katherine Caldwell and carried on a conversation. Katherine seemed determined to get better and was pushing herself, Riley could tell. Her speech was slurred and the left side of her face was a bit droopy. Before she left, Katherine grabbed Riley's arm gently, and pulled her closer. "Thank you for coming in and spending time with me. And, Riley, would you do me a favor? Keep an eye on Linc. I just worry about him, that's all." Riley promised she'd do her best to help Linc, but she added, "You know Linc. He's his own man."

The ride back to the farm was quiet. Linc spoke first. "Thank you for goin with me today. This has been real difficult. I think my father's death was harder on her than anyone else. I was so wrapped up in my own grief, I didn't realize what my mother was goin through. I'm selfish and blind."

"No, you're not." Riley countered. "You're one of the kindest, most thoughtful people I've ever met."

"How many people have you met?" Linc was messin' with her now.

"Hundreds, possibly thousands." Riley played along.

"And, I'm better 'an all of them?" He smiled.

"Yes. And you don't have a big ego, either. That's another fine quality for the list." Riley kept her eyes forward driving. She knew if she looked at Linc right now, she'd not be able to keep a straight face. But she also imagined that her compliment didn't improve his quiet desperation.

When they arrived at the farm, before he got out of the vehicle, Linc touched Riley's hand and spoke in a somber tone. "I don't know what's gonna happen with my mom. I'm scared, Riley. And, I don't know what's gonna happen with Jenna, either."

Brimming with emotion, Riley waited as he got out of her vehicle and closed the door. She couldn't leave him like that, just standing in the driveway, without some sort of hope.

She rolled down her window. "How about stopping by tonight at my place and I'll make you something for dinner?" She offered. My parents are stopping by and Marcus will be there, too. Maybe we can talk it over. You know, your mom's situation, and come up with a good solution."

"Oh, I don't want to impose." Linc responded.

"No, I insist. You need to get off this farm for a few hours and be around people."

"Okay. What time is dinner?" Linc asked softly.

"8:00 PM." Riley waved as she drove off. "And, don't be late. That'll give you time to finish milking and clean-up."

No sooner did Riley drive away, than Sonny ran out of the barn with a drop dead serious look on his face. "Got some bad news." Sonny grabbed him by the arm. "Inspectors were just here. They gave us a bunch of stuff to fix or they're shuttin us down."

"What? You've got the list?" Linc's eyes focused on the paperwork in Sonny's hand.

"Yes. And, we've got to get movin. They'll be back tomorrow. They're givin us twenty-four hours. That's all. And, some of this stuff ain't gonna be easy."

Linc read down through the items. He'd need money, a bundle of it. He was flat broke right now. He didn't want to tell Sonny he was waiting on the next dairy association check to be deposited on the following Monday. He was ashamed of the fact he couldn't seem to pull things together financially. He was hemorrhaging money at a rapid rate. His mind was swimming with desperate ideas. He'd pull Clara out of pre-school for the time being.

Jenna stepped out of the barn. "I can help, Linc. I got a job at the hospital, workin the night shift as a CNA. It's not much, but if you let me stay here, I'll pay you rent." Linc paused for a moment. If he took Clara out of pre-school, he'd definitely need a babysitter for her. Who better than her own mother? Plus, the income from Jenna could keep him afloat just a bit longer.

Sonny yelled from the barn. "Linc. Come on, cowboy. We ain't got all day."

"All right." Linc said to Jenna. "But, you've got to live up to your end of the bargain."

"Which is?" Jenna coyly batted her thick dark eyelashes.

"You've gotta take good care of Clara every day. I'll make sure she gets a bath every night and a bedtime story. But, during the day, you've gotta pull your weight here – make Clara a good breakfast, do lessons with her, take her outside to play, make her lunch. She needs constant attention from a loving mother." There he'd said it. He felt like he just laid some sort of gauntlet before her.

"Sure, Linc." Jenna's hand touched his bicep as her beautiful eyes connected with his. "And, where do you want me to sleep? Are there any requirements in that department?"

"You can stay in the guest room for now." Linc moved toward the barn. Damn, if she wasn't coming onto him right there in the driveway in the middle of the day. What was going on in that pretty head of hers? He had no time to think about that right now. He had to fix things and quickly.

The rest of the day was filled with trying to increase his credit line with the vendors he dealt with on a regular basis. Luckily, they let him charge the parts he needed. He explained about the extra income that would be coming now that Jenna was going to live there. Thankfully, he had kept a great relationship going with those who supplied him. Even though some of his payments were late, he always dropped by and explained things, promising to reconfigure his books so the bills would be paid on time. Since his father's death, just *keeping the books* had been an exhausting new chore.

His phone buzzed and it was the hospital. Katherine Caldwell was being moved to the rehabilitation facility tomorrow. The nurse on the phone informed him about the financial side of things. "Your mother has an insurance policy through Regional Hospital and it's a good one. She has been pre-approved for three weeks of rehabilitation."

"Three weeks?" Linc almost choked on the words. "Then what?"

"Well, if she's not doing better, insurance won't pay for more physical therapy. She has to be making some sort of progress. You understand, Mr. Caldwell?"

The phone call ended and Linc wondered what *else* could happen today – then, he quickly stopped that thought from entering his mind. He said a silent prayer and repaired machinery with Sonny. Chris and Rob came running once Sonny called them. "No charge on the hours, cowboy. We just wanna do what we can to help."

Sweating bullets, Linc mopped his forehead. "Thanks. Much appreciated." They disinfected the clean room and repainted the whole place. Finally, he finished up the list of repairs, after running to and from the store several times. By milking time, Linc was already exhausted. But, he had called the inspectors and informed them they were ready for another look-see. They were backed up and said they'd show in a couple of days. Linc thanked them and hung up. He wished he would've known that before he practically broke his neck trying to get everything wrapped up for them the next day. But he bit his tongue. He tried to be as pleasant as possible. These guys ruled his life.

When 8:00 PM rolled around, he was showered and shaved; his stomach was growling with hunger. He and Scruffy got into the old Chevy and rolled toward Riley's beach house.

He'd seen her dad a couple of times since the funeral. He was nice enough to stop by and offer some of his younger guys as helpers if things got rough. Linc had said he could handle the situation, but appreciated his kindness. A few other friends and neighbors did the same. Lincoln Caldwell was a poor man according to his bank statement, but he was rich in other ways. He was humbled and touched by their compassion. Sometimes it took a tragedy to make you realize what you had. Sort of like when he had Riley all to himself ten years ago. *You never truly appreciate what you have until you lose it.* He vowed not to take anyone or anything for granted ever again. Life was too short. He needed to appreciate this moment, because he'd never get it back. So much for his well-laid plans and his road-map.

Riley saw the old Chevy pull up in the side drive from the kitchen window and watched as Linc removed his hat and ran his fingers through his hair. Gosh, he was handsome. She used to think it was a joke when someone would say, *oh, so-and-so has gotten better looking with age.* But, her cowboy was living proof it was true. She tried hard not to let it show, but she still got butterflies every time she laid eyes on him. She heard his boots on the back porch and ran there to welcome him. Little Scruffy was by his side.

Before Riley got a chance to say hello, Linc had already opened the back porch door. Riley could see he had the situation well in hand. He walked right into the porch, friendly as ever. She heard his deep voice introducing himself politely to her husband for the first time. "Good to meet you, Marcus. I've heard a lot of good things about you. I'm Linc Caldwell."

Marcus was eyeing Linc and extended his hand warmly. "Great to meet you, Linc. So, you're the cowboy I've heard so much about."

Linc gave a little embarrassed laugh. "Nah. I'm not a *real* cowboy, like the guys out West. I'm just a dairy farmer and a poor one at that."

Riley's mother and father were seated and had been talking with Marcus for an hour or so. But as Linc arrived they each greeted him, mom with a hug and dad with a firm handshake and a smile. Dad said what Riley was thinking. "Well, Linc, we view you as a real cowboy. Those are real cows you're taking care of. And, you do have a horse and you even do some blacksmithing."

Riley stepped onto the screened porch before Linc could respond. "Hey, Linc. I'm glad you could make it. How're things at Clear Springs today? How's your mother doing?"

"Oh, things at the farm are just hummin..." Linc gave her that boyish grin. "Mom's making progress, but it's slow. She's in rehab now. But she's a tough cookie."

Riley knew he was trying to minimize the mess he was in. She'd already heard from Sonny what had happened – the surprise inspection, extended credit line, and Linc's decision to keep Jenna there. Sonny said she was paying him rent. At least Clara was happy. But Riley had a sinking feeling about that whole scenario. Tonight she'd try to focus on Linc's business plan and not his personal life.

After dinner, they sat on the porch and tossed around some ideas. Linc was open to any and all suggestions. His lean muscled form stretched out on the sofa as Riley's father talked about equipment repairs needed at Clear Springs. "When things need fixing, I think it would be neighborly of us at O'Neal's Engineering to give you a hand. I can send one of the guys over gratis, if you give us some stuff from the garden from time to time. Would you be okay with that?"

Linc hesitated and glanced down. "I appreciate that, Mr. O'Neal...I mean, Conor. But that's quite an expense for you and I don't want to disrupt your business."

"We *want* to do this for you, Linc. Riley said so, too. In fact, if you don't mind, I could send her over to help out once in a while. She's on a learning curve with mechanical engineering, but she's a quick study. You know, if the manure spreader isn't working right or you need some work on the milking machines, she can do this stuff."

Riley glanced over and smiled as Linc's blue-green eyes connected with hers. "All right, then. But, you gotta let me give you some food."

Riley figured it was a good time to talk about the tree farm permit. "I've made the application for the tree farm. Your permit hasn't yet been approved. If you *do* get approval, your property taxes will be cut in half."

"Well, I'll be damned. That's great work, Riley. Thank you." Linc said softly.

"I'm not done yet." She smiled. "There's more. I've been in touch with five families in the area who needed to board their horses. I've estimated what it would cost you to keep them, and checked around to see what other stables charge for boarding. I've drafted up a contract for you to review. You'll make a good amount of money boarding five horses, as long as Rob and Chris could add them to the feeding schedule. They could do that easily. Just feed and exercise them the same time they do Ranger and Star."

The smile on Linc's face was worth all of the hard work Riley had put into the projects. But she had one more surprise in store for him. She hoped Sonny didn't spill the beans. She knew those two talked about *everything* – intimately. They were like brothers, except Linc was even closer to Sonny than he was his own brothers. They shared a special bond.

Riley inhaled and couldn't help the smile that spread over her face. "One more thing. Thanks to my good friend, Sandy, I've been in touch with eight local restaurant owners in town who'd be more than happy to sign a contract to buy all of your organic produce. No more roadside stand! I've checked around to see what the going rate would be for your vegetables and have a sample contract here for you. This would be a steady income for you, Linc. You might even want to think about expanding the business to hydroponics. I've got a proposal here for a good-sized greenhouse. This would be a project I could sink my teeth into, literally."

Linc was silent for a moment before he spoke. "Wow. I'm speechless. I'm blown away by everything you've done for me, Riley. I don't know if I can ever thank you enough. This is incredible!" She thought she saw the beginning of a tear in his eyes.

In the meantime, Marcus had been taking in this homey scene, and Riley perceived he wanted to help in his own inimitable way. "I can get that tree farm permit pushed through for you, Linc. I'm the head of the DEP here in the state and have connections on the government side of things."

Linc turned to Marcus. "Thank you, sir. From the bottom of my heart. I sincerely mean that." Linc put his broad hand on Marcus' shoulder. "I greatly appreciate it."

By the end of the evening, a gloom seemed to have lifted. It was late, nearly 10:00 PM, way past her cowboy's bedtime, Riley knew. Her parents walked out with Linc to the old pick-up truck and she couldn't hear what they were saying, but Linc got into his truck with Scruffy and drove away. She heard her parents' vehicle leave the driveway.

"That was an interesting evening." Marcus helped her fill the trash can in the driveway.

"Yes. It feels good to help someone, to know you're really making a difference." Riley said.

"I mean it was interesting how you've become so eager to rescue this young man. I don't think I've ever seen you so enthusiastic about anything." Marcus commented with a tinge of sarcasm in his voice. "He's an old boyfriend of yours. Maybe *that's* why you're so interested in him. And, he's divorced, isn't he?"

"Yes. He is divorced. But I learned today that his ex-wife will be living back at the farm. Linc has been raising their daughter, Clara. She's only three years old. His wife has been gone for just over a year, but now she's reappeared and wants to be in her daughter's life."

"Does that mean she wants to be in Linc's life?" Marcus asked pointedly.

"I'd imagine so." Riley twirled her hair around her finger, avoiding his eyes. "I can only guess at this point. I'm not involved in his personal life, only the business aspects of the farm. It's important to Linc to keep Clear Springs. He promised his father."

"Well, I'm sure with your help, my dear, your cowboy will be very successful. Let's hope your charitable work doesn't interfere too much with your obligations at home. I've missed you lately, Riley. We spend very little time together. And, when I am here, you're off with your friends or working for this cowboy's better interests."

"I know. My job as a civil engineer was filled with travel, not my first choice. Working for dad like this now, at his engineering firm, I'll be working normal hours. We'll see more of each other. That is, if you haven't scheduled your climate change conferences back-to-back." Riley's voice trailed off.

"I've got to make a living, Riley. Not everyone can donate their time to a cowboy in need. How do you think everything gets paid for? *I pay for it.* How do you think this beach house got leased? *I paid the lease.* Who do you think pays the monthly bills? *I pay for almost everything*!" Marcus' face was red and he'd had too much to drink.

"I'm sorry, Marcus, if you feel that way. I've always contributed plenty to our expenses. If you want more, I can provide more." Riley offered. But the sting of his words struck her like a slap in the face. He minimized her contribution and went out of his way to demean her. He always did this when he drank too much. It was as if the evil twin of Marcus came out to play, and Riley wasn't fond of him at all. In fact, her reaction to the evil twin was to run and hide.

"I'm going to bed, Marcus. I'm exhausted." Riley announced without looking at him.

"I'll be along shortly..." Riley could hear him mixing another drink as she left the room and walked into the master suite with a breathtaking ocean view. The moonlight was beautiful on the sea and she'd love nothing more than to hold hands and have a kiss under that moon. Instead, she peeled off her clothes, washed her face, brushed her teeth and crawled beneath the blanket alone. Within minutes she was asleep.

It was well past midnight when Riley was awakened and immediately blinded by the overhead light in the bedroom. Marcus was standing next to the bed. "Get up." He slurred the words. She chose to ignore him. It was the wise course of action when he got into these drunken rages where he wanted to argue. "I said get up!" he whipped the covers off her and pulled her by the arm out the bed. Riley pushed him away but he was much larger than she. "Leave me alone!" she tried to pull her arm out of his grasp.

"Ah, yes. That's what you'd like, wouldn't you? For me to leave you alone so you can go off with your cowboy friend? Well, it's not going to happen. You're married to me! You'd better start acting like it. I have needs, you know. And, you're not giving me the attention I deserve." For a moment, Marcus lurched backward, stumbled then caught himself. "Aw, to hell with you." He released her arm with great force tossing her onto the bed like a rag doll. Riley rolled off the bed and made it through the bedroom door to the hallway. She could hear him falling into the bed in his drunken rage. "Yes, go ahead. Sleep elsewhere. You think you're so much better than me."

When she got to the screened porch, she opened the French doors and found a blanket. She wrapped herself up in a blanket on the wicker sofa and took a deep breath of fresh salty sea air. She could no longer hear sounds from Marcus. She knew from experience, he was now passed out on the bed in a drunken stupor. It was late, but she slipped her phone out and called Sonny.

"Hey, it's me. Yes. It happened again. I'm afraid. Okay. Thanks." Riley hung up the phone. Sonny would be in his truck sleeping near the wild roses tonight. It was the only way Riley could sleep.

CHAPTER 19: EVERYONE HAS AN AGENDA

The next couple of weeks passed quickly. Conor O'Neal spent his time at the tail end of his workday driving to the beach house to talk with Marcus, unannounced. But, he soon found out that wasn't going to work. Marcus either kept him on the outside stairs waiting, or, wasn't home at all. He was getting the distinct feeling the man was doing all that he could to avoid him.

Conor had never really gotten to know Marcus at all. Riley's courtship and marriage took place mostly far away from home. Even holidays and vacations were spent in New York City at Marcus' directive. Now with his daughter close to home, Conor O'Neal could see Riley's marriage had lots of problems. Up until now, he imagined Riley had gone along to keep the peace. That's how she was. But, now he wasn't so sure that was a good idea. Riley's needs weren't getting met. And, for a man to ignore a beautiful and intelligent wife like her, there had to be some reason for it. There was dysfunction of some kind, and he was bound and determined to get to the bottom of it.

Today, when he approached the beach house, he didn't ring the doorbell. He walked to the side of the house around to the back. Marcus was on the porch on a phone call. Standing in the shaded part of the driveway near the house, Marcus couldn't see him, but, Conor could hear his words on the phone. "Yes. I want Nicole to meet me there tonight. My flight arrives at 8:00 PM. You stupid bitch. It's Nicole...she's the one I want. Not Vanessa or any of the others." The phone call ended because Marcus hung up in anger with the person he was talking to, or yelling at.

Good timing. Conor stepped up to the screened porch. "Hey, Marcus. I thought I'd stop by, have a beer with you on my way home." Ah, he caught him unaware. Good.

Marcus seemed to need a moment to collect himself. "Sure. Come on in." He opened the porch door and Conor got comfortable in an overstuffed chair on the porch. "Bud Light if you have it."

"Oh, yes, of course. I think we only have Heineken. Is that okay?" Marcus traipsed into the kitchen.

"Sure." Conor answered.

The two sat on the screened porch watching the beach walkers pass by. "Great view here." Conor remarked.

"Yes. We love it." Marcus answered.

Twenty minutes passed with idle chit chat. Conor needed to use the bathroom. "Hey, that beer went through me. Where's the bathroom?"

Marcus answered. "Just down the hall on the right."

In the bathroom, Conor O'Neal noticed the medicine cabinet was slightly ajar. While washing his hands, he touched the door with his finger and it opened wider. Hmm. Viagra. And, he's not had sex with Riley for six months? And, who was Nicole and why was he arguing to have her for tonight? Riley had to be careful. This situation was more alarming than he'd thought.

As he walked past the kitchen table, he noticed Marcus' laptop was open to a website "Fight Global Climate Change." He'd find out what he could about that group. He knew Marcus was deeply involved. He bragged about it more than once.

As he sat back on the porch with Marcus, he noticed his phone rang but he did not answer it. "You going to get that?" Conor asked.

"No. I think it is rude to speak on the phone with you here. So, tell me, how is Riley doing on her projects at your engineering firm? She seems happy to be working there with you." It was clear Marcus had something to hide.

On the ride home, Conor O'Neal got the message. He wasn't welcome there, and if he did manage to get inside, he'd be treated like an unwelcome pest. There were other ways for him to find out about Marcus Reed. Face to face wasn't going to work at all with him.

* * *

As for Riley, she was getting used to a new rhythm in her life. Waking early, she couldn't wait to get out of the house before Marcus when he was there. She'd spend time at the shop with her father on projects other than Clear Springs Farm. But by late afternoon, she'd be at the farm, helping her cowboy at milking time. She fed and watered the herd, then tended to the newborn calves, while she caught up with Sonny and Linc.

It wasn't easy to have a full-fledged conversation while the chores were being accomplished in the barn, but Riley loved to listen to her cowboy sing along to the radio and when he finished, she could talk with him while they cleaned and hosed everything down. That was the only time she got to really converse with him face-to-face, with the sound of running water in the background.

"So, how's things going with Jenna living here? I'll bet Clara loves it."

Linc was filling up the bins with feed. "Good. So far, it's good anyway. She's heading in to work her 7:00 PM shift at the hospital just as I'm finishing dinner. So, we're like ships passing, you know?"

"Yeah, I can imagine." Riley smiled.

"As for Clara, she loves having Jenna here. She keeps asking me when we're going to get married. I just tell her we'll see about that." Linc said with a glum tone.

"Oh, cowboy – I'm sorry. That's gotta break your heart." Riley whispered.

"It's not my heart I'm concerned about." His eyes met hers. "It's Clara's. I don't know how good it is to fill her with hope like this."

"Speaking of hope, I stopped by to visit your mom yesterday. She's doing better..." Riley tried to sound positive, but the prognosis was not good.

"Yup. That's another thing weighing on me. She has sort of hit a wall with her recovery. She's gettin depressed. I've never seen my mother beat like this. She always forges ahead. Right now, I don't think she has it in her. She's given up. I don't know what to do. I feel helpless."

"Think positive, cowboy. Soon there will be some extra income and we'll turn this thing around.....I mean, you'll turn this around." Riley caught herself mid-sentence.

"You said it right. You're in this with me. I'd be lost if it wasn't for your ideas and optimism. Hell, I'd have thrown in the towel long ago if it wasn't for you, Riley. You know that." He was standing close enough to put his arm around her shoulder in a gesture of comradery. Her heart skipped a beat when he touched her like that. It was as if electricity passed through Linc into her. She didn't know if he felt it, but she did. Just seeing his blue-green eyes every day, listening to him sing, watching him work, being close enough to smell his leathery masculine scent -- was enough for her.

A squeaky door opened and the sound of Jenna clearing her throat was audible. "Linc, you comin in for supper? Or, you gonna talk out here all night?" The tone of her voice let them know she was done waiting.

"I'll be right along." Linc yelled across the barn, and they heard the squeaky door slam shut.

"She's pissed right now. She came here with high expectations, thinkin I was gonna take her back with open arms. Jenna didn't expect this arrangement and I think it's bothering her, although it works for me right now. Especially with my mother comin home soon. I'm gettin the small bedroom ready off the kitchen for her and building a ramp. This ain't gonna be easy. I gotta take care of her, Riley. You understand."

Riley listened to him and added a comment now and then, but for the most part she listened to Linc vent. She knew he spoke to Sonny privately, too. They were both worried about Linc – Sonny and her. But, they also knew his decision to get closer to Jenna was his to make. They couldn't advise him on that situation, as much as they wanted to, it just wasn't right.

Pulling out of the gravel driveway, Riley waved goodbye as Linc trudged into the house. She could envision him sitting at the table with Jenna and Clara – a happy little family. On the way home, she spoke into her Bluetooth, *Sonny Black*. The phone rang and he picked it up right away.

"What's up?" Sonny asked.

"You tell me."

"You know – the usual. Jenna's shaking her booty around. Linc hasn't had a woman in a long time. It's not like he's made of stone, you know."

"What do you mean? You think he's getting back with her? For sex?"

"She's putting it out there. I mean really." Sonny exhaled.

"Like what is she doing, exactly?" Riley asked, almost not wanting the answer.

Silence for a moment. Then Sonny told her. "She walks out of the shower naked and in front of him like that, a lot. She wears those short shorts. Ah, damn, Riley. You know the shit women do to get a guy to look at them. You're a woman!"

Yeah. Sonny was right about that. She was a woman, but she was never like Jenna. She was a whole different kind of woman. "Well, do you think it's working? Does he talk to you about her like he's thinking of doing her?"

"Some days he does. Then, other days, he's pissed at her. She's shaking that thing for other guys, too. Linc's no idiot. There are guys down at Bruno's who tell him what she's doing.

Word has it, she's seeing some big deal lawyer in town. And, he's married on top of that." Sonny had disgust in his voice. "When Linc found *that* out, he was angry. He said she hasn't changed. But, like I said to him – man, she's *not yours*. She's screwing around and she's single. I think she's messin with his mind. Trying to make him jealous. That's what I think."

"Okay, I'm home. We'll talk tomorrow."

"Hey, listen, Riley. If you have a bad night – you call me, okay. I mean it." Sonny sounded serious.

Riley read the note posted to the refrigerator. Marcus was back in New York City for another global climate change conference, a two-day affair. He didn't give her much information beyond that. Her phone rang and she heard her father's voice. "Hi daddy."

"I just want you to know...I finally stopped by and spoke to Marcus today, briefly after work." Conor O'Neal swallowed hard. It was never easy to deliver bad news to anyone, especially your daughter. "Honey, I think there's stuff going on. I don't know how to tell you this."

"Tell me, dad." Riley said stoically.

"All right. I went into the bathroom. The medicine cabinet door was open." He said.

"And, there's Viagra in there." Riley finished his sentence.

"So, you knew that?" Conor asked her.

"Yes. His doctor's office left me a message by accident and told me he should stop taking Viagra. It's affecting his vision and he's having other neurological symptoms. When I heard that message, I immediately knew he wasn't having sex with me – so there had to be somebody else. And, dad, there's something else."

Her father's voice took on a tone of impatience, rare for him. "Riley, tell me. I need to know everything."

It pained her to say it, but Riley had to utter the words. It made it all the more real. "Marcus pulled me out of bed the other night, in a drunken rage, after you guys left. I'd fallen asleep, but he stayed up drinking....and, well....he sort of has this Jekyll and Hyde thing that happens when he drinks like that."

"What are you saying? Did he hurt you, Riley?"

"I got out of the bedroom and slept on the porch. He pulled me by the arm. There's a bit of a bruise. Yes, he hurt me. He scared the shit out of me." She hated to utter the words, but it gave her a sense of freedom at the same time.

"Why are you staying with him, honey?" Conor O'Neal was astonished.

"I don't know. I need to confront him. But, he's not an easy guy to get into an argument with. He's an attorney, remember?" Riley exhaled.

"Riley, honey, you and I need to talk – and not on the phone. Him touching you, pulling you by the arm, that's not all right. Has he ever hit you? Oh shit, Riley. You can't go on like this. Yes, he's cheating on you. But that's the least of your problems. He was on the phone with someone when I arrived. I overheard the conversation. All I'm telling you is this: there's someone else. Her name is Nicole. That's all I got out of it. But, it doesn't matter what her name is. You can't go on like this."

Riley knew in her heart he was right. Speaking with Marcus about divorce would be a challenge, but it was something that she had to do for her own sanity. Things hadn't been good between them for a long time, and now this. It was the final straw. "I know, dad. I'll confront him and tell him I want a divorce. It's not going to be pretty. And, you know what the outcome will be. He destroys anyone he gets angry with. He's impulsive and uncontrollable."

"You always have a room here with us, Riley. Please consider this." Her father sounded concerned, almost desperate. "Do you want me there when you talk with him?"

"Thanks, dad. I'll handle it. I love you." She ended the call, but her thoughts continued in a vicious circle.

CHAPTER 20: ANOTHER DAY IN PARADISE

Linc was haying when Riley's vehicle pulled into the gravel driveway at lunchtime. She came early today. She could see his equipment and a group of men in the field, nothing more than a dusty yellow haze on the horizon. The wavy image of men and equipment reflected in the heat of the sun and she imagined how miserable he was at that moment. It was important for him to get the haying done while the weather was good. And, critical that he filled the barns with as much as possible, wrapping the extra and placing it behind the barn under a lean-to for the harsh winter.

Jenna, wearing her shortest shorts, was preparing sandwiches and lemonade in the kitchen with Clara at her side. Riley stepped in, as the door was propped open with a rock. "Can I lend a hand?"

"Riley!" Clara screamed and ran to her. The little girl wrapped her arms around Riley's legs. "Hey, Clara, how are you? Riley responded. "Can I help with anything?"

Jenna glanced back over her shoulder. "Sure. Load those trays into the back of the truck outside. I need to feed the hayin crew right away. I gotta go to work tonight. Linc's mother has run out of insurance money for rehab. She'll be here tomorrow and I've plenty to do gettin ready for her. This is more than I signed on for, that's for damned sure."

"Okay." Riley didn't know what else to say. Jenna seemed to be in a foul mood and when she looked at Riley, it was as if she could feel the resentment radiating from her eyes. Riley piled the trays of wrapped sandwiches and pickles, along with individual servings of potato salad into the bed of the pick-up. When Jenna stepped outside, Riley held up her hand. "It's okay. I'll do this. You've got plenty to do. You can tend to other things. I don't mind."

Before Jenna could answer, Riley got into the old Chevy and started the engine. Slowly, she edged through the freshly cut path straight to her cowboy on the horizon. You'd think she was the cavalry coming to save them from sure disaster. The men hooted and hollered as she approached. Linc pulled his sweat-soaked shirt off and sat upon the hay wagon for a rest. When he noticed Riley driving his truck he sat upright. "Hello – didn't expect to see *you*."

"Well, if you don't want this stuff, I can turn around." Riley said from the truck window.

"No. No. We want it. We want you to feed us." The guys all shouted in unison with a few choice words mixed in. "Hey!" Linc waved at them. "There's a lady here. Let's keep it clean. Eat up. We've got a long way to go."

Riley couldn't keep her eyes off Linc's well-formed abdomen. She'd seen fitness models who didn't look as good as he did. His face was getting red from the sun. She had a tube of sunscreen in her purse and put it in her pocket. When she pulled down the tailgate, the men swarmed her like locusts. Watching them eat and drink, you'd think they'd been working on a prison chain-gang. Riley snapped a few photos with her phone as they ate like cave men.

"Great food, Riley." One of the guys managed to say between bites.

"Delicious." Another said.

"Fantastic." Linc smiled with food all over his face.

She took a rag and wiped the sweat from his brow, but the beads immediately returned. This was the kind of heat that could kill a man. She took a bandana from the truck and soaked it in water and tied it around his sunburned forehead. Then slowly and methodically, while the men whooped and cat-called, Riley dabbed sunscreen on Linc's red face. His eyes met hers and something transpired. She wasn't quite sure what, but it was sensual and stimulating. Then, he said it. He mouthed it really. "Wanna go swimmin tonight?" Under her breath, she whispered. "Yes."

Back at the farmhouse, Linc's mother was returning home. Whatever physical therapy she'd get now would be day-to-day living. Riley parked the truck and got out to assist Katherine Caldwell, as Jenna took one arm and Riley took the other, they settled her into the wheelchair and used the plywood plank Linc had secured to the side of the staircase to get her inside. Linc's small office now had a twin-size bed in it and a nightstand. His computer had been moved to the master bedroom upstairs.

"How about something to eat?" Riley offered. Katherine sat at the kitchen table in her wheelchair. Clara's eyes were big as she sat next to her grandmother. "You can't walk?"

"Not yet." Katherine smiled. "Maybe soon. I'm gonna need some help."

"Oh, I'll help you grandma."

Jenna put a plate with a sandwich and potato salad in front of Katherine. With tremendous will, the older woman used her right side to do everything, including chewing her food. Clara stood next to her and wiped her grandmother's mouth with a napkin a few times. Riley felt her heart breaking, but forced herself to remain positive.

"If you need anything, and I mean anything, you just give me a call. You have a phone with my number in it, right?" Riley asked.

"Yup. Linc got me this phone and he put all the numbers in it for me. The boys are coming home to see me tomorrow. Grant and Madison both will be here. I miss them so." Katherine seemed exhausted and Riley watched Jenna and Clara walk behind her wheelchair as it buzzed into the small bedroom. Riley took her cue to leave.

Before she drove away, Riley looked at her phone, it had buzzed with a text. *Swimmin tonight, pond 8:00 PM.* It was Linc. Riley smiled to herself. Yeah, right. As if he'd have an ounce of energy left after this day. But the afternoon at her engineering job was filled with thoughts of her with a sunburned cowboy, down at Clear Springs Pond, *skinny-dippin*, as he'd say. She smiled to herself.

"What the heck is so funny?" her father asked.

"Oh nothing." Riley answered absentmindedly.

"Have you thought about moving back in with us, separating from Marcus?" Conor O'Neal spoke softly.

"Yes. I have. Don't worry, dad."

***

Jenna had been pushed to the side, at least that's how she felt. Linc running off with Riley to do things aggravated her. When Linc was at the farm, he was working constantly. Jenna had to change things up. She wanted Linc, and she knew deep inside there was still a spark there. She still turned him on. A man with a kind heart like Linc would surely let her back in – *completely in*.

Jenna particularly enjoyed the time she spent with little Clara. It was fun seeing all of the things Linc had taught her, manners and all. And, Jenna noticed the influence of Katherine Caldwell, too, on her young daughter. Clara told her more than once, *that's not what a lady does,* when Jenna snapped gum or cussed or smoked a cigarette.

With Linc's mother moving in, Jenna's duties would be non-stop morning 'til night. The two nights she did have off, she usually spent at The Nova, a sports bar on the beach. It was only a few miles from Riley's perfect beach cottage, which really had no resemblance to a cottage at all. It was more like a mini-mansion. Jenna had spent her life in a trailer park filled with double-wides next to the railroad tracks. It wasn't exactly luxury accommodations, but it was better than the single-wides near the dump on the other side of town. There was a pecking order.

She was a trailer park girl, no doubt, but she was the prettiest one in that town.

Tonight Jenna decided not to go to The Nova. She decided to stick around and get things comfortable for his dear sweet mother, knowing this would impress Linc. She rummaged around in the dressers upstairs and found the sheets for a twin bed. When Linc came in from the barn for dinner, she noticed he was sunburned from haying all day. He didn't even look at her when he spoke. "You off tonight?"

"Yeah." Jenna answered. "I'd like to spend some time tonight settin up your mother's room. She'll be in the small room off the kitchen...used to be your office."

"Yeah. That's the plan. I put a twin bed in there and a nightstand and found an old dresser with a mirror. My brothers are arriving any minute. They just sent me a text. Cows are all milked. Barn's cleaned. Everything's done here. They'll help you with anything you need moved. There's some linens upstairs." Linc served himself a portion of the roasted chicken with biscuits and gravy. Jenna stared at his back. "Has Clara had dinner?" he asked her.

"Yeah. She ate with me a little while ago." Jenna said as she pulled the screen door shut. "She's watchin TV with your mother."

Jenna watched as Linc moved into the living room and listened as he spoke to Clara and his mother. He was a good father and a good son. Jenna wished she could've had a father like him. Hell, she wished he was back to being her husband. He looked handsome with his shirt off, and she found herself staring at him more and more lately, like that, wanting him. Remembering what it felt like to be wrapped up in his arms. Recalling his kiss, and how good he smelled right after his shower. He emerged from the living room, unaware Jenna was transfixed on him. Damn, his ass looked fine in those Wrangler jeans.

As he sat at the table, Linc glanced at Jenna. "Clara's almost sleeping."

Jenna watched as he finished his meal quickly. He seemed distracted, almost as if his mind was miles away. "You said they both had dinner, right?"

"They ate with me." Jenna said, as she watched him pile food into his mouth like he had never eaten in his life.

For a moment, he seemed self-conscious because of her stare. "Sorry. I've forgotten my manners. Just so hungry. Thanks for the chicken and all the fixins. It was delicious."

"Have fun playin pool tonight..." Jenna said tentatively. "Isn't that where you said you'd be? At Bruno's?"

Linc avoided her eyes. "Yeah. That's what I said."

* * *

Linc ate that meal in record time. As he dashed upstairs, there was only one thing on his one-track mind: a cool dip in the pond with Riley tonight. He'd sent her a text letting her know he'd be there at 8:00 PM. It was getting close to that time. Damn. Where were his brothers? He got into a hot shower and scrubbed away the grime and sweat from the day. When he emerged, he felt reinvigorated, filled with energy. Was it the shower, or the thought of seeing Riley? *He already knew the answer to that*.

As he descended the staircase, he kissed Clara and his mom goodbye. "I'll be gone for a couple of hours. Jenna's fixin grandma's room. Uncle Grant and Madison are coming. They'll be here any minute. Aren't you excited?" Linc had the distinct feeling that Clara had been parked in front of that TV set for most of the day while Jenna did whatever it was that she did during the day. Not exactly the agreement they had made in the beginning.

A car pulled into the driveway and Clara ran to the window. "Hey, it's them!" she screamed.

Grant and Madison met on a converging flight and arrived together sharing a white Cadillac rental car. Linc pushed open the screen door and waved them in. "Hey, good to see you guys."

After a few hugs and gentle punches, the brothers settled down to business. "Where's mom?" Grant asked softly.

"Jenna's settin up the small room off the kitchen for mom. We figured it'd be better for her because there's a bathroom right there and the kitchen is close, too." Linc explained. Both of his brothers tentatively peeked into the bedroom.

"Jenna's in there. She needs some help, so maybe you guys can shake a leg and help her..." Linc stated the obvious.

"Where the hell are you going all shaved and smelling good?" Madison asked. "Shouldn't you be here with Jenna, helping her yourself?"

"Nah. It's not like that. Jenna is sleeping in the guest room. She's takin care of Clara during the day. I can't afford the preschool any longer. She'll be takin care of mom now, too. Damn, what am I doin? Tryin to get you to understand? I'm headin out to see a few buddies of mine. You guys make sure Jenna gets some help. I have this long standin appointment down at Bruno's. You understand – it's a pool game, I've gotta win my money back. Sorry to run out like this. Clara will take care of you, won't you honey?" Linc looked at his daughter's big blue eyes. "Sure, daddy. Will you be back soon?"

"Yeah. I won't be gone too long. Maybe a couple of hours." He reassured her. Then he moved onto the back porch and into the old Chevy. First he pulled out into the roadway, so his brothers would think he was heading for Bruno's. But once he made it around the corner, out of their line of vision, Linc drove onto the freshly mown hayfield and headed in the direction of the pond.

Inhaling the sweet summer air, Linc felt a sense of freedom he wasn't accustomed to. It was rare for him to leave the farm for two hours. But the farm was the furthest thing from his mind right now. Riley's big blue eyes consumed his thoughts. Riley and every detail about her was imbedded in his memory like a special photo album. Whenever his mind was quiet, his thoughts would automatically drift back to her and everything about her. The smell of her hair, the sound of her laugh, her quick wit, her expressive face, how feminine she was, even in muck boots in the barn.

His hopes ran high on this night. He'd be in heaven if he could wrangle a kiss from her. Heck, she was a married woman. He couldn't expect her to give of herself to him as she once did, although he dreamt about such things. The memories of Riley with him were special. He'd made love to other women since, but no one could compare to Riley. It wasn't just what she had on the outside, that elegant lean feminine form, but it was what she had inside that intrigued him. The closer he got to the pond, the more his excitement grew. He tried to steady himself, but he so wanted to get there before she arrived. Riley. He'd be with her tonight for two hours alone. Oh God. It was as if he'd died and gone to heaven.

***

With Marcus already gone on his trip, Riley took her time getting ready. She shaved her legs and other parts of her body meticulously. She took a long time in the shower, soaping from head to toe. Then, rinsed her long blonde hair and towel dried. A tiny bit of make-up well placed, and lipstick. She decided to leave her hair damp. She was going swimming, after all. As she stared at herself in the mirror just before leaving, she realized the giddy anticipation that was running through her veins. Her heart was pounding. She felt like a kid at Christmas time. The dormant sexuality inside her body had been awakened. The memories of her cowboy were warm and clear. She would never forget a single detail of his face. Linc's strong jawline, handsome

smile, deep set blue-green eyes. It was his face in her dreams –
always -- smiling, serious, thoughtful.

Riley got into the Subaru and drove to meet her cowboy
for a nighttime swim. She hadn't done this for a long time. Now
that she was thinking of it, she couldn't remember the last time
she swam on a hot summer night. It was probably with Linc ten
years ago. A twinge of excitement swept over her as she
remembered the look he gave her all sweaty and sunburned
while haying that afternoon. The sexy image of his lean athletic
body, shirtless, stayed with her. The message in his eyes was
not subtle. He excited her and he knew it. *Somehow he just
knew.*

She rolled the driver's side window down and allowed the
breeze to blow her hair around. Humidity hung heavily in the
atmosphere. The heady odor of wildflowers freshly blooming
moved past her. As she turned down the field toward the pond,
the full moon lit her path. It seemed like it took her forever to
get there, she drove slowly, carefully, dodging occasional ruts
and wild animals. Finally, after what seemed like an eternity, she
crested the hill that looked down upon Clear Springs Pond. Her
eyes traced the form of his '50 Chevy in the dim light and as she
got closer, her heart almost stopped as she viewed the tall
rugged figure leaning against the truck.

She shut off the engine and got out of the Subaru, but
before she could close the door, Linc had her in his arms. He
held her for a long moment and she felt him let out a sigh of
relief. "I didn't know if you'd come." He buried his face into her
hair and his breath felt hot against her ear.

He pulled her into his core and her arms automatically
encircled his sturdy waist. Gosh, he was made of rocks, she
thought for a moment. His biceps and forearms were hardened
from lifting endless bales of hay. His cheek felt hot against hers
from the sunburn. As she turned her head to speak to him, he
covered her mouth with his. She was engulfed with a burning
passion, only having dreamt of kissing Linc like this. His soft full
lips touched hers, gently at first. Sweetly, his tongue probed her

lips, as if pleading. Riley's lips parted and their tongues danced together in unison. She tasted peppermint.

Linc's large rough hands were on her rear, pulling her against him. He stopped kissing her and exhaled excitedly as one hand moved to unbutton her jeans. The built-up anticipation was almost unbearable. She took his lead and began unzipping his fly at the same time. His mouth moved to her neck, as he unfastened her shirt. "You sure you want to do this? I've dreamed about you for ten long years. But, then, you know that, don't you? It had to be obvious."

She was breathless as Linc paused and looked into her eyes, waiting for her to give him a sign, any sign. "Yes, I want you." She exhaled weakly. Spellbound, Riley couldn't seem to speak as Linc slipped her shirt off. She heard him murmur. "Good, no bra to bother with. Damn, you're gorgeous." Every inch of her body was affected by his skillful hands. Her breath became erratic. Her nipples grew hard as Linc's thumb skimmed them. "You're even more beautiful than I remembered." He pronounced. His shirt was open and she placed her cheek against his chest and listened to his heart as it pounded wildly. Riley placed her lips on his chest gently kissing his sunburnt skin. Lord, he smelled so good, she felt as if she could eat him up. The scent of his skin, leather, soap, whatever it was – it got to her. The smell of a working man. That's what it was. No Ralph Lauren here. This was so sexy, you could never bottle it. And, if you did, you'd have to name it cowboy sexy.

Then, without warning, as their clothing dropped to the ground in a heap, Linc scooped Riley into his arms. When he did that, she felt as light as a feather. In one swift leap, he jumped into the pond holding her, making a terrific splash. They both were underwater for a moment, then emerged gasping and laughing. She felt Linc behind her, his hands on her breasts and his lips on the nape of her neck. "Skinny-dippin...is good for the soul." He whispered.

Riley turned to face him in the water and felt his hardness against her body as he held her close. "Feels good, doesn't it?"

he said quietly. "Yes." She uttered, hardly able to regulate her breathing. Whatever Linc was doing with his hands was making her lose control. She couldn't think straight. She couldn't think at all when he touched her tenderly like this. His mouth was on her neck as his hands were underwater on her hips, her rear, between her legs. His touch was sensitive, delicate, gentle, and she didn't want him to stop. If he was trying to arouse her, he was doing the trick.

They pulled themselves out of the cool water and onto the old quilt on the ground. Riley exhaled with a shiver as she sat on the blanket; Linc was on his knees in front of her. His hands cupped her face as his lips touched hers softly, but with great eagerness. He knew how to make her shudder with expectation. Riley flashed back to the first time they kissed. He was a good kisser. No, he was a *great kisser* – gentle but firm – he kissed like he really meant it, as if the passion was ripping his heart out. As if he'd die right there if she didn't give him what he needed.

***

Linc couldn't believe he was kissing Riley – how many times had he had this dream? Possibly thousands. Now she was here with him, naked and kissing him – he felt like he should pinch himself. But no. If this was a dream, he never wanted to awaken. *She loved him, he knew it.* He didn't care if she was married or if she lived on Mars. Right now, he'd love her as if there would be no sunrise in the morning, as if this was the last day of his life. When he wrapped Riley in his arms and kissed her, he had no control over his feelings. He was wide open. There was no stopping this. Whatever there was between them, it was strong and sweet. No regrets. He wanted her. She knew it now. She always knew he wanted her. It seemed as if Riley was the air he needed to breathe and he'd been waiting for ten long years to inhale the joy of life again. Her lips parted and her tongue welcomed his. Oh, she felt so good. This felt so natural.

The mosquitos were buzzing and he picked her up, quilt and all, and put her into the bed of the pick-up onto the mattress. He chuckled. "It's a new one. She giggled and he beamed. "I'm breathless with you, Riley. I can't stop thinking about you." He sensed she wanted to slow things down and sat facing her. Visible in the moonlight, her pale blue eyes focused on him. He knew she was aroused as she leaned forward and climbed into his lap facing him, her arms around his neck, her legs wrapped around him. Oh yes! A shot of adrenaline rushed through him, mixed with testosterone and a feeling of reckless abandon. She took his face in her soft feminine hands and kissed his forehead, nose, and cheeks. He couldn't stop his erection as it strained against her soft wet thighs. Instinctively, his hands moved to her shapely rear. He felt her inhale sharply and murmured. "I want you, baby. I hope you want me."

"Yes." He felt her exhale and his heart pounded. Her hands were all over him, everywhere, it seemed. She brushed her fingers over his neck and arms, as if savoring every inch of him, trying to memorize every curve. Her lips were on his, and her kiss caused a tingling sensation through his entire body that lit a fuse right between his legs. *Don't stop, he pleaded silently.* "I need you, Riley." He whispered between kisses. She was moving his arousal between her legs rhythmically, methodically, and arched her back. Her breasts were right there in front of him and he suckled each nipple as he felt a wave of pleasure engulf her. She held her breath for a moment, then exhaled and whimpered. But, her movement didn't stop. With his hands on her rear, he guided her above him slightly. As he entered her, he began to move automatically, thrusting inside of her. She had him, all of him, and her mouth covered his as he lost control. Instinctively, he held her while they both rocked together with a wild rhythm. Her breathing was erratic, wild, he let out a low growl as he felt a shockwave of pleasure go through him like a freight train.

For a long time he held her like that. His hand stroked her hair. He said it first. "I love you, Riley." Her face was against his and he felt her smiling. "I love you, too, cowboy."

"You okay?" he murmured. When he brushed her hair back, she looked more beautiful than ever. Her eyes locked with his in the moonlight.

"Yeah, I'm all right. Actually, I feel wonderful."

"I'm astonished, amazed, thrilled ...ecstatic...." Linc stammered. "I never believed you'd love me like this again....ever."

"Wanna wash up in the pond?" Riley gazed at him in the moonlight.

"Hell, yeah." Linc bounced out of the truck and helped her down.

They plunged almost soundlessly into the water together. When they emerged, Riley heard her cell phone ringing, but by the time she got to her bag in the bed of Linc's truck, the ringing had stopped. She noticed there was a message and it was from Marcus.

"What're you doin?" Linc was approaching as Riley climbed into the truck bed.

"Marcus left a message on my voicemail. He's at a meeting. Should I?" Riley's eyes sought permission, it seemed.

"If you want my opinion, Marcus can wait."

"He's not patient, like you." Riley said, then gazed down at the phone again.

"What is it, Riley?" Linc asked innocently, knowing full well the marriage had problems.

"Nothing." Riley answered. "In fact, I'll ignore his call....just this once, even though I'll hear about it later."

"Really?" Linc almost laughed, but she was dead serious.

"I'm listening to this damned voicemail." Riley's voice changed to a serious tone.

Linc watched as she held the phone up to her ear. Her face changed. Riley's eyes were cast downward. He couldn't tell what she was listening to and felt it would be invading her privacy if he asked, but she had become visibly angry.

"I don't dare to ask you what's wrong." Linc offered. "Can I help?"

"He's just pissed. He wants to know where I am."

His heart sank when he heard those words and watched the anguish twist Riley's face. "He likes to keep track of you. Is that out of love or is that just how it's always been between you?"

"He's always been like that with me, from the very beginning. I have to tell him everything. He tells me nothing."

Linc feigned surprise, but figured Marcus was a slime ball from the moment he laid eyes on him. "I'm sensing you're not exactly happy with him lately. I'm sorry. I shouldn't have said that."

"It's okay." Riley exhaled. "I accidentally received a message from his doctor. It was the physician's assistant, actually. She advised him not to take Viagra, especially since it was causing headaches and vision problems." Riley paused. "We haven't had sex for months. So, why would he be taking Viagra? I thought I *knew* Marcus, but there are obviously things I *don't* know about him."

Linc wrapped the quilt around her and listened as Riley spilled her emotions onto his shoulder. "My father stopped by to talk with him and overheard a phone conversation. Her name is Nicole. He's in New York with her now. The pieces of this horrid little puzzle are falling into place, cowboy. The signs have always been there. I was either too blind or too stupid to see them. Why?" Her voice broke off and he knew the tears were coming. "Why did Marcus do this to me?"

Betrayal. Yeah. He remembered that feeling. But this wasn't about him. It was about her dealing with the fact that her marriage was disintegrating before her eyes. And, more than anything, Linc wanted to be the one to pick up the pieces when and if it happened. Riley leaned against him as she sobbed. He stroked her hair. He felt her chest heaving and reached into his backpack for a bandana; it was the one she tied around his forehead earlier that day. As he dabbed her tears with it, he spoke softly. "There, now. It's gonna be okay. I'm sorry, Riley."

Wait – what was he saying? *He wasn't sorry.* He was thrilled that Marcus had shown his true colors. This guy didn't *deserve* Riley. He deserved a kick in the ass, and Linc was just the guy to do it. Then, reason prevailed. No. Kicking her husband's ass would only get him into trouble. "Listen. We've gotta be smart about this." Linc urged. "You need to talk to him about this stuff."

Riley's tears had stopped. "Well, yes, I suppose need to, but I have to choose a time when he's not drunk."

"What do you mean?"

"When he's drunk, he can become *forceful* with me." Riley looked away as shame swept over her.

"You sayin he's getting physical with you, like pushing or slappin you around?" Linc's voice was filled with concern. His finger gently lifted her chin so her eyes were level with his. "Riley, you've got to tell me *everything*."

"The other night was the first time he ever laid hands on me. Usually, he just yells a lot. He grabbed my arm and pulled me out of bed. I was sound asleep. It was the night you came by for dinner. He was in a drunken rage. I slept on the porch." Her voice stopped. Then, she swallowed hard and continued. "He's gone right now on one of his many trips."

"Don't worry. This is gonna stop." Linc embraced her tightly. Riley had no idea what he had up his sleeve, but she wished right now it was a 9mm Glock fully loaded and she could blow Marcus away with it. *Not an option.* She had to stop thinking like an idiot and listen to her cowboy. He was talking like her mother, who was the district attorney for the county. When did he become so thoughtful and rational? *So mature?* Her cowboy had learned a lesson or two.

"Everything is going to be okay. You know that, right?" Linc embraced her. The softness of the quilt and the hard muscles of his body felt wonderful. Riley soaked in the moment, not knowing if she'd ever have this chance again. She felt like a fool dumping all of her problems onto him like this. Lord only knew, it was her cowboy who was struggling with the loss of his father, his mother's health issues, financial stuff, and now she put this on him, too. Not fair of her.

"I know it will be okay, cowboy." Her voice faded to a hushed stillness.

"I'll make it okay." He leaned forward and lowered his voice.

His kiss was slow, thoughtful, and sent spirals of excitement through her once again. His lips moved to the hollow at the base of her throat. "I love you, Riley." He sighed. His hands moved gently down the length of her back. "Riley, I've missed you so much."

Aroused again, she drew herself to him. "I love you, cowboy." His callused hands explored the lines of her back, her waist, her hips. The moonlight highlighted her ivory breasts and he outlined her nipples with his finger. The feeling between them was much more than sexual desire. His expression stilled and grew serious. She felt her breathing almost stop as his fingertips gently moved her legs apart. He stared at the pink folds between her thighs and inhaled sharply.

His hand moved between her legs as he whispered, "So soft and sweet and sexy." His lips traced a slow sensual path down her abdomen. She arched her back and whimpered as his mouth descended and covered the warm wet spot between her legs. Gasping with desire, her fingers clutched his hair. She cried out in ecstasy as he expertly delivered a sensation that was pure pleasure. Her whole body ached with longing. She exploded with exhilaration several times before he moved his body above her.

"Ready?" he asked.

"Yes." Her eyes met his, and his lips covered hers hungrily.

She tightened around him, throbbing, tingling, as he moved inside of her with a steady rhythm. She quivered with a desire she'd never felt before. He was hot, hard and magnificent. As pleasure coursed through them simultaneously, she felt him let out a long heavy breath. As he collapsed next to her to his breathing began to regulate. His hand touched hers and he brought it to his lips and kissed her palm lovingly.

"I can't get enough of you, Riley."

"Oh cowboy. What have we gotten ourselves into?" Riley exhaled, out of breath.

"Somethin really good." He answered. "And, Riley – "

"Yes."

"Sonny told me about the other night, about Marcus. That ain't gonna happen again. I promise." Linc sounded certain.

She wished she could feel so confident. Pulling on her clothing and saying goodnight was one of the most difficult moments Riley had experienced for a long time. She had just been in the arms of the one man she always wanted, but was too stupid to realize until it was too late. Kissing her cowboy tonight, making love to him, was overwhelming. Her heart skipped a beat when Linc kissed her goodbye. As she opened the door to get into her vehicle, he pulled her back to him. In that last embrace, when his hand clasped hers, he lingered as if he didn't want to let her go. He kissed her forehead and whispered. "I love you," into her ear. She had all she could do to get into the Subaru and drive away. In her rearview mirror, she saw his silhouette in the moonlight against the pond. The last cowboy.

She loved him so much her heart felt like it was going to jump out of her chest.

* * *

Sonny Black heard a truck start and rode the four-wheeler out into the field behind his house. From there, he had a partial view of Clear Springs Pond. He brought the night vision glasses up and focused on the departing SUV and picked out the truck in the distance. Sure enough, it was Linc's truck and Riley's vehicle, too. He'd had a strong feeling all along this might happen, but this was sooner than he had expected. He also knew all about Marcus Reed's attempts to stop the tree farm permit. He'd told Linc about this shit, but now he felt compelled to do something to stop Marcus Reed. It was imperative. Linc and Riley were back together, in love.

Linc Caldwell was more than his best friend, he'd saved his ass more than once in his lifetime. From grammar school on, Linc had become Sonny's benefactor, his bodyguard, of sorts. Back in the day, it wasn't so cool to be Native American and Sonny lived through all sorts of bullying and teasing. Every person, big or small, who slurred Sonny in any fashion was quickly taken out with a glance or a beat down by Lincoln Caldwell. More than once, Linc went home from school to work in the barn with a black eye or a pulled muscle. But, he just pushed through the pain. Sonny knew. He worked right alongside him. Once or twice his father had noticed the bruises, and Linc waved the subject off. "Aw, I ran into a door, or fell down the stairwell at school. No big deal." Sonny always suspected the old man knew, because he'd smile. Not a grin or a full smile, but a little smirk would curl the edges of his mouth, and he'd make eye contact with Sonny for a moment with those deep-set blue eyes with that shrewd look. Then he'd get right back to business.

By the time Linc drove away from the pond that night, he was seriously concerned about Riley's safety around Marcus. Anyone who'd do stuff like that to his own wife wasn't to be trusted. It nearly killed him to watch Riley drive away. It was 10:00 PM, well past his bedtime, but he didn't care. He'd just lived through the most incredible night of his life. If he died right now, driving home, it wouldn't matter. The love he experienced with Riley filled him up. He was reliving every moment in slow motion. Riley's touch, the words she spoke, her smile, her giggle, the soft touch of her hair. Every detail buoyed his spirit as he drove back to the farmhouse. Although he was physically exhausted, his mind was alive with possibilities. Riley. She *could* be his, *maybe*.

As he pulled into the driveway, the lights were on in the kitchen. He'd imagined his brothers would still be up, talking, and felt a twinge of guilt leaving them in the lurch like that with his mom just getting home. But he figured Jenna and Clara would tell them where everything was and they would somehow get through two hours without him being there. As he opened the kitchen door, he realized he couldn't have been more wrong.

The scene was chaotic. His mother was sitting at the kitchen table with tears in her eyes. Clara was still awake. It was way past her bedtime. Grant and Madison were making tea and had served a piece of pie to mom, and had cut it into small bite-sized pieces. Clara was helping grandma eat by getting her napkin ready to wipe her chin. As Linc walked in, he heard his mother say, "This isn't how Linc does it."

"You guys are up late, aren't you?" Linc tried to be nonchalant about the whole matter.

"We didn't realize we'd arrive and have to set mom's room up..." Grant started.

"Yes. And, she needed a shower because she had an accident on the floor." Clara blurted.

"We...helped mom take a shower. It's okay, Clara." Madison explained. "Just now, Jenna took a pie out of the oven. We're ready to eat. Yes, it's late. But, we're doing fine."

Linc had the distinct feeling that everything was *not* fine. In fact, the way his brothers were exchanging glances, he wondered what really happened. "Time for you to go to bed, young lady." He picked Clara out of the chair and put her under his arm. She squealed, "Read me a bedtime story, daddy!"

"No story tonight. It's way past your bedtime. You need your rest if you're gonna grow big and strong." Linc walked her upstairs slung over his shoulder. "We'll do your bath in the morning. Just wash your face and brush your teeth."

In ten minutes, Linc had Clara in her pajamas and tucked into bed. He kissed her forehead. "Sleep tight, buttercup. I love you."

Back downstairs, his mother wanted to go into the parlor. "I just want to see the late news." She managed to communicate with a slight slur.

"Yup." Linc helped her with the buttons on the electric wheelchair. "This one will back you up." He knew she was still getting accustomed to her new means of transportation. He walked behind her watching, then turned on the television. "Okay, how's this?"

"Good. Thanks." She glanced at him with gratitude. How was it that Linc was so thoughtful, so kind, and his two brothers so distant and downright helpless? Katherine Caldwell thought back over the last twenty years of her life. Grant and Madison sucked up all of her time and attention, always getting into trouble, taking the car without permission, out with girls all hours of the day and night, drinking alcohol, pushing their father to the absolute limit. They were star athletes, therefore, managed to escape many of the farm chores. They were always running off to a game or practice. *But Linc was always there.*

It dawned on her that Linc was so quiet and well-behaved, he received much less attention. But, in spite of that, he grew into a sensitive, intelligent, responsible human being. For the last two hours, all she had listened to was Grant bragging about his high tech job and how he jetted around the globe to technology summits, he called them. The girl he'd been dating broke up with him. He seemed not to care. He said he had no time for a relationship anyway. His work was all that mattered, and making lots of money. He was a millionaire, he bragged to his mother. *Wonderful*, was her reaction.

Madison seemed to feel the need to one-up his brother. "Technology is a flash in the pan. New gadgets coming and going every day. Aviation will always be here to stay." Then, Grant would counter, "But, technology is what keeps *your* industry alive!" Madison lived a busy life, constantly picking up extra shifts, working the maximum number of hours an airline pilot was allowed to fly, sixty hours a week. When you figured in time for eating, sleeping, and traveling to and from terminals – Madison virtually had no time for anything except flying. His eyes were red-rimmed and he looked older than his thirty years. Katherine Caldwell noticed he was hunched over, too.

Her two sons who had seemed to be so successful were arguing with one another in the kitchen, as Linc put his daughter to bed. Jenna sat, like an alley-cat, and enjoyed the quarreling.

***

"Well, I'm goin to bed. Goodnight guys." Jenna rose and walked upstairs. "Comin Linc?"

"I'll be up in a bit. I wanna talk to my brothers." Linc gave her a look. "Oh, and you've got a list of chores for tomorrow."

"Yeah, I've got that." Jenna gave Linc a sheepish look and moved past him. "I'm headin to bed now. Is Clara asleep?"

"I think so." Linc responded.

When Linc returned to the kitchen, his brothers noticed he acknowledged Jenna, but not the way a lover would. More like an employer would a subordinate. His two brothers asked in unison. "What's *she* doing here?"

"She's livin here...in the spare bedroom for now. She wanted to take care of Clara. So, I took Clara out of pre-school, to save money. Jenna works at the hospital nights. She's gonna look after Mom during the day here. Jenna's paying rent. I need the extra income right now."

"Damn, Linc. You're really scraping the bottom of the barrel." Grant said.

"Yes. I'd say you're beyond desperate, if that's the case." Madison joined in.

Katherine Caldwell had maneuvered her wheelchair into the doorway of the kitchen. "He's doing all that he can do to keep this place going. I think Linc deserves a little respect instead of your constant criticism." She added sternly. Silence settled over the room.

Grant and Madison exchanged a look that spoke volumes.

Linc finally spoke. "Hey, I'm goin to bed, guys. I'm up way past bedtime. Gotta get up early." As he passed his mother's wheelchair, he coaxed her gently. "Reckon it's time for you to be tucked in, too."

Grant and Madison watched as Linc followed their mother to the bedroom off the kitchen. They listened as he patiently spoke with her while he slipped her nightgown over her head. They heard the toilet flush and the water running for a few minutes. They listened to their mother's voice, but couldn't make out her words. Linc left a nightlight on, and their eyes followed him as he quietly moved out of her room and left the door ajar.

"Goodnight, guys." He nodded. Linc turned and walked toward the staircase as his brothers stared in awe of the man before them. "When the hell did he turn into Superman?" Grant asked Madison. "I don't know, but I noticed the smile he had on his face when he waltzed by us just now. All of his money troubles, taking care of mom, Jenna, Clara....he was glum a short time ago. Now something's changed, that's for damned sure. That bounce in his step, there's a woman, somewhere in all of this. It's not Jenna, that's for sure. But, there's only two reasons he ever smiles. He just got laid or he just kicked the shit out of someone – and I didn't notice any bruises." Grant added. "Yeah, me either."

At 4:00 AM, with four hours of sleep under his belt, Linc Caldwell was milking the cows and performing all of the other chores associated with the farm, including getting ready for the inspectors due to stop by in the next few days. Thank goodness there had been a delay in their return. Sonny arrived bright and early, Rob and Chris showed up as usual, and surprisingly, his two brothers were on the threshold of the barn door. "Can we help?"

Linc pulled them aside. They had on Versace shoes and some designer clothing that probably cost more than Linc's truck. He couldn't imagine them helping with barn chores. Hell, they'd be more in the way than anything else. "Tell ya what...Ma gets up right about 6:00 AM, like clockwork every morning. You guys wanna please her? Cook something like bacon and eggs or make one of those fancy omelets you like. That would make her so happy."

His brothers went back into the kitchen to rifle through the cupboard and refrigerator for breakfast ingredients. One of them headed to the grocer's. Good. That was something he could use right now, help in the kitchen. Although, he wished Clara was old enough to help with the weaning of the baby calf, they'd named Tootsie. The calf was crying and her mother was bellowing in the stall. It was time to milk the colostrum off and put it into the bottle. He'd do that right away.

As he turned to go back into the barn, Sonny gestured toward the calf pen. Riley was already there with a huge baby bottle, Sonny had just milked the mother for her to feed the calf. The sight of Riley feeding the baby touched his heart in a way he couldn't explain. It was as if she had read his mind and somehow appeared, once again, out of nowhere to help him. He reached down to stroke her thick blonde hair. "Hey, Riley, thanks. I mean that. I was just thinkin...."

"Yeah. I was just thinking, too." Riley beamed up at him. "Thinking about how much fun this was and how much I wanted to do this in the morning and evening. You don't mind?"

"Hell, no...I'm so...grateful, Riley." His eyes met hers and stayed locked there way too long. Last night flashed through his mind like a movie in fast forward. *Pleasure.* That's the feeling he associated with Riley -- pure pleasure. God, he felt lucky to have her. But did he *really* have her? She was married to Marcus. Just because he'd made love to her last night, things still remained the same. Except, he wanted her more than ever, now. And, he knew her marriage was on the rocks.

Sonny broke the spell. "Let's go, guys." And, milking resumed. All things resumed. But, every time Linc walked by the calf pen and caught a glimpse of Riley, he couldn't help but scrutinize her. She was so calm and serene there with the calf. His memory drifted back to Riley at fifteen, Riley at sixteen, Riley at the pond, Riley in his arms last night. The thought of her sustained him through anything. He decided right then and there, his life wasn't worth living without Riley. *But, what about Marcus?*

He didn't dare to talk with her about what happened last night. They had both lost control. *Or, was it just the opposite?* They both knew exactly what they wanted and took it. For once, Riley, the kind, helpful, selfless woman took a chance and loved him. For once, Linc, the good ol' steady boy, found himself with the woman of his dreams and embraced her before she could slip away again. He had imagined she'd text him something -- but nothing. The thought stayed in the back of his mind. Maybe she had a talk with Marcus on the phone and they'd patched things up. He looked at her Facebook page and the only photo she posted was one of them eating the lunch she served in the hayfield yesterday. Oh damn. He looked like a savage, covered with food and sunburned. But the photo made him smile. Is that what I really look like?

CHAPTER 22: LIES

Jenna had agreed to meet Marcus the next night at The Nova. She wanted to screw Linc as much as he did, just in a different way. Marcus was well aware that Linc was sweet on Riley. Trouble was brewing and Jenna wanted in. She only had one meeting with Marcus thus far. He'd stopped by the hospital while she was working and talked with her on her lunch break outside while she had a cigarette. There was no question in her mind that Marcus was dead set on taking Clear Springs Farm out of commission.

"You understand, it's nothing personal." Marcus had lied to her. "He's not going to make it, anyhow. So, it's no big deal if you help me end this now."

"Yeah, I know. I don't give a shit if Linc is a dairy farmer or not. I'm leavin town anyhow. Just not yet. I need more money to make the move on my own. That's why I'm helpin you out. I need the money, that's all." She was lying to Marcus Reed, but why not? He could fall under her spell just like many men had before him. She'd have him eating out of the palm of her hand in a short time.

"We seem to be on the same page, then." Marcus leered. He had perfect teeth, Jenna noticed. A good looking guy, she was amazed that Riley was ignoring her handsome dark-haired husband. Jenna would jump at the chance to be with someone as handsome and successful as Marcus Reed. But then, Riley was a spoiled rotten bitch. She always got what she wanted, when she wanted it. Riley was one of those girls who lived a perfect little life, went to church, didn't cuss, and was treated like a princess. *It was time to take her off her throne.*

"Here's the plan." Marcus leaned closer. "Just contaminate the raw milk tanks before the inspectors come. All you need to do is dump some of the run-off water into them. You know the stuff with manure in it. The inspectors will shut him down."

"I'll see what I can do. Let me think on it." Jenna had said. That was the gist of the first conversation. She wondered how deep Marcus would go with her tonight. Jenna had worn a tightly fitting Lycra dress with a floral pattern. It highlighted her bottom perfectly. She took extra time applying make-up and blow-drying her long dark hair.

When she gazed at her pretty little self in the full length mirror in her bedroom, she knew she would turn heads. At this point, there was only *one* head she wanted to turn, but he wasn't interested because he had Riley on his mind. After tonight, maybe Riley would be out of the picture. That was her goal.

When she walked through the door of The Nova, she spotted Marcus in the back corner and stopped at the bar to order a drink. She did as Marcus had ordered her. He came to the bar and sat on the chair next to her. "Come here often?" he asked, eyebrows raised.

"Once in a while." Jenna grinned and stirred her drink. Within two minutes, she had sucked the entire mixed drink down.

Marcus put his arm over the back of her chair. She could feel his eyes on her. Jenna was beginning to think he could be flirting with her.

"You want another drink, honey?" He asked as his lips curled into a smile.

"Sure." Jenna beamed.

Marcus licked his lips and ordered another drink. She was beautiful. Linc Caldwell sure had great taste in women. Jenna was a sultry dark-haired beauty with a body that was amazing. Her ample breasts were revealed every time she moved, her dress was low cut and he couldn't keep his eyes off her assets. Marcus couldn't help but notice her curves. She had exotic eyes, too. And, such a lovely mouth. He appreciated those details. And, he was relatively certain if Jenna had a few more drinks, he'd be able to charm her into a hotel room nearby. If she showed any sign of hesitation, he'd offer her more money. He had to find out everything he could about Lincoln Caldwell. She was living under his roof and she knew every move he was making on the farm and all about his money troubles.

The gin and tonic arrived and a clinking sound came from her glass as she stirred the ice cubes around. "Well, I've got about another two hours to kill." Jenna spoke in a soft feminine voice. "You wanna help me kill it, mister?"

"How'd you know?" Marcus locked eyes with her. "You're so beautiful, Jenna. I don't think you realize how sexy you are."

"No. I don't." Jenna kept stirring her drink. "Why don't you tell me?"

Persuading Jenna to join him in the hotel room on the beach was easier than he'd thought it would be. Two drinks later, Marcus was jiggling the key in the lock and Jenna did a clumsy little dance across the threshold. For twenty minutes she answered every question he asked about Clear Springs Farm -- where things were located, what Linc's plans were -- every little detail.

Decorated in soft beach colors, the lamplight in the room was just enough for him to relish the undressing of Jenna.

The taste of gin was strong when he took her into his arms and thrust his tongue into her mouth. But, she grabbed his ass and pushed her hips against him. Damn. He didn't have any of the little blue pills, or did he? "Excuse me a moment..." he awkwardly peeled Jenna off him as he went into the bathroom. For a frantic moment, Marcus fished around in his jacket pocket. One! He found one! He filled the bathroom glass with water and swallowed it. In twenty minutes, he'd be able to make Jenna beg him to stop. But, he wouldn't stop.

When he opened the bathroom door, Jenna was lying face down on the bed. As he approached her, he suddenly realized she had passed out. How many drinks did she have? Four? As his eyes took in her shapely form naked on the bed, the medicine began to aid his arousal. Marcus figured Jenna didn't need to be awake for him to enjoy himself. He pulled his necktie off and unbuttoned his shirt. Yes, the next two hours were going to be very enjoyable for him.

***

In the morning, Grant Caldwell helped to feed his mother breakfast. He was twenty-eight years old and knew mom fed him this way at one time. Although he couldn't remember that, he looked at the photographs today. The old albums were taken off the dusty shelf every time he arrived home for a visit. Now a successful top tier manager in a high-tech giant in Silicon Valley, he never imagined he'd be spoon-feeding his mother oatmeal. He wondered how Linc managed to take care of mom, plus everything else. But then, Linc had always been his big brother who seemed to be capable of anything. Grant felt insignificant next to Linc. It might have been the fact that he was the baby of the family, but it could've been because he was living a lie.

"Yes, mom, I'm dating a girl. You'd love her. Her name is Sarah, really sweet. She wants a family and all of the same things I want. She's an actress. Only bit parts so far in a couple of television shows and one movie, but she is going to hit it big someday." Grant prattled on. Lies. All of it lies. Sarah had broken up with him months ago. But he hadn't been able to talk about that with anyone except his therapist. Everyone in California had a counselor or a life coach. Grant had been with this one for six months now and his depression hadn't improved.

"Where are you living, now?" his mother asked, haltingly. Her left side definitely affected by the stroke. He wondered if she would ever improve. She was only sixty-four. He'd pray she would get better, but he hadn't been in touch with a higher power since he left Clear Springs Farm. It seemed he'd left everything behind, including the values his parents had instilled in him, truth, honesty, kindness, sharing. No. He started with a fresh slate and couldn't wait to distance himself from the family he called hayseeds, rednecks – the family who embarrassed him. Now he was talking with a stranger, a psychotherapist, to find out *who he was*. One thing for sure – his brother, Linc, knew who he was. There was never any doubt about that. Linc was his father, personified, and comfortable to be just that.

"I'm living in Malibu, mom, in a multi-million dollar house. Here are the pictures on my phone. I want you to come out to California to see me sometime. I know you're busy here at the farm, but I wish you'd come to visit." Grant smiled. *Another lie.* He hoped his mother would never take him up on that invitation. And, he was pretty certain she never would. She loved her job at the hospital, loved her friends, and wanted to help Linc raise Clara. Even though she'd had a stroke, his mother's life had more purpose and deeper meaning than his.

Later, Madison strolled into the kitchen. "Would you like me to take you outside, mom?"

"Sure." Her eyes lit up. "Let's go down to the garden. Mostly flat land from here to there."

Her electric wheelchair buzzed and moved toward the ramp. "I need a little help with this part." Her voice wavered. "Got you, mom." Madison stepped right up. The sun was shining on a beautiful warm summer day, and a dragonfly flitted by. "I like to sit down there by the garden. Sometimes when I'm just sitting there quietly, it's as if I can hear your father there, weeding and humming away. I like to watch the dragonflies. They're out now." She struggled to speak, and Madison had tears in his eyes as he listened to her words. But, at least she experienced true love for the majority of her life. That was more than he could say for himself. As an airline pilot living in Arizona, he had little time for relationships or anything close to love. There was plenty of sex, but even that was getting old.

"What's your girl's name? I forgot." Mom asked.

"Suzanne." Madison told her. "She is a nice girl, mom. I hope you get a chance to meet her."

"Bring her here to the farm next time. I'd like to see her." Mom answered.

"She's really busy right now." Madison lied. At the age of thirty, he'd served two tours in Iraq, then got hired as a commercial pilot. Suzanne was a married mother of two, someone who he slept with on and off whenever he was back in Phoenix. When he wasn't with Suzanne, he was with Marabelle. When she wasn't available, there was Lucinda. So many girls, so little time. That was always his motto. But he'd never realized how lonely his life really was until he tried to talk with his mother about his future.

"What's she so busy with?" mom asked.

"Oh, she's a top executive in a big insurance company. She works a lot of long hours. But, she told me she'd like to get married and have a family. Three kids, maybe. She even has the wedding planned, but I can't seem to get a vacation right now." Madison turned away. He really didn't like lying like this to his mother, especially at this time. But, he justified it with the thought that she needed to hear something cheery. So, he provided that.

For the first time in his life, Madison envied Linc. He and Grant used to laugh at him, saying he was the dimwit hayseed brother who didn't make it to college, still shoveling cow shit and baling hay. However, he now realized Linc was doing exactly what he *wanted* to do. He was his own boss. His fate was in his own hands. He was the last cowboy, trying to save the only family dairy farm left in the state of Maine. Hell, he didn't even realize it until dad's funeral, but Linc was a local hero to the townsfolk.

But there was more to Linc than being a struggling businessman. He was a good person with lifelong friends who loved him. Madison always felt dwarfed by his older brother. When they were younger, he sometimes resented him for telling him to straighten up. Now he wished he would have listened more.

It was obvious to Madison that Jenna was not Linc's type. Linc's failed marriage was not his fault. He married Jenna out of a sense of obligation. He tried to make it work. That was much more than he would've done. Beyond that, Linc was raising his little girl, loving her, trying to be the best father he could be. Hell, he'd even taken Jenna in so Clara could have daily contact with her mother. *That had to be painful.* Taking in the bitch that left you high and dry, left her little girl for a whole year. His brother was a gentle, selfless man, a good person.

As Madison spent the afternoon in the garden with his mother, it seemed his eyes were opened for the first time. Not only did Linc resemble his father physically, but he had many of his characteristics. Admiration swelled in him as he understood what Linc's day-to-day life was like. Besides caring for mom, Linc had the weight of the world on his shoulders. Yet, you'd never suspect it. He was happy, genuinely comfortable in his own skin. Linc gave of himself freely. Madison hadn't yet known the exhilaration of true love, and wondered if he ever would. He had a lot of women, all along his flight paths, but nothing that even resembled love. Linc had his feet firmly planted in more ways than one. He ignored the extraneous stuff of life and focused on the things that really mattered.

CHAPTER 23: A KIND GESTURE

The next morning at the breakfast table, Grant and Madison were deep in discussion. Grant, being the tech wizard that he was, realized there was a parting gift they could leave with their worn out brother. "It's simple, really, just a few cameras -- it's like a nanny-cam. Linc can see mom on his iPhone. I can install a few of these in the house...one in her bedroom, one in the kitchen, and one in the living room. Those are the places she spends most of her time." As he scrolled through a website on his phone, he remarked. "These are really small and you can put them right into a plant or on a bookcase. They blend in with the décor."

"I don't think Linc's going to care about the décor..." Madison chuckled.

"But, seriously, bro. This would make his life a little bit easier, especially while he's in the barn or even at the feed store. He can view this from just about anywhere." Grant was insistent. "There's a store not too far from here that sells the components. I'll have to install a powerful router, but that's no big deal. Come on." The two took off in the Cadillac to do a good deed, a kind gesture, for their older brother who was juggling caretaking priorities on a daily basis.

Two hours later, they were putting things into place, testing the router and cameras. When they asked Linc if they could borrow his iPhone, he looked at them as if they were kidding. "Don't you guys have phones?"

"We're not using your phone as a phone." Grant started. "Look..." He tapped Linc's iPhone and downloaded an app. Then waited as the app detected the router and handed the phone back to Linc. "Now watch mom on this. We installed a simple system. It's really neat." Linc stared at the screen on the phone and viewed his mother in her wheelchair in the kitchen. "Wow. Thanks! I had no idea you were doing this. This is great!"

"Nah, don't mention it." Grant touched his shoulder. "You're carrying a heavy load on these shoulders. This was the least we could do for now."

Madison added. "I want you to take this check, Linc. It's not much, but will get you through the next month or two." Grant had his checkbook out, too.

"Look, you guys. You already gave dad money. I can't take this from you. I can make things work, if I can get that tree farm permit, and a few other things going." Linc noticed they were writing and not paying attention to what he was saying. They handed him the checks.

"Cash these. Do it for mom. Do it for Clara. But, just do it. You're a good man. Gee, I never thought I'd be saying this to a guy who's kicked the crap out of me --- I don't know how many times!" Grant laughed. "Me either." Madison chuckled. "We've got to catch a plane. We'll be in touch. Take care."

Linc watched as they tossed their bags into the white Cadillac and rolled out of the driveway beeping and waving. He looked at the two checks in his hands. Fifty thousand dollars. That was enough to pay off what he owed right now, plus ten grand for those needed repairs. But he tore them up. There was no way he could take advantage of his younger brothers. He imagined they probably had their own problems, financial and otherwise, and decided his success would rise and fall on his shoulders.

* * *

Marcus Reed was getting comfortable in his leather chair as the head of the DEP in Maine. A pile of paperwork on his desk awaited his signature and he sorted the big pile into three separate ones. Approved, Not Approved, and Needs Further Scrutiny. When he got to the Tree Farm permit for Clear Springs Farm, it went into the "Needs Further Scrutiny" pile. Marcus held the permit in his hands and reveled for a few minutes in the feeling of complete and total power that he had. *Riley's cowboy's fate was in his hands, literally.*

There were many obstacles for her cowboy to overcome. Vernal pools, an endangered species on his land, the Bureau of Land Management regulations -- the list was growing by the minute. This would tie his permit up indefinitely, while his money dwindled down to nothing. Then, once a deadly bacteria was found in the dairy's clean room – well, that would shut down the operation for a full investigation. The risky part was getting Jenna to contaminate the clean room. It was easy enough to do. Tossing in contaminated water mixed with manure would do the trick. Also, turning down the temperature on the cooling tanks that held the raw milk. This was almost too easy.

The contamination plan was well thought out, but Jenna hadn't committed to actually doing it yet. That gave him pause, but what really pissed him off was he couldn't stop Riley from setting the cowboy up with restaurants who wanted to buy his organic produce. That deal was already in progress and Marcus was fuming. She worked quickly, his wife, on things that mattered the most to her. The horse boarding was going forward, too. But the revenue wouldn't quite be enough to keep the cowboy going. *Marcus Reed would take out the last cowboy without using a bullet. He'd just sharpen his pencil and kill him with regulations. It would be a quiet death, really. There wouldn't be a sound, just suffocate the farm with regulations and roadblocks.*

* * *

Jenna knew the opportunity to do what Marcus asked of her was a one-shot deal. If she got caught, she'd be the one going to prison. Then she would never see her daughter again. She put out her cigarette and moved back inside the hospital. She loved the night shift. Most of the patients were sleeping or on medication and in a pretty good mood. She had worked hard to get her Nursing Assistant Certification. All of that would be for nothing if she got caught contaminating the clean room at the farm.

Tonight was the night she was supposed to do it. But now, she was having second thoughts – actually third and fourth thoughts, too. Linc wasn't in love with her, but he had been forgiving and kind – all of the things she wished she could've been with him. She hadn't been in love with him when she gave birth to Clara. She hated what the pregnancy did to her body. But Linc told her she was beautiful, even then when she was nine months pregnant. Since running away and being horribly abused for the last year, Jenna had come to the realization that she loved Linc. She'd returned with the hope he would remarry her. But she knew that wasn't going to happen, especially now with Riley hanging around.

When she got off her shift in the morning, she knew she had to make a phone call. She wasn't going to contact the local police or anyone as lowly as that. Jenna was taking this to the top. She had to save her own skin, now. Marcus Reed was a powerbroker. He'd used Jenna for sex and information gathering. He had paid her well to perform the contamination. To go against Marcus now would be suicide for her. She had to play the few cards she had carefully.

The information she had garnered about the corruption in the DEP under Marcus Reed was mind-boggling. More than once, she'd been in his office waiting for him to finish a meeting. She saw the folder on his desk marked Clear Springs Farm and took it upon herself to read through it. She even photocopied a couple of things. *Insurance.* That's what she called it. Just in case Marcus became unmanageable. And lately, he had become more than that. He had become downright abusive with her. She couldn't take it any longer. She searched for the phone number of the local county district attorney. "She won't be in until 9:00 AM, ma'am. Hello. Are you there?"

"Yeah, I'm here. Listen. You call the district attorney and have her contact me at this number. I'll be waiting. If you can get word to her to call me now, as soon as possible, that would be best. I've got information for her – she's gonna be plenty interested in this – I'm just sayin' – this ain't no prank."

Jenna listened as the person on the other end of the phone took her first name and phone number and said she'd get right on it. Within ten minutes, Jenna's phone vibrated. Unknown caller. The district attorney was calling her from a private cell and blocked the number – that was to be expected. Sitting in her car at the edge of Clear Springs Farm, she told the lady on the phone she'd need to meet with her in person – it was urgent.

"What's this about?" the district attorney asked.

"It's about someone high up in the federal government trying to ruin someone financially and in every other way. Just pure evil. That's what it's about. I have proof. Names, phone numbers, details, documents. I'm scared to death of this guy."

"Can you come down to my office? I'm in the town of Stockton, about ten miles from Clear Springs Farm. My office would be a good secure place to talk."

"I just got off my shift. I'm beat. Yeah, I can meet you there." Jenna said. She started her car and headed in the direction of Stockton. Might as well get this over with as soon as possible.

* * *

Linc was in the barn watching Jenna on her phone. He thought it was odd that she drove away in her car instead of coming directly into the house. She had been acting strange lately. He couldn't quite put his finger on it, but if he didn't know better, he thought she might be dating a guy. He figured she'd been lonely. Things would never be the same between them. She knew it, he knew it – but he wanted Clara to have the chance to be with her mother, to get to know her, as much as possible. That relationship was so important to a young girl. He knew Jenna was no angel, but she was Clara's mother. He went out of his way to praise Jenna every chance he got and treated her with the utmost respect and kindness. It was important that Clara saw this, as it would leave a lasting impression on her young female mind. He wanted to set the tone for guys she'd consider later on in her life; he wanted Clara to see a respectful relationship, if nothing else.

It was Saturday. He finished up the morning chores in the barn and walked down to the stable. Chris and Rob were grooming the horses.

"Goin ridin today." Linc announced as he walked through the paddock.

"Great day for it." Chris said as he went about his business.

"Going alone or someone joining you?" Rob asked.

"Riley's gonna ride Star. I'm takin Ranger." Linc smirked.

"Like the old days." Rob laughed.

"Yeah. Somethin like that." Linc couldn't stop the grin taking over his face. "Two old horses and two old friends goin for a ride."

"She's damned pretty." Chris added. "Even prettier now than she was ten years ago, if that's possible."

"You talkin about Star or someone else?" Linc shot a glance his way.

"Riley, of course!" Chris rolled his eyes.

"Yup. That, she is." Linc agreed. "I've gotta get myself cleaned up a little. See you in a few." Linc strode up to the farmhouse and remembered he'd left his phone in the barn. As he walked by what used to be a tack room, he witnessed what he considered to be a small miracle. Ellen Turner, Riley's friend, had taken him up on his offer to set up her pottery shop in the ancient tack room off the side of the barn. It was being used for storage at the time, most of which got hauled to the dump. Riley had installed an upgraded circuit for the kiln and for the first time Linc saw his mother sitting in her wheelchair at the pottery wheel -- and, Katherine Caldwell was smiling. Not a crooked half smile. The left side of her body seemed to be coming around. Ellen was bent over standing behind his mother, helping her throw her first vessel.

Ellen glanced up when she saw his figure in the doorway. "We're doing great."

"Yeah! I can see that. Keep goin and don't let me interrupt you." Linc grinned.

He hadn't seen his mother that excited in a long time. She was making a contribution. That's what she had told him earlier. It was what drove Katherine Caldwell all of her life. She didn't want a free ride. He grabbed his phone and ran upstairs to the bathroom.

He laughed to himself in the shower, and sang a song he'd heard on the radio, that reminded him of Riley. Lately, things were lookin up. But, the inspectors were coming on Monday, and he wanted to make sure everything was in perfect order. He'd check the raw milk tanks for bacteria, as he did every day. He had a test kit that was sensitive for other contaminants, too. He'd use that just to make completely sure everything was up to snuff.

As he brushed his teeth and put talcum powder in his boots, he thought about how long it had been since he'd ridden with Riley. When she first came to the farm, she was interested in horses, so he taught her everything he knew about them and fell in love with her as he did so. She loved Star, the old mare, and she was still going strong. Good stock. Ranger was getting older, too. But, hell, they all were. Linc was beginning to notice that thirty-two was a helluva lot different than twenty-two. He was feeling sore from working all day.

He heard Riley's vehicle pull up and scrambled down the staircase with wet hair. He met her on the screened porch and pulled her to him. "I missed you." He murmured in her ear. The smell of her hair was intoxicating. He wanted this to be a day just for them, filled with romantic notions. There were so many things he wanted to tell her. How happy she made him. How much he loved her, even now, after all these years. How he didn't care a hoot about Jenna, or any other woman for that matter. The only woman he'd ever wanted was Riley.

"I'm glad we're meeting today." Riley took his hand and plunked something into it.

"Where'd you get that? It's Jenna's. I gave that to her when she gave birth to Clara. Sonny's wife made it special for her."

"It was in Marcus' jacket pocket. I brought his stuff to the drycleaner for him. The lady at the counter always fishes through the pockets and she put this in my hand." Riley stared into Linc's eyes hard, as if willing him to say something.

"Jenna's seeing Marcus?" he said it, but then realized the two of them just didn't seem to match. Marcus, the big city, super-wealthy playboy and Jenna was...well, just Jenna. Pretty, yes. But not in his league, especially since his league was probably high-end hookers, wanna-be models and movie stars. He'd heard rumblings about Marcus ever since he moved into the area. The townsfolk could be brutal with gossip, but sometimes they knew what they were talking about. He was a city slicker with an eye for the women, lots of women.

"I'm a little surprised, too." Riley sighed. "What's she doing with him? That's nothing but trouble, right there." At that moment, Riley received a text. "It's my mother. She said Jenna waltzed right into her office this morning and said Marcus wanted her to do some awful things here at the farm to put you out of business."

"Awful things? Like what?" Linc asked, shocked.

"I don't know. She wants me to call her right away." Riley dialed her mother's private number. "You alone?" Riley asked.

"Yes. I've only got a minute, but here's what Jenna told me. Keep this to yourself. I don't want to damage the case in any way. But, I've got to let you know this for your own safety. Marcus wanted Jenna to contaminate the clean room at Clear Springs Farm. When I asked how, she said he wanted her to put some of that water run-off in there, you know the stuff contaminated with manure. She was going to do this just before the inspectors came on Monday." Riley put her mother on speaker, and she continued. "Don't know if I should believe her. She has a record, minor stuff, but I don't have enough to arrest Marcus. Riley, we need to talk. Make sure Linc is on guard there. Jenna's headed back."

"We need to act like we don't know any of this." Linc stared into Riley's eyes. "We've got to pretend we're goin for a ride on the trail. I can watch things on the cameras from my phone."

"But we don't have a camera in the clean room." Riley said.

"Better 'n that. We've got Chris and Rob. Come on." He tugged her toward the stables, and sent a text to Sonny letting him know he'd be stopping by real soon.

Rob and Chris agreed to watch over the clean room, without being obvious. They had some things to do in preparation for the coming inspection, anyhow.

Riley put an old worn blanket onto Star's back and rubbed her mane. "Gosh, she's still beautiful. I missed her so much. She remembers me."

"You're not ridin bareback, are you?" Linc seemed worried.

"Sure. Why not?" Riley's eyes narrowed. "You're not getting bossy with me, are you, cowboy?"

"Just sayin', ridin bareback – it's a challenge. You have to hold on with your knees and thighs, just so."

"I know that, silly." Riley said as she swung her leg over Star's back and the mare barely moved. "See, she remembers me."

"How could anyone forget you, Riley?" Linc smiled as he saddled Ranger and hopped onto him. "Git up..." The two horses moved side by side along the trail into the meadow. Butterflies appeared now and then, and they interrupted a horde of bees feasting on a patch of clover. "Quiet out here, ain't it?"

"Yes. I miss this, cowboy. I miss you." I don't want to go home to Marcus. Especially, now that I know all of this. The prostitutes and all of that was just one layer of corruption. I never would've thought Marcus would go this far to ruin you."

Sonny's homestead loomed in the distance. "Come on. Keep up." Linc glanced back at Riley as Star pranced along the trail. "No fancy stuff, now."

"She's doing that on her own. I'm not making her do it." Riley giggled. One moment she felt sheer terror thinking of Marcus and his horrible plan; the next she was filled with serenity and laughter riding a horse in the middle of a field. Riley was frightened, deeply so. But something way down inside kept telling her everything would be all right. Call it hope or wishful thinking.

Sonny was standing outside working in his garden and shielded his eyes from the sun. "Hey. What brings you here?"

"Somethin you mentioned a while ago. You were right." Linc said as he moved off his horse. "There is somethin rotten goin on – and Marcus Reed is at the center of it."

"He's using Jenna." Riley added.

"Yes, I knew that." Sonny said avoiding their eyes.

"I've been watching things from afar." Sonny waved them over. "Let the horses have a drink here in the shade. I didn't want to tell you this until I had further proof, but Marcus is using

Jenna. They're having sex. He's paying her money for something."

"Well, Jenna's gone to the district attorney and told her everything. Just happens to be my mother." Riley sighed.

"What should we do?" Linc asked with genuine concern. "Damn. I don't want to have this inspection go sideways. I've got Chris and Rob guarding the clean room now. The place is locked up tight as a drum and they're the only ones with keys other than me."

Linc, Riley and Sonny sat together for an hour. Meanwhile, Linc watched the camera on his phone. Jenna arrived. He viewed her in the kitchen. It seemed she went to bed. Linc could see his mother from time to time. She'd started gaining strength in her arms and was using a walker; she dragged her left leg a little bit, but every day brought slight improvement. She was in the kitchen for a few minutes. There didn't seem to be anything out of the ordinary.

* * *

Jenna's phone was vibrating and wouldn't stop. Someone was calling her over and over again. Groggy from sleep, she put the phone to her ear. "Yeah."

"You were supposed to call me at 2:00 PM and it is well past that time." Marcus sounded angry. "Did you do what we talked about? I told you I want to be informed every step of the way."

"What are you talkin about?" Jenna mumbled.

"You know what I'm talking about." Marcus yelled.

"Well, no." Jenna mumbled, rubbing her eyes. "I didn't get the chance. Damn, calm down. I just woke up."

"From now on, I want you to inform me about everything. Do you understand?" Marcus hissed into the phone. Jenna could envision his contorted face, his red, puffy eyes bulging. She had to pacify him somehow. "I'll get to it tomorrow. The inspectors ain't comin until Monday."

"Don't give details on the phone. We talked about that." Marcus sounded furious, but maybe he'd leave her alone. She hoped. She had said what he wanted to hear.

"Okay, I'm hanging up now." Jenna uttered.

"One more thing." Marcus said with a strange tone to his voice.

"What?" She replied as she sat up in bed.

"Everything, and I mean *everything*, has been recorded. You won't be able to tie me to this in any way. If you say a word about this to anyone, *you're* the one who'll be doing time. Not me. I have people watching you, tracking you. I even know who you call on your phone. So, don't try anything stupid." Marcus was threatening her, yet again.

"Well, if that's true, and everything has been recorded, you'll be in the recordings, too. You don't think I'm that stupid, do you?" Jenna couldn't help herself.

"Don't kid yourself. You're dealing with someone way out of your league. Recordings can be altered. I'll not be implicated." Marcus argued.

"You told me I'd be protected. You said I wouldn't get in trouble. That was the deal. That's it, Marcus. I'm through with you and this crazy idea of yours to shut down Clear Springs Farm. I'm sick and tired of being treated like some sort of robot, programmed by you to do your bidding. Go to hell." She disconnected the call, then took a deep breath and exhaled slowly. A few minutes passed as Jenna lay on the bed, her heart beating wildly. Her phone vibrated with a text. Just one word. "Good."

CHAPTER 24: MARCUS PLUS THREE

Marcus rolled over in a drunken stupor. Nicole and Yolanda were there, Savannah had left. He was having trouble taking a deep breath. The evening had been full of fun and games – the kind of games he loved. He now had a new favorite playmate: Savannah. But she had already left and he was vastly disappointed. The throbbing pain in his head wouldn't stop. He moved from the bed to the bathroom, not wanting to wake the girls still sleeping. If he could only get a pain reliever. He found a bottle of over-the-counter pain medication and popped the pills into his mouth and drank a glass of water.

The girls were stirring. Nicole was hungover and had problems even opening her eyes. No wonder. Nicole had done some amazing gymnastics last night. She was learning quickly and didn't seem so innocent and nubile lately. Yolanda, however, was fully awake and stretching. "It's time to take a shower." She murmured sleepily. "Who wants to take a shower with me?"

Marcus decided he couldn't miss this opportunity. Yolanda wasn't even that pretty, but he liked doing it in the shower. He knew Yolanda would do anything he wanted, and she knew exactly what he wanted. But, at the moment the lower half of his body didn't feel like it was functioning. He searched through his pants pocket on the bathroom floor and found the Viagra and washed two pills down with the remainder of the water.

When he stepped back into the bedroom, both girls were whining for breakfast or coffee. A soft click at the door drew his attention to Savannah entering. "Ah, a vision of loveliness, and she has a food cart with her." Marcus responded. He loved the food at the Ritz-Carlton. But he loved looking at Savannah even more. His erection was already starting just at the sight of Savannah fully clothed. The Viagra helped. He knew it would be wild once she was naked.

But right now, the girls were rushing the cart, pouring coffee, and eating voraciously. They were hungry, he imagined, as was he. The sexual romp they had last night lasted into the wee hours of the morning. All four of them did more drinking than eating. The more Viagra he took, the longer he lasted. Four or five hours sometimes. And the girls – well, they loved it. They also loved one another, which made the whole thing even more stimulating for him. But, once in a while they almost left him out of the action – he wanted to make sure that didn't happen this morning. Yolanda wasn't going to steal Savannah away from him this time. No, he would have her first. Yolanda could work around him.

After eating breakfast, he showered with the girls and got exceptionally excited. In the large walk-in shower, they soaped him up and worked his erection until he as hard as steel. Savannah stepped out first and Marcus was right behind her. Yolanda and Nicole were enjoying the shower a bit longer. Ah. The perfect opportunity for him. Savannah's long blonde hair was wet and covering her body. She sprawled her shapely body on the bed and dangled her head off the side. He slid his erection between her lips and placed his hands on her beautiful breasts.

As he got closer to the wonderful rush of pleasure, something bizarre happened. Marcus felt as if he could not take a breath. A sudden searing pain shot through the middle of his chest. Clutching at his torso, he felt a tight squeezing sensation and cried out in pain. Savannah seemed to think he was crying out in delight, and continued pleasuring herself as she worked him with her mouth. But his erection disappeared and Marcus couldn't stop himself as he slumped to the floor. Savannah screamed. "Oh my God! Hey...Yolanda, Nicole, get in here, quick."

Marcus Reed's skin color had turned blue. His breathing had completely ceased for well over five minutes. His eyes were open and his mouth agape, but nothing was coming out. Yolanda knelt beside Marcus. "Damn. I think you killed him, Savannah." Nicole gathered her clothing. "I'm getting the hell out of here right now." Savannah and Yolanda debated about calling 911, as Nicole slipped out of the room. "There's no sense to call anyone. He's not even breathing." She held a compact mirror under his nose. "See, nothing." Savannah said. "Plus, I don't want to be implicated in any way."

"Good point." Yolanda agreed. She rifled through his wallet and took the $4,000 in cash he had.

When the housekeeping staff let themselves into the room, they called 911. But, it was too late. Marcus Reed had been dead for over an hour by then. His body was brought to the morgue in New York City and a phone call was placed to Riley O'Neal, the next of kin.

CHAPTER 25: ALONE

It was mid-morning when Riley got the phone call from a
New York City police detective. Marcus' body had been found at
the Ritz-Carlton. Her father accompanied her to the morgue for
identification. "How did this happen?" her father asked the
mortuary attendant. "Looks like a heart attack. That's what the
medical examiner has written here. But if there's an autopsy
performed, we'll give you more detailed information. That would
be up to a Ms. Riley O'Neal, she's his wife."

Riley was sitting outside in the room where family
members waited to identify a loved one. As her eyes roamed
around the room, she noticed some folks were crying, others
were just numb with shock or grief. She didn't feel anything.
She fell into the numb category. Her father was inside getting
more information, but Riley had a pretty good guess as to what
killed Marcus. The ominous warning from the doctor that she
mistakenly received gave her a hint. The fact that he was
drinking heavily at the Ritz-Carlton gave her another clue. And,
she noticed the mortuary report indicated he had Viagra and
alcohol in his system, too. The police report revealed he was not
alone in the room, however the names of the other people who
might have been there were not in the details. She'd seen
enough to make her stomach turn.

Her father emerged and they flew home immediately.
Riley wanted to stay at the beach house, even though her father
kept insisting she shouldn't be alone at a time like this. She
hugged her father and thanked him. "I don't know what I
would've done without you, dad. I'm okay. I just want to sleep
right now. I know you probably think I'm going through some
deep grieving, but it's just not happening. I'm not shocked or
surprised, really. Marcus was playing with fire."

"Okay. I'll check in with you in the morning. You want
me to come by and help you clear out some stuff?" Her father
asked softly.

A wistful expression settled on Riley's face. "I don't know. I might just collect his things and bring them to Goodwill. At least someone could benefit from his expensive clothing and Rolex watches." He hugged her tightly. "Okay. We will talk in the morning."

Her father drove away and Riley locked the door and set the security alarm. She closed the drapes and stripped off her clothing and took a long, hot shower. The entire day had been exhausting. Before going to bed, she looked at her phone. She had the ringer turned off and there were several voicemail messages. The first one from her friend Sandy, then one from Martha, and another from Anita. The fourth one was Linc's voice. "Hey, Riley. I'm sorry about...Marcus. If you feel the need to talk, I'm here anytime."

Craving sleep, she curled up into a fetal position and pulled the sheets over her. She didn't wake until 9:00 AM the next morning. After brushing her teeth, her phone was ringing again and going to voicemail. More messages from well-meaning friends. Her father had called and Linc again.

She called her father back. "Hey dad. I'm fine. Just slept a lot and putting piles of stuff into boxes today. I think that might be all I'm capable of right now."

"Take your time, honey. Mom and I will be over this afternoon to help you with that." Her father said.

Riley had to call Linc back. She knew he was concerned. He picked up on the first ring. "Riley – are you okay?" For a moment she just listened to the concern in his voice. "I can have Sonny watch things here and come over to help you. Would you like that? Scruffy misses you, too." Riley hesitated, but responded. "Thanks, cowboy. My parents are going to come over this afternoon. I've decided to just box his stuff up and donate it to a good cause." There was a long silence on the other end of the phone. Then Linc made one more attempt. "If you need me, I'll be there in a heartbeat. You know that, right?"

Riley's parents came as promised, later in the afternoon. It was good timing because Riley had a chance to take the moving boxes and fill them with everything that had belonged to Marcus. Her parents helped her take it all to a local charity. She had dinner with her parents that night, then returned home to walk on the beach alone. The exhaustion was overwhelming. Insurance policies, paperwork, phone calls, she couldn't seem to cope with anything else right now.

After three more days of being alone, walking on the beach, and putting away the old photo albums of her with Marcus, Riley felt ready to be with someone. Martha stopped by and they had a good talk about everything over a take-out dinner. The next day Sandy stopped by with some food from La Belle and they ate on the porch.

Linc called her every day and spoke with her on the phone. "We miss you here at the farm." He said. But, Riley knew it was more than that. Sonny stopped by and took a beach walk with her. "You're going to be okay, Riley. You have plenty of people who care about you, including me and Linc."

The following day Riley found herself at her father's shop. O'Neal's Engineering was the type of place that could get you out of yourself. The guys were glad to see her but didn't make a big deal out of Marcus' sudden death. It felt good to drink coffee with them and talk to her father throughout the day. She jumped right into some projects that needed her attention which caused the day to whiz by.

That weekend, Riley found Clara in the pottery shop with Ellen Turner and Katherine Caldwell. Clara had been unusually quiet in Riley's presence. "Where have you been, Riley?" Riley knelt down and put her face close to Clara's. She thought for a moment before answering. "Someone close to me passed away and I had to take care of things." Clara's clear blue eyes met hers. "You mean like my grandpa going away?" Riley managed a little smile. "Yes, like that."

Clara tugged Riley's hand. "We have a new baby in the barn. Come on, Riley. It's time for you to feed them." Riley took her hand and they walked together to the barn. Riley helped Clara hold the oversized baby bottle to feed the new calf. Linc walked by and said. "Good job, buttercup." Riley felt his hand on her shoulder and her eyes met his. "Stay for dinner?"

She nodded. "Okay." Riley turned her attention to the eyes of the calf as they met Clara's. The little girl was bonding with the newborn and thinking of nothing else, except scrutinizing those long thick eyelashes surrounding the calf's huge brown eyes.

Jenna walked by and her little daughter didn't notice her. The child was hypnotized in the moment with the calf. Riley noticed Linc talking with Jenna in the driveway. She'd heard that Jenna purchased a condo with the money Marcus had given her.

The agreement between Linc and Jenna had been a good one for little Clara, but things were changing. Jenna's new condo was only a few minutes away. Linc had told her she could come to the farm as often as she wanted to see Clara.

Fall pre-school was starting soon. Linc explained it was better for Clara to be there. She needed the preparation for kindergarten. Jenna took it well and silently drove away. Riley noticed Jenna didn't even stop to say goodbye to Clara. But then, she imagined she had a lot on her mind right now. Riley turned her attention back to feeding another new calf, as Clara fed Tootsie, who was getting bigger every day. She didn't howl for her mother any longer and the mother cow didn't bellow incessantly for her baby.

The milking and chores in the barn brought a semblance of order to what had been a chaotic time in Riley's life. Linc walked by her as she gave the calf some feed. The late August day was sweltering and he bent down to kiss her cheek. "It's going to be all right, Riley. Just keep goin."

That was what her cowboy had always done – he put one foot in front of the other no matter what life threw at him. Riley noticed that the hydroponic greenhouse had been delivered and installation would begin immediately. Soon, Linc would have automation taking care of feeding and watering his vegetables. The money would start rolling in from the restaurants eager to buy his food. The inspectors had come earlier in the day and he got the green light on everything. In fact, Riley saw the inspector shake Linc's hand. "Fine job. Damn fine."

At the dinner table that night, Linc insisted she sit next to him. He held her hand beneath the table and was incredibly sensitive to her feelings about Marcus and his sudden death. She knew Marcus was corrupt, but all of the information that was coming out now had her mind reeling. It was difficult to sleep at night. The worst part was planning a funeral for Marcus. Riley had no idea he'd written his wishes to have his remains cremated and sprinkled into the Hudson River. She traveled to New York City and stayed at the Ritz-Carlton in Battery Park. It had a lovely view of the Hudson River. Her father wanted to come, but she told him she felt this was something she had to do alone.

Riley arranged to take a private boat to a place in the river where regulations gave her permission to dump the ashes of her deceased husband. None of Marcus' relatives were available to join her. They were all busy at some corner of the globe. How sad, she thought, as the sack of ashes was opened and what remained of Marcus floated away on the river.

When she returned to the dock, two women were there, smiling and talking to one another. They called out to her. "Hi." The dark-haired one said. "I'm Vanessa. You were married to Marcus Reed, weren't you?" Riley's eyes traveled over her. Attractive, but too much make-up. Designer clothes, high end jewelry. If she didn't know any better, she'd guess she was a call-girl. "Yes, he was my husband. He just passed away." The other girl standing next to Vanessa was quite young, blonde, and looked like she'd just seen a ghost. She shook Riley's hand and spoke somberly. "I'm Nicole. We worked for Marcus when he came to New York for his conferences. I was the hostess for his meetings, you know, the Fight Global Climate Change meetings?" Riley swallowed hard. "Um, yes. I remember those conferences." The conversation seemed to be over, but Riley had the distinct feeling lots of people knew Marcus there at the Ritz. More than one young girl dressed to the nines with false eyelashes gazed at her and whispered to her friends. These were his Viagra girls, she realized. Flying home Riley fell asleep on the plane.

The beach house seemed different that night...comforting, quiet, peaceful. She found herself spending extra time at La Belle with Sandy, Martha and Anita. They came to the beach house for walks. It all helped. They often went shopping or to a movie. But, Riley knew little Clara needed her and so did Katherine Caldwell. And, she knew Linc was chomping at the bit to get her alone. But, Riley wanted to be alone, by herself, right now. There was so much to digest and absorb. Time would heal her wounds, her mother had told her. Yes. She believed that to be true. *But how much time?*

Sonny proved to be a comfortable shoulder. He encouraged her to come to the farm and talk with him regularly. Right now, things seemed to be moving in slow motion. Every small moment of every day was moving by her, and Riley noticed things she had taken for granted before. Silly things, really. Like the beads of rain on a leaf after a storm. Or a dragonfly flashing by in the late afternoon sun.

After working at her dad's shop she'd leave in the late afternoon. She began riding Star down to Clear Springs Pond alone. It was always a slow meandering ride, bareback. Once at the pond, she'd take the old blanket and smooth it out on the ground as the horse fed on the grasses nearby. *Solitude.* It was quiet and soothing. For weeks she visited the pond and thought about all of the events of her life over the past ten years. How her life had come full circle. How everything she'd wished for had been granted. But she felt numb inside.

Little Clara started pre-school. Riley threw herself into the hydroponic greenhouse project with a vengeance. She ate dinner with Linc some nights at the farmhouse and played with little Clara. But, more often than not, Riley found herself in the pottery room off the barn with Ellen and Katherine. Sandy, Martha, and Anita would often stop by and they'd make pottery and talk. Some used the wheel, some fired in the kiln, while others painted or glazed a new piece. A canning jar by the door began to fill with money as word got around town that there was a pottery class for women at Clear Springs Farm.

Tonight, Riley tossed the blanket on Star, as she always did after dinner, and took a slow ride down to the pond. September had brought an extended summer, which turned out to be even more beautiful than springtime. Plants and flowers were reinvigorated by the lingering warmth, insects buzzed, birds sang. Riley was at one with nature in this quiet place. It was familiar, yet wild and forgotten by the rest of the world. *Her sanctuary.*

She heard something stir and turned. "Oh, hey there, Sonny."

"How are you doing?" he asked in a subdued tone.

"Better. But I'm still having nightmares." Riley confessed.

"They'll go away after a while. You've been through a lot. You're strong, Riley." He said with sincerity. Riley's pride swelled momentarily to receive such a compliment from Sonny. She admired him so much.

"You know my relationship with the cowboy." Sonny started. This was hard for him, Riley could tell. "We're brothers. He bleeds, I bleed. He's happy, I'm happy. It's like that."

There was silence, as Riley watched a water bug skim the surface of the pond. Then her eyes drifted to Sonny's. "Yeah. I've always known that. He talks about you often to me."

"He is lonely, Riley. You've got to know that." Sonny continued. "He talks about you often, too."

She allowed her eyes to meet his dark brooding ones. "You worried about the cowboy or something?" she asked.

"Not worried so much as having a heavy heart." Sonny was standing at the edge of the pond, not ten feet away.

"Why?"

"It's him." Sonny exhaled and turned away.

"What about him?"

"He misses you. Not just a little bit. He said there's like a light that went out in your soul. That's how he described it. He feels responsible, somehow, for your sadness."

"Oh, gosh. No. None of this is his fault. In fact, I'm the one that showed up on his doorstep when his father died in May. I involved myself in his life. I can be very overbearing, you know." Riley felt a lump in her throat and was suddenly thirsty. Sonny got up and handed her a bottle of spring water."

"But, the cowboy said you saved him. You're the one who brought him back to life, made the light come on in *his* soul. He wants to do that for you. But, he said you turn away from him now. Are the memories too painful?"

Riley looked at the bottle of water Sonny had just tossed to her. She had caught it in mid-air. Her lips curved into a smile. "That's it!"

"Yes, I know." Sonny smiled. "Your work is not done here, is it? Go do what you have to do. The rest will fall into place. You need to trust yourself, Riley. And, I want to personally thank you. Many people here love you. In fact, one person adores you. He is waiting for you to heal. I just stopped by to remind you."

The sun slanted in the late afternoon sky and she could only make out the silhouette of Sonny as he receded. The hydrogeologist she'd met with her father that day in Bingham, Winston Foss, was on her mind as she rode Star back to the stable and put on her barn jacket. When she reached into her pocket for her keys, his business card was there. "Eureka!" Riley screamed.

The next morning Riley bounced out of bed at the crack of dawn. She sent a text to her cowboy. *Do you have some free time this afternoon?* He responded rapidly: *Yes, what do you have in mind?* She laughed at his question, then sent a message back: *I've got a guy you need to meet. He's a hydrogeologist.* Nothing. While she waited for his response, she showered and brushed her teeth. Then he answered: *Had to look that word up. Yes, come by, I'll make time.*

Riley rushed to the farm and worked with the crew finishing the hydroponic greenhouse. In the next few days, plantings would be started and lots of tests needed to be performed to make sure growing conditions were optimal. Programmable logic controllers and switches needed to be installed, too, plus, a back-up generator in case electricity failed.

Linc stopped by to check their progress. "Wow, this thing is going up much faster than I anticipated." He was excited, joyful. Riley was caught up in his happiness for the moment. "Oh, Mr. Foss will be here in a little while. Hey, cowboy, would you like to have lunch on the porch together today?" She definitely had his attention. His head snapped around and he replied. "I thought you'd never ask."

On the porch, they watched the crew from afar. The daylight was still providing long afternoons. Riley lingered on the wicker sofa with Linc. He had eaten his lunch in maybe four bites. She was still nibbling on her sandwich. "I'm sorry, cowboy. I've been so distant lately. It's just that – I don't know – I can't explain it. I needed time to think. Time to be alone. I feel better now."

Linc's blue-green eyes locked with hers. "After this guy comes today, I was hopin that you and I could drive down to the pond. You know. Do some star gazin, like we used to do, back in the day? There's a meteor shower comin tonight. It's gettin chilly -- I'll bring a couple of blankets." Linc held his breath as he waited for her response.

"Okay. Sounds like fun. I've been going to bed really early the past few weeks. Don't know why I'm so tired.

"I know." Linc whispered.

"Hmm – you know?" She added with a slight smile of defiance.

"Yes. You need some lovin to wake you up. You're becoming a zombie, a loner."

"Ha, really?" Riley got a kick out of his description of her. She was anything *but*. Her time had been spent in the company of a mob of women in a pottery room, or feeding calves with Clara. Linc was missing her, no doubt. He deserved her attention. She hadn't stopped thinking about Linc for one moment. His face was in the back of her mind through all the tough moments. She felt as if she had been beaten down and now was building herself back up. She was more than ready to be alone with Linc. Star gazing – yeah right. She imagined he'd be gazing at something, and it probably wasn't going to be stars.

"Sorry, didn't mean to insult you or anything. I just miss you – is all."

Damn, he looked like an innocent little boy when he said things like that. She had raspberry pie for dessert and took her finger and stuck it in. Then pulled out the sweet gooey stuff and smeared it on his lips and kissed him. Linc seemed shocked at first, but she felt his lips cover hers as if he'd just awakened from a coma.

The truck of Winston Foss pulled into the driveway at that moment. Riley took Linc by the hand, raspberry pie and all, to meet him. He was a tall gray-haired man with clear blue eyes and small rectangular glasses. "Pleased to meet you, Mr. Caldwell." Linc seemed eager to get him to the pond.

Winston Foss was businesslike. "We'll take my truck if you don't mind. I've got a bunch of testing kits in there and some other equipment." Linc beamed. "Sure. You can just follow me.

It's a few miles away." Foss got into his vehicle and followed the 1950 Chevy with Linc and Riley leading the way.

"I'm excited about this." Linc shot a glance her way. "Well, that's good." Riley touched his hand. She noticed he smiled when she did that. A simple touch made him so happy – he was her cowboy and always would be. She loved him, for better or worse, richer or poorer, till death. That's how she felt at that moment riding in a bumpy meadow for three miles in an antique pick-up truck.

Once at the pond, Winston Foss set up his testing kits and plotted a place for the drilling rig to do its work. "I appreciate the topographical maps, Riley. These will be helpful. Also, the historical piece. That was pretty interesting, I must say."

"What historical piece?" Linc turned to her. "You didn't tell me?"

Riley rolled her eyes. "That'll be your star gazing story, cowboy."

After an hour or so, Winston Foss finally spoke. "I think you might have something here....something very good."

Riley pressed him. "What's the purity, if I may ask?"

Foss peered over his spectacles. "Actually, I've never seen water this clean and pure and I've been doing this for over twenty years."

Back at the farm, Foss set up a time and date to get the drilling rig out to Clear Springs to see if he could drill into the aquifer. "You'll need to sign some paperwork for us to do that, Mr. Caldwell." Riley took twenty minutes to review the contract. It was identical to the ones she had researched and she told Linc to go ahead and sign it. "Okay, see you next week." Foss flashed a smile and drove away.

"Well, I'll be damned." Linc gawked at her. "I had no idea you'd been working on this all along."

"Actually, I almost dropped the ball. It was Sonny who gave me the idea." Riley admitted.

"Sonny?" Linc laughed. "I doubt that. He's busy making cabinets and raising three kids. He's tuckered out most of the time. I don't imagine he's plotting my land for aquifers."

"Well, I had it all laid out. Just some things got in the way. Took up my time. Sort of derailed me, you know?" Riley asserted. "But, we're back on track now, cowboy."

"How about dinner. What are your plans tonight?" Linc asked softly.

"After chores?" she pondered. "Nothing, really."

"Let me take you to La Belle. Make it a special night. Then, we'll go star-gazin afterwards. How about it?" Linc was winning her over.

"Yes!" But, I'll need to take a shower after chores. Can I clean up here?" Riley asked.

"Sure. Maybe we can shower together to save water." Linc poked her.

"Yeah." Riley giggled. "That would not be a great role model to provide little Clara."

"I know. You're right. I'll let you go first." Linc agreed with the beginning of a smile.

After two brief showers and some primping, Riley and Linc were ready to go out to dinner. She wore a soft cotton sundress with a cardigan thrown over her shoulder. Linc wore his usual plaid shirt, freshly laundered, and a clean pair of jeans. Riley's eyes gave him the once-over. "Damn fine, if I don't say so myself."

"Seriously? I look okay to take you to dinner?" Linc sounded unsure of himself.

"Yes, you look clean and neat." Riley answered. "I like the white cowboy hat, too."

"But not handsome?" Linc was fishing for compliments now.

Riley got close, really close and wiggled her eyebrows. "You're good-looking and you smell good, too. That's a dangerous combination, cowboy."

Linc grinned half-heartedly thinking she might be messin' with him. But then realized she was giving him a genuine compliment.

"Come on. I want to drive that fancy vehicle of yours. Would that be all right?"

"Sure." Riley tossed him the keys. He opened the door for her and adjusted her seatbelt and fastened it. She didn't know why he did that until he leaned in and gave her a kiss.

"There." He said with a twinkle in his eyes. "All good now."

In the driver's seat, Linc was like a kid in a candy store. "Holy smokes. Look at all of the bells and whistles on this thing." Riley explained where things were, but being a car-guy, he figured it out pretty quickly.

Pulling into the parking lot at La Belle, Riley noticed it seemed busy tonight. "We might not get a table. This place is crowded tonight, Linc."

He found a spot in the parking lot right behind Sandy's vehicle.

"You sure you want to park here, behind Sandy? She's the owner. What if she needs to go somewhere?" Riley asked.

"Nah. We're okay." Linc was smiling a lot tonight. He seemed more excited than usual. But, she knew he had waited a long time to be alone with her...really alone. Sort of like an old-fashioned date – just a guy and a girl. No baggage.

As soon as Linc opened the door of the restaurant, a hundred people must've shouted, "Surprise" all at one time. Martha and Anita were there, Katherine Caldwell, and other women from the pottery class, little Clara....Linc's buddies from Bruno's --well, it was half the town, or so it seemed.

"What's the occasion?" Riley whispered. She smiled and waved to everyone, as redness crept over her face and she felt a hot flash coming on.

But Linc was down on one knee and everyone's eyes were on them. In the palm of his upturned hand was the ring he'd purchased for her from Pratt's a decade ago. It was her original engagement ring. "Riley O'Neal – will you do me the honor of marrying me?"

As soon as she realized what was happening, Riley swallowed and felt as if she couldn't speak. She was shocked, overwhelmed, and felt an unexpected teardrop roll down her cheek. "Yes." She exhaled nervously. Her hand trembled as she touched his holding the ring. Linc stood up, proud as could be – "Hey, she said yes!" The crowd cheered.

He held her hand ever so lightly and slipped the ring onto her finger. It was as beautiful as she remembered. Now tears were brimming in everyone's eyes, and her friends ran up and embraced her.

"Drinks for everyone!" Linc turned to Sandy as he waved his arm. Then he handed her a quarter and Sandy pushed the button on the old juke box in the corner. A Chris Cagle song came on, "I'd Find You." This was one song that Linc sang in the barn many times. He'd had this dream every time he sang the words. A hush fell over the restaurant as everyone watched with bittersweet joy as the handsome young couple embracing on the floor clung to one another tenderly. It seemed as if the song could've been written especially for them.

https://www.youtube.com/watch?v=XiWgNczQqe8

Riley couldn't stop smiling or crying. But these were tears of joy and relief. She was in the arms of the man she loved. For the first time she felt completely safe and accepted. When Linc's eyes met hers, she saw nothing but affection. All of the pain she'd suffered to get to this place didn't matter any longer. Being here, accepting Linc's proposal, affirming her love for him openly amongst her dearest friends, she savored the moment. This she wanted to remember for the rest of her life. Friends took many photographs and promised to send them to her Facebook page.

After having a plate of appetizers and a beer, little Clara climbed onto Riley's lap.

"You're happy, Riley. I knew my daddy loved you. I could tell." Clara beamed. "And, now you'll be my mommy, too."

Riley couldn't speak due to the lump in her throat.

Scruffy was begging for attention at her feet and Linc put the small terrier right in Clara's lap. "I want a picture of my girls with good ol' Scruffy." He captured several photos and winked at Riley. "Time for us to go for a ride. Clara, you take care of Scruffy for me. We'll be back in a little while. I wanna show Riley somethin she hasn't seen for a long time."

Everyone laughed when he said it, but Linc swept Riley out through the door in a matter of minutes. The crowd was eating, drinking, and playing songs on the juke.

"Gotta stop home and get the pick-up for this." His eyes met hers.

"Star gazing, huh?" Riley snickered.

"Yeah, heck, there's a meteor shower tonight. Didn't you know?" Linc's eyes glinted with mischief.

"Cool, I haven't seen one since...I can't remember!" Riley laughed.

Clear Springs Farm seemed quiet. A few lights were on in the farmhouse and the barn. Sonny, the ever-present sentinel, stepped off the porch to greet them.

"Congratulations." Sonny murmured as he embraced Riley warmly. He shook Linc's hand and pulled him in for a brotherly hug. "Good job, brother. Go have some fun. I'll keep my eye on things here."

Linc held the door for Riley and she slid into the Chevy, as she had done hundreds of times before. But, tonight it took on a special meaning. Linc started the old reliable engine and the truck glided slowly down through the meadow toward the pond. The further into the darkness they went, the brighter the stars seemed to shine. Linc believed it was Riley who was shining tonight. He'd never seen her so animated and just plain joyful. He inhaled the coolness of the autumn air filled with the scent of the last throes of summer's wildflowers. He felt fortunate to be alive with her beside him right now. He was living in the moment and his spirits were high.

After cresting the hill, the truck glided down to a spot next to the pond, which felt calming compared to the excitement earlier. A gentle wind blew through Riley's blonde hair as she stepped into the truck bed.

"Ah, you have a couple of different quilts..." she ran her hand over the soft cotton.

"Yes. I found them in the attic. They were in my mother's hope chest." Linc looked happy.

"Do you think she was hoping for this?" Riley snickered.

"Yes. I do." Linc's features were serious. His arm encircled her beneath the quilts. "She told me to take them tonight. She said she hoped I'd been lucky enough to have found the one who could make me as happy as she was with my dad."

Riley was silent for a moment. "They were so happy, your mom and dad." She whispered. Linc's hand cupped her upturned face. "Yes, they were. I want that, too." His lips brushed against hers as he spoke. "Is this what you want, Riley?" A shiver of delight shot through her. "Yes. You're exactly what I want."

She pressed her open lips to his and the sweet tenderness of his kiss caused her to quiver. Her soft curves molded to the hard contours of his lean body. His hand moved under her dress and skimmed her hips and thighs. She pulled the dress off over her head and exhaled softly as he laid her down. His tongue explored the rosy peaks of her breasts.

For a long time, they took time to explore, to arouse, and to give mutual pleasure. She yielded to the searing need which had been building for months, years. She had never known such passion existed within her.

Afterward, she laid in the drowsy warmth of her cowboy's embrace, wrapped in the quilts watching the meteor shower. "That's a good one, right there." Linc pointed out. When he spoke like that, he reminded her of a down-to-earth country boy. There was a goodness about him, something plain and true. She silently made a wish upon a falling star as she watched the excitement on his attractive boyish face.

His eyes studied her with a curious intensity. "What...you're supposed to be lookin at these shootin stars!" He laughed self-consciously.

"Oh, don't worry, cowboy. I am enjoying the view." Riley smiled. "Yes, I am."

* * *

A simple early October wedding was being planned and Riley sought the help of Katherine Caldwell and her three best friends, Sandy, Martha and Anita. Little Clara would be the flower girl, and to say she was excited would be an understatement.

Meanwhile, drilling produced an aquifer at Clear Springs Pond that had proven to be an amazing source of revenue. Once the checks started rolling in, Linc felt the choking grasp of debt removed from his throat. He was breathing easier now.

One other surprise was unearthed, however, and neither he nor Riley saw it coming. It started with a phone call from the law firm handling Marcus Reed's estate. The lawyer who contacted them said he was planning a vacation trip to Maine and would meet with them at the farm.

"I don't know about this." Riley said with a troubled look on her face. "Marcus was into so many things that were – well, just not above-board – if you know what I mean. I'm worried this guy could serve me with some sort of unpaid bill or something."

"Well, he will be here tomorrow." Linc tried to calm her fears. "Let's hear him out. It's all we can really do."

"Yes. I know. It's just that I don't like surprises." Riley said anxiously.

"You liked my surprise when I took you star gazin, didn't you?" Linc raised his eye brows. At least he got her to smile.

"Yes. I loved your surprise."

"Then, let's not worry until we know the whole story." Linc thought he sounded sensible, but he was a tad worried, too. Lord knows, Marcus was into some shady things. "We'll know tomorrow. He'll be here at 11:00 AM."

"Yes, I'll steel myself for the worst and hope for the best." Riley sighed. As she collected the dishes off the kitchen table and put them into the dishwasher, Linc stood to help her. "Here, let me do that." He put his hand on her shoulder and brushed the hair from her neck. "If I do this, you can give Clara a bath. Then, I'll read her a bedtime story and we can be alone – just you and me." A mischievous look danced in his eyes as he assessed her.

Riley looked at him with amused wonder. "You are such a good planner."

"Schemer, is more like it." Linc grinned. She found it impossible not to return his disarming smile. Riley snapped the dishtowel against his rear as she headed to the small bedroom off the kitchen.

Katherine Caldwell was reading a book to Clara. The two had eaten earlier and were getting ready to settle in for the night. Riley paused in the doorway for a moment before entering. Katherine's speech was improving daily. Reading aloud was a laborious process for her, but Clara insisted upon it. Riley viewed them from behind, grandmother and child huddled together over a Peter Rabbit story. As soon as the story ended, Riley softly spoke. "Time to get ready for bed, Clara. How about a bath?"

"Yes!" Clara slid off the bed and moved toward Riley. "Wait, I need to hug grandma." She ran back and sweetly embraced Katherine. Riley watched her smile in the lamplight. "Goodnight, Clara."

As Riley took Clara upstairs, Linc spent time getting his mother ready for bed. Riley heard the water running in the bathroom downstairs as she got Clara's bath ready upstairs. Riley collected Clara's bath toys, a magnetic fishing pole with plastic fish and a rubbery shark and a whale that floated. Clara liked to linger, so Riley set the timer. "When this alarm goes off, it's time to put our pajamas on."

Clara never questioned Riley's methods. It was much easier to set a timer and have the clock make the determination for her bath to end. Riley picked out Clara's pajamas, the ones with funny bunnies on them. As she listened to Clara singing in the tub, playing with her toys, she wondered what it would be like to have a child with Linc – a little cowboy – a miniature version of him. As her hand touched the soft cotton pajamas, she imagined him. Blond and masculine, but a good little boy, well-behaved and smart like his daddy.

She almost jumped out of her skin when the alarm went off. Riley got Clara dried off and dressed for bed. Linc appeared in the doorway of Clara's bedroom. "Which story tonight?" he asked softly. "This one, daddy." Clara handed him the book she wanted. His eyes were gentle, compassionate, understanding. "Sure, honey. Let me tuck you in."

Riley pulled the door almost shut as she left the room. She listened to Linc's voice and marveled how she got to this place. She lay in the cozy warmth of his bed thinking. This would soon be the bed they'd sleep in as man and wife. She didn't stay overnight and wouldn't until they were legally married. But, once or twice he had locked the door and made passionate love to her without Clara's knowledge.

Out of the corner of her eye she spotted the old steamer trunk that was Linc's time capsule. Curiosity got the best of her and she moved off the bed and sat on the floor in front of it. It had to be a hundred years old, or more. She touched the lid and it lifted. Ah, it was unlocked. The first item that caught Riley's attention was a bundle of papers tied with a string. She lifted them out and started reading them. Each one was written in Riley's handwriting to her cowboy. Goodness, he was organized. He even had them in the order in which they were written.

At age fifteen, she knew she was in love with her cowboy. Her handwriting was the same, but the note included doodles and sketches in the margins.

Dear Cowboy,
Thanks for hiring me on at Clear Springs. I hope I don't disappoint you.
The work is hard, much harder than I imagined, but you make it fun.
I look forward every day to seeing the calves and feeding them. And the cow

manure doesn't bother me. I'm a lot tougher than I look. Thanks for being
so patient with me. - Sincerely, Riley

At age sixteen, she made love to him for the first time. The note she left for him in the barn reminded her of the emotions that were churning through her.

Dear Cowboy,
Last night was incredible. No, it was amazing. Amazingly incredible.
I've never felt this way before. I hope you don't think I'm the sort of
girl who does this with just anyone. In fact, I've never done anything
like this ever. But being with you last night was wonderful. I can't
stop thinking of you. – Sincerely, Riley

Oh God. She sounded like such a dork. She wondered what Linc saw in her. She turned and he had entered the bedroom. He held his finger up to his lips and turned to slide the bolt on the door. Crouching next to her, he pulled out the six-foot two-inch gum wrapper chain. "This is my favorite." He whispered. Then, he rummaged in the chest and pulled out a teddy bear with a sign around his neck that said, "Take me to bed with you." Riley started to laugh, but put her hand over her mouth.

He pulled out an old photo album filled with pictures of a gangly version of Riley at age fifteen. That first picture in front of the barn. "Oh, gosh, cowboy – what did you see in me? I was a skinny, goofball with braces!" Riley giggled quietly.

"Oh, damn. You were a super-model in my eyes." Linc confessed. "I fell in love with you the day you started workin here. But you were fifteen and my father told me to back off. If it's meant to be, then you can wait. He told me the first year, we could only be friends. It wasn't proper for a guy to date a girl under the age of sixteen. But, I have to admit, you looked much prettier when you had your braces removed." Linc flipped to a photo of Riley the first day she smiled without them. She was sixteen then.

"Let me see that..." Riley took the photo album from him. "Gosh, I never realized how awful those braces looked."

Then her eyes spotted a calendar. It was big with lots of notes scribbled on it. "What's this?" Riley inquired.

Linc pulled it out of the trunk. "It's sort of a journal I kept in my bedroom. This calendar hung on the wall next to my bed. I kept track of things." As Riley's eyes swept over the pages, she saw where Linc had recorded their first kiss, their first walk, first everything.

"Sort of makes you realize how much I love you, doesn't it?" He exhaled softly.

"Yes. I have one just like this." Riley replied. Her face was close to his and she felt his lips brush her cheek.

"Need to be quiet. I don't know if Clara is sleeping yet." Riley closed her eyes.

"I can be very quiet." Linc said softly. "A ninja couldn't be this silent." He gathered Riley up and placed her upon the bed. The soft lamplight softened his features and she watched the play of emotions on his face. His lips slowly descended to meet hers. She drew his face in with her hands, welcoming his advances.

As he kissed her, she felt his hands as he unbuttoned her shirt. Then he removed his and tossed it onto the floor. Riley's eyes roamed over his chest and abdomen, and he guided her hands to his belt buckle. With slow precision, she removed his belt and unzipped his jeans. His eyes were filled with a deep longing. After he tugged off her jeans, Linc was above her, his mouth planting kisses in the hollow of her neck. Then the knock on the door stopped them cold.

"Daddy, I want a drink of water." Clara's voice sounded sleepy.

"Be right there. Just changing my clothes." Linc responded.

Riley and Linc leapt off the bed and dressed in record time. As he opened the door, Clara was rubbing her eyes. "I want Riley to give me a drink."

Riley put her arm around Clara and walked her back to her bedroom. "I'll get you a drink." Clara tilted her head and looked up at Riley. "Are you sleeping over tonight?"

"No, Clara. I've got to go home now. "I'll run downstairs and get you a drink." Riley shot a quick glance at Linc, as if to say *we almost got caught*. He rolled his eyes and shrugged, *oh well*.

At precisely 11:00 AM, Robert Barrington pulled into the driveway at Clear Springs Farm. Linc and Riley were sitting on the porch with mixed feelings of anticipation laced with dread. What if Marcus died and left her a bunch of unpaid bills? That would be so like him, Riley thought. The attorney stepped out of the rental car, casually dressed, carrying a leather briefcase. In fact, it was Marcus' personal briefcase, Riley noted.

"Hello. You must be Riley O'Neal." The gray-haired man extended his hand as she opened the porch door.

"Yes." Riley swallowed. "This is my fiancé, Lincoln Caldwell." The two shook hands.

"Are you comfortable right here on the porch sofa?" Barrington asked.

"Sure." Riley answered and they sat down. A pitcher of iced tea was on the table next to the sofa. "Would you like a drink?"

"Yes, thank you." Barrington opened the briefcase on the sofa and paused. He took a long drink of iced tea. When he spoke, he directed his comments to Riley. "I don't quite know how to tell you this, Miss O'Neal, but Marcus left you as his sole beneficiary. He ran a charitable foundation which he sold just before his death. The proceeds of the sale have been designated to pass to you."

Riley sat with her mouth open, surprised, shocked, and slightly nervous. "Exactly what are the proceeds?"

Barrington handed her a sheet of paper. "Two million, five hundred thousand, to be exact. And, that's tax-free."

As she looked at the transfer of wealth imprinted upon the sheet of paper, she tried to wrap her head around the thing. "Why? How? Where did Marcus get this money?"

"FGCC." Barrington explained. "Fight Global Climate Change – he sold the foundation to a Chinese company. It's all totally legitimate. It was the very last deal he signed just before...his untimely death."

A myriad of feelings washed over Riley – but after the torrent of emotion finished, she gathered her thoughts. "What should I do now?"

"I'm not a financial consultant, but you might want to think of investing this and living off the income it makes for you. Even if you only earned 5% interest, you'd get $125,000 a year." Barrington said slowly. "In the meantime, I need to find a notary so we can get your signature on these documents. The money needs to be in your name until you decide which account you want to transfer it to."

The rest of the day was a blur. After a trip to city hall and some photocopying of paperwork, Riley O'Neal was an heiress. This was not what she expected, but embraced the windfall with unadulterated joy. She parked the money into an investment account that yielded a fair amount of income. For the first time in her life, Riley felt free to do as she pleased. She visited her father's engineering shop regularly, but spent more and more time at the farm with Linc. A new farm hand was hired to help with the milking.

Riley was walking on air for the next few days. Although she had an unexpected windfall, she and Linc agreed that their wedding plans would remain unchanged. They were to be married in a small Methodist chapel a short distance from the farm. Hoping the weather would cooperate, the reception was to be at Clear Springs Farm in the side yard under a large white tent. Riley's best friend, Sandy, insisted on catering the affair.

CHAPTER 29: TO HAVE AND TO HOLD

In search of the perfect wedding dress, Martha traveled with Riley through the back roads of the county and the malls of the city in search for *the one*. Most of the modern dresses did not appeal to Riley. She wanted something different. As she told her friends, it was one of those things: she'd know it when she saw it. After a long day of shopping, Riley and Martha stopped by La Belle for refreshment.

"Find anything?" Sandy asked.

"No. We came up empty. I want something vintage – if I can find it." Riley sighed as she sipped a pineapple and rum drink made by the talented Santos.

"Hey!" Anita yelled from the other side of the table. "Bingo! What size did you say you needed? Size 10? I just found the dress of your dreams on Craig's List."

The girls all clustered around the screen of Anita's laptop. There it was, the dress Riley had been searching for. It was a 1930's gossamer and lace replica. It was a steal. "That's the one!" Riley squealed. "Oh, we just have to go get it." The four friends traveled together to watch Riley try on the dress, and it fit perfectly. The dress was purchased for a bargain price.

Piece by piece, the wedding plans fell into place, as if it was meant to be. The dress for Clara was made by a family friend. Clara looked like an angel in it. Katherine Caldwell found a beautiful green dress. Lately, she had been walking with a cane and the use of her left side seemed to be stronger every day. Her therapy had been the pottery shop in the barn, filled with women on Monday and Wednesday nights. Ellen managed to grow the business into something profitable. Katherine Caldwell spent many hours making pottery. Townspeople and tourists stopped in to purchase the pieces she created. In the past couple of months, the newspaper had done an article on the fresh new artist at Clear Springs Farm. Katherine had found a sense of purpose.

As the date of the wedding drew near, Riley refused to let Linc see her dress. She kept it at the beach house and spent time there planning and walking on the beach with her friends. Linc kept joking that she had some sort of surprise she was going to spring on him. The more she tried to keep him out of the beach house, the more he wanted to go inside. It had become a game with them and many nights she'd push him away after a few kisses on the back porch. "Ah, no, you can't go inside. My stuff is all laid out in there. No peeking!"

Finally, October 4th had arrived. Around mid-morning, the sunlight filtered through the misty morning haze. Birds were singing, and the moderate temperature was just right for a wedding day. Riley's group of friends came to the beach house and everyone got ready there. Clothing, hair accessories, jewelry, mixed with fast food wrappers and half-filled cups of coffee covered every horizontal surface in the house. The ladies were primping as Riley stepped into the vintage-inspired dress for the last time. She had it on before, but without hair and make-up. This time when she slipped into the gossamer sheath, her friends fell silent for a moment. Then, there were oohs and ahhs galore.

"Wow, Riley. You are stunning!" Sandy uttered.

"Yes, breathtaking!" Martha added.

"You're a real honest-to-goodness bride!" Anita breathed.

"Aw – don't make me cry..." Riley begged.

Riley's blonde hair was tied into a loose chignon with a simple ribbon. A dusting of powder gave her skin a translucent glow. The slightest hint of eye make-up enhanced her big blue eyes. A soft rosy lipstick gave her a perfect pout.

The limo picked the bridal party up and delivered them to the chapel at 4:00 PM, where Linc and his groomsmen awaited inside. The chapel was filled to capacity with many people spilling out into the front yard. As a cool autumn breeze blew over her, Riley stepped out of the limo and made her way to the front door of the building where her father was waiting. Tears were already streaming down Conor O'Neal's face. He didn't have the chance to attend Riley's first wedding, and now he understood why. The hasty marriage to Marcus wasn't the real thing. *This was*. He'd hand his baby girl over to the guy who really loved her all along. These were tears of joy, not regret. He took Riley's arm and tucked it under his. He couldn't utter a word.

Walking through the chapel door, Riley saw Linc standing at the small alter. His hands in front of him, holding his white cowboy hat. He'd found a tuxedo and looked damned good in it. Riley smiled as the cameras focused on her. Sonny stood next to Linc and had a big grin on his face. As the traditional wedding march played, she gracefully walked step by step down the aisle toward Linc, and her father's arm left hers. She was standing at the alter facing the minister.

Linc couldn't seem to stop staring at her. Maybe it was because she was wearing make-up. Maybe it was because he was shocked and amazed they were really doing it, tying the knot, making it legal. She'd be his wife in a few more minutes. Riley Caldwell.

During simple wedding vows, the ring was placed on her finger. She couldn't stop the tears stinging her eyes when she heard the words, "You may kiss the bride." Linc cupped her face in his hands as he touched his lips gently to hers. She observed a single tear trace a path down his cheek. The devotion in his eyes said everything she needed to know.

A late afternoon reception started under the white tent at 5:00 PM. When the bride and groom arrived, soft music was being played by a DJ and the bar was open. Two hundred people filtered into the space and the reception was filled with fun and laughter. Riley and Linc danced, off and on, for two hours as the sun got lower on the horizon.

As the guests tapped their silverware against the glasses, Linc leaned in and kissed Riley. "Hey, I like this idea." He smiled.

Right after the kiss, Riley stood and a hush came over the crowd. She walked to the edge of the tent to the newly planted cherry tree, removed the white ribbon from her hair and tied it around a branch. There was a moment of silence as everyone in the crowd thought about Timothy Caldwell. It was a simple gesture, really, but she didn't want to finish this day without remembering him.

"Would the bride and groom come to the floor for a final dance?" the DJ requested. "This song was selected by the groom for the bride."

https://www.youtube.com/watch?v=Je_24df8BZs

Linc swept Riley into his arms and held her close. The moment she heard the words to the song, she recognized it immediately – Linc often sang this while doing chores in the barn. Thoughtful and romantic, were the words she'd use to describe her cowboy. But right now her cheek on his shoulder made her feel like she was floating on a cloud. She had never been so happy and feared something could happen to spoil it.

After the dance, Riley escaped into the silence of the limo with Linc. As the door shut, Linc took Riley's hand and pressed his lips into her palm. "I love you. I'm sorry it's a one-night honeymoon."

"Every night will be a honeymoon with you." Riley sighed.

Linc closed the window behind the driver for privacy as they changed into comfortable clothing. The limo dropped them at a path that lead to a small cabin on the outskirts of Clear Springs Farm. "You folks all set?" the driver asked.

"Yes. I've got everything we'll need. Thanks." Linc handed the driver a fifty dollar bill and the chauffeur smiled and drove away.

"It's gettin dark." Linc muttered as they walked along a winding trail through the forest. Twenty minutes later, after turning at the big rock and traipsing through a hayfield, Linc shouted, "We're here!"

The sun had slipped beneath the horizon and the cool night air ruffled through Riley's hair. "Don't know why I lock this door – there's no one out here but us and some wild animals."

When he opened the door, Riley was pleasantly surprised. The small one-room cabin was clean and had fresh sheets on the bed. A vase filled with fresh flowers sat on the primitive kitchen table. An old bathtub was in the corner of the room, next to a sofa and a chair. Along with a woodstove, a small propane stove and fridge along with handmade cupboards and an old slate sink made up the corner that would be used as a kitchen. Linc struck a match and lit the gas lanterns. The light cast a warm golden glow on his handsome features.

"Oh, cowboy, this is beautiful – I never expected this." Riley murmured. "This is Sonny's old place, isn't it?"

"Yeah. He lived here for a while as a child. That was just before his parents died. Gosh, that was twenty some odd years ago now." Linc's voice trailed off.

"Your father loved him." Riley added.

"Yes, he did. And, thank you, by the way, for remembering my dad tonight like you did. That sort of caught me by surprise, but was so perfect."

Linc had opened the woodstove flue and got to work building a fire. "Gonna be on the cool side out here tonight. Might as well get this thing goin now." In a few minutes, the fire was crackling and snapping and he stoked it with a bigger piece of wood. "There, that'll keep us warm."

"I have you to keep me warm." Riley teased him.

"Hey – let's get this party started...I've got beer in the fridge." Linc's eyes sparkled with mischief. He removed his shirt and Riley started to unbutton her shirt, but paused for a moment. "Is there a bathroom here?" she asked, hoping he'd say yes.

"Well, there's a bathroom – but it's outside."

"An outhouse?" Riley smirked. "Oh, God – I guess I'd better buck up."

"It's all clean and everything -- really." Linc was trying to sell her on the idea. He handed her a spa robe and she slipped it on.

"Take this flashlight." Linc smiled.

"I'm tough. I can handle it." Riley said. She stepped outside and it was dark. The outhouse was about 100 feet away. About half-way along the path, she heard something rustling in the underbrush and flashed the light upon it. Damn – it was a skunk and he immediately put his tail up and sprayed Riley. She screamed, "Oh damn it!" The strong odor immediately soaked into her robe and skin and her eyes started watering. She made it to the outhouse, choking and coughing. The smell was unbearable.

As Riley made her way back to the tiny cabin, she tapped on the door. Linc opened it and said, "Holy cow – what happened – oh, don't tell me. I *know* what happened! Stay right there – don't come inside. We've got to clean you up outside."

Linc dragged the large tin bathtub outside and heated up water on the both stoves. It took him a good hour to fill the tub up with several kettles of hot water. "Soap ain't gonna do this." Linc held his nose. "We need tomato juice." He tapped his phone and called Sonny. "Yes, tomato juice and a ton of it."

By this time, it was getting chilly outside and Riley was nude in the big tin tub. Now Linc was laughing and she was giggling. "This is surely an exciting wedding night!"

Sonny arrived forty minutes later with sacks filled with cans of tomato juice. "I've got something better." Sonny said. He put hydrogen peroxide, baking soda, liquid dishwashing soap and a plastic spray bottle on the table with a pair of rubber gloves. "Okay, this is what you've got to do...spray Riley thoroughly with this mixture. Let it saturate her skin for five minutes. Then rinse her off. I mean really rinse her off 'til you can't do it any longer. I'll help you pump more water."

While Sonny made the mixture and put it into the spray bottle, Linc drenched Riley in the tub. The two of them couldn't stop laughing. Sonny was pumping water into the kettle and had stoked a good roaring fire in the woodstove. Another hour passed, as Riley was drenched with the magic formula and rinsed with lots of warm water.

Always a gentleman, Sonny looked away while Linc did the spraying and rinsing. Finally, Linc handed Riley a towel and she wrapped herself in it. "We're gonna have to burn that robe you had on." The thought of it made them both laugh.

Before Sonny left, he looked at the two of them and erupted with laughter. "Damn. I don't know about you two." Then he noticed he had the skunk smell on his clothing. "Ugh. I smell bad, too! I'm getting out of here." Sonny took off into the darkness.

Riley came inside wrapped in a towel with Linc right behind her. "That's done. Oh, babe, I'm sorry about this. You're shiverin." Linc dragged the sofa a bit closer to the woodstove and cradled Riley in his arms. The warmth of the stove made her sleepy. Before long, Linc had fallen asleep, too. As a log popped loudly, Linc woke momentarily. He carried his sleeping beauty to the bed and covered her up. Then, climbed in next to her and promptly fell asleep.

CHAPTER 30: RETURN TO SENDER

As if Riley and Linc's wedding night wasn't enough of a disaster, Sonny got into his truck to drive out to pick them up the next day after morning chores with a worried mind. He let them sleep late, but knew Linc would be up early because that was his habit. Sonny wasn't sure why Riley's mother was waiting at the farmhouse to talk with her, but from the look on her face, it was something serious. As he pulled up to the cabin, Linc was standing in the door way.

Sonny hopped out of the truck. "Did you two lovebirds have a wonderful evening?" Linc rolled his eyes. "Yeah, right. We both fell asleep shortly after you left. We were exhausted from the wedding and the skunk thing, you know?" Sonny and Linc laughed for a minute.

Riley appeared. "Okay, I'm ready to go."

Sonny leaned over and sniffed in an exaggerated fashion. "Oh, Riley, phew!"

They climbed into the truck and Sonny had a serious tone. "Your mom is waiting for you this morning at the farmhouse. She looks like she has something on her mind. Just letting you know."

Riley wondered what her mother wanted. She hadn't called her or given her any warning. That certainly wasn't like her. As the truck pulled into the driveway, Riley walked into the kitchen. Clara hugged her and ran into the pottery studio with grandma.

Erin O'Neal pulled Riley and Linc aside. "I've got to talk to you about the money that Marcus left to you. I dug into it, as you requested, and the sale of the charitable foundation wasn't legal. The whole thing was a scam, one of many Marcus was embroiled in. I'm sorry, Riley. But the federal government has been investigating Marcus for quite some time. The money will be confiscated while the investigation continues."

Riley glanced down at her hands, then back at Linc. "Wow. I'm glad I didn't spend a dime of that money. I always had a strange feeling about the whole thing."

"What's that smell?" Riley's mother asked.

"Oh, we had a run in with a skunk last night." Linc murmured. "A special wedding night for us, you know?"

"Yes, I imagine it will be memorable." Riley's mother stood. "I've got to get to the office. I'm sorry about this bad news."

Riley's phone vibrated and it was her father. "Hey dad."

"Your mother told you the news about Marcus' money venture."

"Yeah. It's okay. The money from the spring water company will sustain us." Riley was upbeat.

"I was wondering if you'd be willing to take on a few projects here. We've gotten pretty busy." Conor O'Neal waited for her answer.

"Sure, dad. I'll stop by this afternoon to meet with you. Is that all right?"

"You don't have to come today. Next week is fine. Just wanted to touch base with you. How was your night at the cabin? Good, I hope."

"Oh, yes, it was lovely." Riley said. "Except for the skunk."

"Skunk? That doesn't sound good."

"It's a night I will remember, that's for sure." Riley chuckled.

"Oh, I got a moving truck to get your stuff out of the beach house for you. I scheduled that for tomorrow. Do you have most of your stuff boxed up?"

"Yes. I'll pack the rest of it right away. Thanks for the help, dad."

Riley had a tummy ache and slipped into the downstairs bathroom. Sick to her stomach, she had a few minutes of dry heaves. Must be all of the excitement of the wedding and the skunk night. She washed her face and got a bottle of ginger ale out of the fridge to calm her stomach. Coffee had no appeal.

"You all right?" Linc was at the doorway when she came out.

"Yes. Just an upset stomach." Riley dismissed the incident.

"Back to the barn for me." Linc kissed her forehead and moved onto the porch.

"Wow, I think I'm going to be sick again." Riley returned to the bathroom.

By evening, Riley was starving, or so it seemed. She prepared dinner which consisted of salmon, rice and a salad. As Linc came in to eat, he asked her how she was feeling. "I'm starving." Riley said.

Katherine Caldwell and Clara were sitting at the table, too. Everyone enjoyed the meal. As Riley started cleaning up the kitchen, her tummy felt upset again. Oh no. She didn't want to worry Linc. But while he was helping his mother get ready for bed, Riley ran upstairs and lost her dinner. She decided to stop by the doctor's office tomorrow to see if she had a stomach bug or something.

CHAPTER 31: OR SOMETHING

Without telling Linc, the next day Riley made a quick visit to her doctor's office. Her physician was nice enough to fit her in at Noon. She arrived a few minutes early to fill out paperwork with her new married name, then watched the minutes tick by on the wall clock. "Mrs. Caldwell" the nurse called her name. After the nurse took Riley's vitals, she parked her in an examination room and she waited for the doctor.

"Hey, Riley." Dr. Stanton came in. "Sick to your stomach? How long has this been going on?"

"Just started." Riley answered.

"Are you taking any birth control?"

"No."

"Well, you're having morning sickness. According to your urine sample, you're pregnant."

"Oh wow, I am?"

"When was your last period?"

"I had one last month."

"Normal?" Dr. Stanton asked.

"Now that you mention it, it was lighter than usual." Riley was deep in thought. *Pregnant.*

"I'd like to schedule an ultrasound to determine how many weeks you've been pregnant. How about later this week? I'll set it up....and congratulations!"

"Sure." Riley's mind was swirling. She hadn't had sex with Marcus for six months. It had to be Linc's baby. She wondered if she was having a beautiful dream. Linc's baby. She wanted to tell him and couldn't wait to get back to the farm. She was thrilled with the news and thought about calling her parents. But first she had to tell her cowboy.

Riley drove straight back to the farm. Just as she walked inside, she remembered the moving truck was coming to the beach house today to bring her things to the farm. She was supposed to be there at 2:00 PM. She drove to the beach house and got to work inside. The timing was perfect. The box truck arrived thirty minutes later. She ran through the house and tossed everything that wasn't packed into trash bags and piled them up for the movers. She instructed them to take all of the furniture and trash bags to Clear Springs Farm. As they emptied the house efficiently, Riley walked through one last time. The fridge was empty, everything was packed. She tapped her phone to call Linc. "Hey, it's me."

"Where'd you go? I've been lookin for you."

"I need to talk with you." Riley exhaled.

"This sounds serious. You usually don't sound like this. What's goin on?"

"I'll be there in a few minutes. The moving truck is bringing my stuff."

"Okay, sweetheart. I'll be right here waitin for you." Linc's voice was tinged with concern.

As Riley pulled into the driveway, the moving truck was pulling in behind her. Damn, those guys were fast. She explained where to put the furniture and other items, as Linc waited in the background.

Finally, Linc coaxed her into the barn. It wasn't milking time yet, but Sonny was ringing the bell for the cows. "Riley, please tell me what's goin on..."

"I don't know how you're going to take this." She started.

"Just tell me, babe. I'm a big boy." Linc's eyes were intense.

"I'm pregnant." Riley whispered.

"Seriously? How do you know?" Linc smiled.

"I was at the doctor today. My urine test was positive. There's no question. I'm having an ultrasound later this week."

Linc stepped forward and held her. "Oh God, I'm so thankful. I thought you had something awful to tell me. I was prepared for anything. This is fantastic!"

Riley wrapped her arms around him, clutching his strong back. Her face was pressed into his chest. "You're really happy?"

He moved back and cupped her face with his hands. "Are you kiddin? Damn, Riley, I'm the happiest guy on the planet right now. I wanted a baby with you, in fact, thought about bringing the subject up last night, except the skunk interrupted things. Oh, God, baby, I'm thrilled!" His lips were on hers and she felt him smile as he kissed her. "Oh, Riley, I'm so excited – this is terrific news. I've gotta tell Sonny, my mother, your parents."

Riley let out a sigh of relief. She imagined Linc would be positive about the pregnancy, but she had no idea he'd be this happy. As he moved into the barn to prepare for milking, he paused in the doorway with a lingering gaze. He was exuberant, beyond happy.

Riley stood on the porch alone for a moment. Her hand lightly skimmed over her abdomen. She didn't *look* pregnant. But, then she had no idea what pregnant looked like on her. She didn't care how she looked. The only thing that mattered was having a healthy baby. She decided to tell her friends and family. This was a momentous occasion, one she couldn't keep to herself.

She walked into the barn and saw the women in the pottery room busily working away. Turning, she saw Linc talking with Sonny in the barn. She knew he told him she was pregnant because Sonny was smiling and slapping Linc's back, hugging him. Her attention was drawn to the produce truck pulling up to the greenhouse. The men were loading fresh vegetables into it and would stop up to hand her a check in a few minutes. In the field, Riley noticed three of the young women who boarded their horses there riding. One of them was riding bareback and it made Riley smile.

As she stepped into the office, she noticed the water company had made a large deposit into the Clear Springs Farm account. When she checked the Facebook page, she clicked on the Fund Me project to upgrade the farmhouse. Somehow, the number had grown to $70,000 – a testament of the loving family and community that embraced the Caldwell Family. She smiled and realized how lucky she was to be a part of this unique group of homesteaders. Tonight she'd share the historical maps with her cowboy. He would be interested to know how far back she traced his lineage.

THE END

Note from the author:

Thank you for reading my novel.   I appreciate you as a reader!

I welcome you to follow me on Facebook: www.facebook.com/AuthorAvaArmstrong

I love to answer questions from readers. Please don't be shy!

If you liked "The Last Cowboy", please leave a review on Amazon for me.

Please check out my other novels:

Deep Blue Truth – Romance

http://www.amazon.com/Deep-Blue-Truth-Ava-Armstrong-ebook/dp/B019WI0RCQ/ref=sr_1_1?s=books&ie=UTF8&qid=1451317331&sr=1-1&keywords=deep+blue+truth

THRILLER | ROMANCE | BLACK-OP STYLE

"A Sense of Duty"

http://www.amazon.com/Sense-Duty-Dark-Horse-Guardians-ebook/dp/B00VAWBIYO/ref=sr_1_1?ie=UTF8&qid=1429142523&sr=8-1&keywords=ava+armstrong

"Encountering Evil"

http://www.amazon.com/Encountering-Evil-Dark-Horse-Guardians-ebook/dp/B00N2E77N4/ref=sr_1_6?ie=UTF8&qid=1409170965&sr=8-6&keywords=encountering+evil

"Flawlessly Executed"

http://www.amazon.com/Flawlessly-Executed-Dark-Horse-Guardians-ebook/dp/B00QBFEMRK/ref=sr_1_1?ie=UTF8&qid=1417233334&sr=8-1&keywords=flawlessly+executed

"Hard Man to Kill"

http://www.amazon.com/Hard-Kill-Dark-Horse-Guardian-ebook/dp/B00WT1E88S/ref=sr_1_5?ie=UTF8&qid=1430513953&sr=8-5&keywords=ava+armstrong

SWEET ROMANCE ~ NOVELLA CLIFF HANGER SERIES

"Fallen for Her" Book One

www.amazon.com/Fallen-Her-Ava-Armstrong-ebook/dp/B00R0HYZY8/ref=sr_1_6?s=books&ie=UTF8&qid=141
8598003&sr=1-6&keywords=ava+Armstrong

"Fallen for Her" Book Two

http://www.amazon.com/Fallen-Her-~-Book-2-ebook/dp/B00RQO77RM/ref=sr_1_7?s=books&ie=UTF8&qid=142
0547907&sr=1-7&keywords=ava+armstrong

"Fallen for Her" Book Three

http://www.amazon.com/Fallen-Her-Book-Ava-Armstrong-ebook/dp/B00THUMCIM/ref=sr_1_6?s=digital-text&ie=UTF8&qid=1423704601&sr=1-6&keywords=ava+armstrong

CHILDREN'S NOVELLA SERIES - "THE GARDEN SHED"
LIFE LESSONS, VALUES

Book One - 5 year old Zoe meets a garden gnome named Edmond.

http://www.amazon.com/Garden-Shed-Ava-Armstrong-ebook/dp/B00QSEUNEA/ref=sr_1_1?s=books&ie=UTF8&qid=141
8219093&sr=1-1&keywords=the+garden+shed+ava&pebp=1418219098197

Book Two – 5 year old Zoe goes on an adventure with Edmond.

http://www.amazon.com/Garden-Shed-Book-2-ebook/dp/B00T2H84DC/ref=sr_1_2?s=books&ie=UTF8&qid=142
2884100&sr=1-2&keywords=the+garden+shed+ava+armstrong

Book Three – 5 year old Zoe receives a gift from Edmond and visits the world of gnomes.

http://www.amazon.com/Garden-Shed-Book-Edmond-
surprise-
ebook/dp/B00ZGUBN3C/ref=sr_1_9?s=books&ie=UTF8&qid=143
4124097&sr=1-9&keywords=ava+armstrong

Made in the USA
Columbia, SC
14 January 2021